BAD BOYS
of SUMMER

BAD BOYS
OF SUMMER

LORI FOSTER
ERIN McCARTHY
AMY GARVEY

BRAVA

KENSINGTON PUBLISHING CORP.
http://www.kensingtonbooks.com

BRAVA BOOKS are published by

Kensington Publishing Corp.
850 Third Avenue
New York, NY 10022

ISBN 0-7582-0934-7

First Kensington Trade Paperback Printing: June 2006
10 9 8 7 6 5 4 3 2 1

Printed in the United States of America

CONTENTS

LUSCIOUS

Lori Foster

To Sergeant Paul J. Scowden with the Westerville Ohio Division of Police. For all the questions you answered, the fun anecdotes you shared, and the great insights you gave, you have my sincere thanks.

SWAT guys make great heroes!

P.S. Any bloopers in the book are entirely my own.

One

Lucius Ryder took aim at the front porch area of the home where Mary Seeder's son held her at knifepoint in the six-hour standoff. Lucius didn't want to shoot the dumb-ass punk—but he would if it came to that.

Beneath the IIIA vest, ballistic helmet, and various pads, sweat gathered, making him itch. Material clung to his flesh. The friggin' athletic cup started to chafe. Even before daybreak, the August heat rose and humidity sweltered. But on the chance this could resolve peacefully, he'd wait another six hours before taking an impatient shot.

Unless the kid started to move that knife.

Until now, the son hadn't been visible. He'd hidden in the house, and only phone calls and reports from neighbors told them how critical the situation might be. Then suddenly, under grayish daybreak and emergency lights trained on the house, Steve Seeder dragged Mary onto the rickety front porch.

Out of the corner of his eye, Lucius detected a low, slinking movement at his right. He didn't take his eyes off Steve; he didn't dare. He trusted his backup to alert him to any additional danger.

Through his radio headset, he heard, "Just a dog, Lucius. A mangy mutt, big as a horse, but it doesn't seem threatening."

A stray dog. Just what this day didn't need. If the animal got too close to him, he'd probably end up with fleas.

"Get the hell off our property or I'll kill her! I swear I will."

Speaking of animals . . . Lucius narrowed his eyes over the son's rabid warning. According to neighbors, Steve Seeder had a temper, yet Mary Seeder always took him back in. This time, however, she accepted him back with conditions, which included no smoking. She'd even gone so far as to throw out his last pack of cigarettes.

To a nicotine addict like Steve, it took only that to push him over the edge. Now, thanks to his rage, Steve had added a new slew of charges to his parole revocation warrant.

Despite the expertise of the SWAT team, standoffs were always iffy. Someone could die. Lucius would do his best to ensure it wasn't Mary.

The dog leaned against Lucius's leg. "Easy, bud." Lucius didn't have the heart to nudge it away, but he couldn't divert his attention to it, either.

It circled Lucius, putting itself in his line of vision. With one quick glance, Lucius took in the bone-skinny structure with short, chocolate-brown fur that darkened to black on its face, tail, and feet. Scars, ticks, and burs marred what otherwise would have been truly beautiful coloring.

The animal smelled Lucius from every angle. Because Lucius didn't want his position pinpointed, he said to the dog, "Go on now."

That black face turned up to him, and for a split second, Lucius looked into the dog's eyes. So much expression shown there that Lucius felt oddly connected.

With an eerie vigilance, the dog turned its head and made

note of Steve and Mary on the porch, then began inching forward. Oh shit.

"Come here, dog," Lucius whispered, but to no avail. The dog continued forward.

Lucius waited—tense, alert. The knife Steve held at Mary's throat would also be good for throwing. He wanted Mary safe, but not by sacrificing a dog, damn it.

The second the mutt hit the clearing, Steve stared in disbelief. To no one in particular, he shouted, "What the hell is that hound doing here?"

Lack of fat left lean muscles exposed all along the dog's frame—muscles now taut with readiness. Steve yanked on Mary, and the scruff on the dog's neck rose in warning.

"You call that a police dog? What a joke." While scoffing, Steve inadvertently eased the knife a scant half inch away from Mary's throat.

The dog quivered in anticipation before slowly sinking back on his haunches in a semi-crouch. He could have been cowering—or taking a stance.

Lucius put his money on the latter.

Gleeful at the prospect of causing more pain, Steve dragged Mary a few feet toward the porch edge, raised his booted foot, and prepared to give the dog a vicious kick.

He wasn't quick enough.

A sudden, ferocious snarl made Lucius's hair stand on end and in the next second, the dog attacked. He caught Steve's pant leg, ripping the material while jerking and growling, forcing Steve off balance.

Mary bolted, throwing herself off the porch in awkward haste. She landed on the weeded lawn, screaming and hysterical. With Mary free of the threatening hold, the SWAT team swarmed in, and Steve Seeder had no choice but to give up. The dog released him and eased away.

In seconds, the standoff ended without bloodshed.

No one touched the dog. No one had to. Black ears perked

in interest, he watched the proceedings until everything calmed, then started to saunter off the same way he'd come in.

With everything now under control, Lucius gave all his attention to the animal. The poor thing had the look of a greyhound—but Lucius suspected it was starvation, not breeding, that exposed the dog's rib cage. Patches of abuse showed through the dark, matted fur. Head down in a posture that epitomized sadness, the dog retreated.

Hell, Lucius had never seen such a long face on a mutt. He couldn't bear it.

Soft and low, he whistled. The dog halted, ears perked.

Lucius hunkered down to one knee. "C'mere, boy."

Sharp shoulder blades flexed as the dog looked back with heart-wrenching hope in his mournful brown eyes.

And on that sizzling-hot August dawn, Sergeant Lucius J. Ryder became the owner of a very heroic pooch.

The knock on the door startled Bethany Churchill so that she almost fell off the couch. With blurry eyes, she squinted at the kitchen clock on the far wall. Barely seven A.M.! Another glance at her sister's bedroom door showed that Marci slept on.

Wrapping herself in the borrowed sheet, Bethany hauled herself off the couch and went to the door. She put one eye to the peephole, and moaned at the sight before her.

Big, tall, sexy male.

No, no, no. She didn't need this, not today, not right now, not before caffeine.

Without opening the door, she called out, "What do you want, Luscious?" Her teeth snapped down on her tongue and she mentally cursed. "I mean, *Lucius.*"

At the sound of his deep laugh, her head hit the door with a thump. Damn the other women in the building for giving him that ridiculous nickname. So he was SWAT. And brave. And he looked downright luscious. Luscious Rider, they called him, a name that seemed strangely apropos to her sleepy brain.

Not that Lucius, the egomaniac, ever complained over the endearment. Nope, he soaked in female adoration as if it were his due.

"Bethany, I take it?"

How could he always tell them apart? More than one guy had been confused over time. More than one guy had insisted he didn't have a preference, as if she and her twin were interchangeable, especially if Marci proved unavailable.

But not Lucius.

He behaved very differently with each of them.

Issuing an obvious challenge, Bethany said, "Yeah, so?"

"Open the damn door."

"Why?"

His head hit the wood this time. "I need to see Marci. Now open up."

Of course he wanted to see Marci. The men always wanted to see Marci. Her twin had a charisma that somehow hadn't entered Bethany's gene pool. "No. She's asleep." And I'm in my underwear, and I haven't yet recouped enough from a bad week and a long night to face you.

Another couple of hours sleep, at least three cups of coffee, *then* she might be ready to square off with the hunky landlord.

A hesitation, then, "When did you get in, Bethany?"

Uh-oh. She knew that tone of his, a tone he never used with Marci. "Midnight. Why?"

"You realize you're breaking the rent agreement by imposing on your sister so often?"

Go screw yourself, Sergeant, she mimed to herself—but she didn't dare say the words aloud. After all, he was the landlord, and Marci really liked her apartment. "I'm only here for a few days." Or weeks. Maybe even forever, if she didn't find her backbone. "No big deal."

"It will be a big deal if you don't open the door."

"It's early."

"And I have an emergency."

Now more awake, Bethany put her eye to the peephole again. Lucius looked rumpled and tired, but in a good, cozy and warm way—not panicked. Definitely not injured. Her suspicions rose. "What kind of emergency?"

From behind Bethany, Marci yawned, then said, "What's going on?"

Well, shoot. They'd awakened her sister. "I don't know." She glanced over her shoulder at Marci. "It's Lucius. He wants in for some reason."

"I have an emergency," Lucius yelled, proving the paper-thin walls did little to protect privacy.

Also in a T-shirt and underwear, Marci strode forward and edged Bethany aside. As if Lucius Ryder saw her in a state of undress every day, Marci opened the locks, removed the chain, and swung the door wide without a hint of modesty.

It was then that Bethany detected the beastly howling coming from Lucius's apartment across the hall.

"What is that?" Bethany asked, at the same time Marci said, "Oh my God. That's a dog, isn't it?"

"A dog?" Wrapped in the sheet, Bethany joined Marci in the doorway so that they stood side by side.

Lucius started to explain, but his mouth snapped shut. He went on alert. His exhaustion disappeared. From Bethany to Marci and back again, his gaze went up and down one, then the other.

Finally, one brow raised, he said, "Yeah, see, I brought a dog home and—"

Shoving past him, Marci ran to his apartment, yanked open his door, and disappeared inside.

Lucius flicked one more scorching look over Bethany's sheet-covered frame, then started to follow Marci across the hall.

Without thinking it through, she snagged onto his upper arm. "Oh no, you don't." No way was she leaving "Luscious Lucius" alone with her sis—Wowza. The man had very impressive biceps. She couldn't even get her fingers around him . . .

He stared at her hand up to her face, a question—or maybe a suggestion—in his green eyes.

Recalling herself, Bethany scowled. "You," she said, filling that single word with warning, "are waiting for me to come with you."

"I'm a gentleman." He leveled a very hot look on her. "I always wait for the lady to come."

Her mouth dropped open. Visuals crowded her brain. She started to speak, and squeaked instead.

Oozing satisfaction at her reaction, he grinned. "But in this instance, I can't. You see, the dog—"

Flustered and somewhat feverish, Bethany pulled him inside. "I'll only be a minute." With that dismissal, she raced the few feet across the teensy living room into Marci's bedroom.

Hurrying, so he wouldn't leave without her, she dropped the sheet and bent to fetch her jeans from the floor.

Lucius spoke right behind her. "This could be a wet dream except that I'm wide awake and there's a dog pissing all over my floors."

Squawking, Bethany yanked the jeans up so fast she tripped herself and landed on the side of the bed. She bounced right back up again—no sense in testing things—and turned to fry him with a glare.

He stood with one muscled shoulder propped in the bedroom doorframe. His jeans looked well worn and comfortable, and his T-shirt read: *I quit the band. Now I just play with myself.*

She sneered at the shirt. "I bet that's appropriate."

"Wouldn't you like to know? Maybe fodder for some dreams of your own?"

Absolutely . . . not. Well, okay, maybe a little. Bethany drummed up a convincing snort, pretended disinterest, and rummaged in a drawer for more clothes. If the apartment weren't so minuscule, she might have found a smidge of privacy. But Marci liked the small place, the inconspicuousness of it, and the anonymity it afforded her.

"What are you doing?"

Grumbling as much to herself as to him, Bethany said, "I'm getting Marci some clothes, too."

"Not on my account, I hope."

Don't look at him. Don't look at him. Her teeth locked, making speech difficult. "She probably doesn't even realize what's she's wearing."

"Or not wearing?"

Obviously, he'd noticed. "She wasn't trying to entice you, Sergeant. It's just that Marci's never understood her own sex appeal."

That made him laugh, but not in a ha-ha way.

"What's so funny?" she demanded.

"You think your sister is sexy?"

"You know she is." Good grief, he'd all but swallowed his tongue when he saw her.

"She looks exactly like you, Bethany."

Heat crept up her neck. "No—"

"Exactly like you."

Clutching another pair of jeans, Bethany straightened. Damn it, so they were identical twins. That's not what she meant and he probably knew it. "There's a big difference."

"How?"

"It's an attitude thing."

The second she turned, his gaze skipped over her again, lingering in inappropriate places before settling on her face. "You wanna explain that?"

She didn't, but since she'd talked herself into a verbal corner . . . "Men have always noticed Marci, while she remains oblivious to them."

"And you think they don't notice you?"

How the heck had she gotten herself embroiled in this stupid conversation at such an ungodly hour with the stud of the complex? "Look, forget I said anything."

"Not on your life."

Pigheaded, stubborn, macho . . . "You've eyed Marci, haven't you? You're aware of her as a woman. I know it's true, so don't try to deny it."

"I've eyed you, too." His voice sounded like rough velvet. If rough velvet could talk. "And trust me, babe, I know you're all female."

"I am not your babe."

"More's the pity."

"Lucius," she warned, but her heart tripped at the way he said that, as if he actually wanted to get something going with her. Which he didn't. At least, she didn't think he did.

Did he?

He shrugged. "I'm not blind, gay, or too old to fantasize, so yeah, I've noticed you both. But Marci is a fruitcake and you've formed some grievance against me, so I mind my manners."

Those words, in that particular tone, left her mute for an extended moment. He'd sounded almost complimentary. Then she kick-started her brain and stiffened with affront. "If you consider your current behavior mannerly, I'd hate to see you being rude."

He melted her with a long, hot, dark stare. "I haven't mentioned that enticing lace I saw on your panties, now have I? Or the fact that you're not wearing a bra and it's pretty damned noticeable. Or that you look like a woman who's just rolled out of bed, all sexy and warm and soft."

His mouth quirked at her wide-eyed stupor. "If that's not polite, I don't know what is."

She had to get out of the bedroom.

It had always been that way with Lucius. From the first day she'd met him, they shot sparks off each other. Marci adored him, but according to her sis, their relationship remained strictly platonic. He teased Marci, and Bethany had seen him flirt with every female that came into his vicinity.

But it seemed different with her. Somehow ratcheted up a notch or two.

She didn't know how to take him, given he'd known Marci first. Had her sister been oblivious to Lucius's amorous attempts, so he chose to focus on her instead? Wouldn't be the first time. She should be used to it by now, but no way would she ever accept being second pick. Ever.

Not even for Lucius Ryder.

So despite the sparks, she did her best to keep their relationship platonic, too. Her efforts often seemed antagonistic, but then, she'd never had to deal with such an awesome case of admiration before. Sergeant Ryder was a walking dream of a man.

On the way out of the bedroom, Bethany snagged his arm again. "I don't harbor any grievances against you," she felt compelled to admit.

She just resented the fact that he had an earlier association with Marci, and that women seemed to gravitate to him. Most of all, she resented the easy camaraderie he had with her sis. She couldn't admit any of that, though, so she said instead, "It's just that I don't appreciate how you always poke fun at Marci."

He stopped, which meant she stopped. In fact, the sudden brakes nearly took her off her feet.

Frazzled, she turned to him and snapped, "What?"

"Your sister claims to be a pet psychic."

Stunned, Bethany stared at him. "She told you that?" But her sister never told anyone. Disbelief and ridicule had taught Marci to keep her special talent to herself.

"You can relax. No one else in the building knows. But you gotta admit, that's a little . . ." He made a "cuckoo" gesture with one finger.

Bone-deep protective instincts shot to the fore. More than anyone else in the world, Bethany loved her sister. Crossing her arms over her chest and bracing her feet apart, she faced off with Lucius. Since he stood six-two and she stood only five-seven, she had to tip her head way back, but she didn't let that stop her.

Her smile taunted. "And yet, here you are, Sergeant, anxious for my sister's help. What was it you said? Oh yes, you have a dog pissing all over your apartment. Did you expect Marci to clean the messes—or tell you why the dog is so upset."

He grumbled, dropped his arms to prop his hands on his hips, stared down at his feet. "Okay, so I was hoping she could maybe help."

"And you called her strange."

"I did not! I said being a pet psychic was strange."

"Ha!" Bethany pivoted on her bare foot and marched out. She felt Lucius hot on her heels, and when they entered his apartment, they both stopped dead in their tracks. Lucius bumped into her, clasped her shoulders to keep her from stumbling—and then didn't step away.

She felt his broad chest against her narrower shoulder blades. His hard thighs against her cushy rear.

Marci sat on the floor just inside the door, in her T-shirt and panties, legs crossed yoga style. A long, painfully skinny brown dog draped across her lap.

"Marci?"

Tears glistened in her sister's eyes. "Poor baby, it's okay now. No one will ever hurt you again. Luscious is a good man. He'll keep you safe." She rubbed her face on the dog's scruff, sniffled and nodded. "I know, baby."

Dropping the clothes next to her sister, Bethany sank to her knees. She loved animals as much as Marci, but she didn't have Marci's talent. She started to pet the big dog, but he flinched when she lifted her hand, so she retreated. "Is he okay?"

Marci nodded. "I need a hammer."

"Okay." Trusting her sister one hundred percent, Bethany didn't ask questions. She climbed back to her feet and turned to Lucius. "Got a hammer?"

His green eyes narrowed. "What the hell does she need a hammer for?"

Bethany shrugged. "All I know is that she needs one." And that was good enough for her.

He turned his piercing gaze down on Marci. "I don't want him bludgeoned out of his misery, damn it. I brought you here to—"

"Oh, puh-leeze." Bethany shoved his shoulder, unable to credit the course of his imagination. "You should know her better than that. She's lived in your building for how long now? More than a year."

"So? It's not like we've been intimate." He took a step closer to her. "I've talked more with you than her."

He had? She shook her head, dislodging the wayward thoughts. This was no time to start daydreaming. "Aren't SWAT guys supposed to be astute about people?"

Dark stubbornness replaced his uncertainty. "Yeah, but being around you dicks up my instincts."

She gasped. "You're blaming me?"

"You—and my libido." Gaze bright, he looked at Marci. "What's the hammer for?"

"We have to take off your closet doors."

Because Bethany watched Lucius, she saw his jaw go slack. "What? Why?"

"He's afraid of closets."

Lucius turned to Bethany for help. She shrugged again and repeated, "He's afraid of closets." If her sister said it, then it was true.

"Well . . . can't he just get over it?"

Bethany looked to her sister to answer that one.

Tears spilled down Marci's cheeks. She hugged the dog tight. "No," she said in a broken croak. "He can't just get over it. He's been locked in closets. They terrify him."

Silence fell like a sledgehammer.

Bethany turned to Lucius. She started to reiterate what her sister had just said, but he appeared . . . poleaxed.

Then he looked really, really pissed off.

Muscles flexed all over his big body and he locked his teeth. "Someone locked him in a closet?"

Gifted in a way that allowed her to feel an animal's suffering, to understand it, Marci nodded sadly. "It was horrible for him."

"Son-of-a-bitch." Lucius's fist hit the wall, leaving behind a dent.

Bethany jumped. Marci jumped.

The dog stared at Lucius with worshiping eyes.

Touching his arm, Bethany said, "Lucius, calm down."

"Calm down?" he demanded. "You heard him."

"Him?"

"The dog."

Talk about whacko . . . "Uh, no, I didn't."

"Someone abused him," he reminded her. Then, to Marci, with evil anticipation, "Can he tell you who?"

Bethany blinked at him in disbelief. "Can he tell her who? What, are you out of your mind? He's a dog, Lucius."

Disgruntled, he thrust his face toward her. "He's telling her other things."

"No, he's not. Marci can feel what he's afraid of, but he's not a talking dog. He's not carrying on a conversation with her."

The comical expression that came over Lucius's face made it worth waking at dawn.

His empathy for the dog shredded her last bit of resistance and completely stole her heart.

Not that she'd let him know it.

She dredged up a credible smirk. "I guess if you had the name of the abuser, you'd go charging off in search of vengeance?"

For several seconds, Lucius just stared at her. Then he rubbed his face. "Yeah, something like that. And stop harassing me, damn it. It's been a helluva day." He waved a hand. "Or night. Whatever."

"Yelling and punching walls won't help to reassure him."

"Actually," Marci said, "he's more fascinated with Lucius's reaction than anything. But he also thinks you're both nuts, that's for sure."

Lucius looked down at the dog. The dog stared back, his face arrested in anticipation. Bethany could almost swear the creature smiled. His long, skinny tail began thumping hard.

"He likes you," Marci told Lucius.

"Is that right?" Lucius crossed his arms over his chest. "Is that why he soiled ever inch of my floors?"

"Part excitement at the prospect of having a home, and part fear at being put back out. Plus he hadn't eaten in a while. His system is fragile." Chiding, she added, "You shouldn't have fed him so much."

"He was hungry, damn it."

"I understand." Marci shared a look with Bethany, one that said, *Isn't he wonderful?*

Lucius saw that look, and for some reason, took exception to it. Furious again, he strode past them into his kitchen, rattled some drawers, returned with a hammer and screwdriver, and went to work on the closet door in the entryway.

Marci hugged the long-limbed dog closer. "There, you see? You're safe, baby. I promise."

"He's not a baby," Lucius said. "I named him Hero."

"Really?" Bethany walked over to lean on the wall and watch while Lucius used the hammer and screwdriver to tap the hinges apart. "How come?"

"He saved a woman today." Showing off those impressive biceps, he worked the door loose, hefted it onto a shoulder, and carried it over behind the couch, where he stowed it away out of sight.

Bethany followed him. "How's that?"

"He gave us the opportunity we needed." Lucius eyed the dog, who eyed him back with keen expectation. "'Course, then he proceeded to destroy my apartment. I've already cleaned no less than seven messes. Everything he eats comes right back out."

Bethany wrinkled her nose. "Lovely description. Thanks for sharing."

Marci said, "He couldn't help it."

Lucius sighed. "Yeah, I know." He crouched down in front of the dog and rubbed an ear. "All's forgiven, big guy."

The dog's tail started thumping again.

Charmed, Bethany said, "You should take him to a vet right away."

Lucius stretched back to his feet and turned to stand in front of her. He gave her all his attention, putting her temperature on the rise and making her toes curl. "Got one you recommend?"

Those words, accompanied by that look, didn't mesh.

Bethany stared up into intense, glittering green eyes. Gorgeous, strong, heroic—and kind to animals.

He couldn't be real.

What he said finally registered. She cleared her throat. "So you plan to keep him?"

"Yep." He stared at her mouth.

Lucius could be tragic to her emotions at the best of times, and this was not the best of times. "I thought you had a no-pet policy for this place?"

Without seeming to move, he eased closer until the heat of him hugged around her. "I have a no-roommate policy, too, but you're here." And he added: "Again."

So she visited her sister often. They were close. Twins, for crying out loud. And this time, she wasn't just here for the fun of it.

But what did he care, anyway? Just because she sort of gave him a hard time whenever she came around didn't mean he should kick her out. Antagonizing him was her way of protecting her heart. Even if she didn't lust after him, she'd still refuse to gush like the rest of the ladies in the building.

Chin raised, expression haughty, Bethany informed him, "I'm a sister, not a roommate. It's an entirely different thing."

"If we're getting specific, you're a pain in the ass." His grin went crooked, removing any insult, and he reached out to pinch her elevated chin. "But I suppose, since you're Marci's twin, I'll try to tolerate you." He dropped his hand and walked off, whistling, to tackle another door.

Two

With that parting remark, Lucius made his escape, putting much-needed distance between him and Bethany.

When he'd first bought the apartment building of six units, he hadn't figured on renting exclusively to women. Yet that's what he'd done. He'd surrounded himself with ladies.

Was he nuts? A masochist? Or too damn partial to those of the feminine variety? Probably the latter. He did love women, all ages, all professions, all sizes and personalities.

Fellow cops ribbed him endlessly over his circumstances. They nicknamed him Sultan, which he supposed was better than Luscious. If they knew about the twins, he'd never hear the end of it, because they weren't just twins. They were really hot twins—and one of them currently wore only panties and a T-shirt.

But oddly enough, it was the other twin who had him twitchy in the pants.

The one with the smart mouth and quick wit.

The one with the attitude.

And those big blue eyes . . . Of course, they both had

pretty blue eyes. And silky, baby-fine brown hair. Lean bodies with understated curves. Soft, full mouths . . .

On Marci, he appreciated the beauty, just as he liked the scenery in the park. Nothing more.

On Bethany, the combination made him wild with lust.

Lucius held his breath. If he didn't, he breathed her, and he couldn't deal with that on top of no sleep and a traumatized, newly adopted dog. Bethany smelled warm, and spicy, and she left his insides churning.

She also made it clear that she didn't want to get too cozy with him, and just as he loved women, he respected their decisions. Even when it pained him to do so.

Bringing the dog home had been a spur-of-the-moment decision prodded by some inner Good Samaritan heretofore unrecognized. Now, dead on his feet from exhaustion and, thanks to his eccentric neighbor's sister, tweaked by horniness, he . . . still didn't regret the decision.

One look at the dog and he knew he couldn't have done anything else. Hero deserved a cushy life. He deserved regular meals and pats of affection and security. No way could Lucius have left him behind, or dropped him at a shelter.

However, he could ignore Bethany. And he would. Somehow.

She only showed up about once a month. She'd stay a few days, and then take off again. Surely he could last that long.

But . . . this was August. And a school secretary probably didn't work during the summer. So how long would she be around this time? Long enough to make him completely insane?

He'd just gotten another closet door off the hinges when he sensed her presence. In his bedroom. Real close.

He stiffened—in more ways than one.

Without looking at her, Lucius asked, "What do you

want, Bethany?" And he thought, say me, me, me. Tell me
you want me, tell me—

"I was thinking . . ."

"Yeah? About me?" He lowered the door and shoved it
under his bed, then moved to stand right in front of her, as
near as he dared without getting smacked. "I figured as
much."

"No—"

"Don't fight it, Bethany." He tried to look serious, but the
expression on her face made him want to laugh. She riled so
easily. "It'll only make it harder on you." And harder on him,
too.

"You are so—"

"What?" He made his tone intimate, provocative. "Tell
me."

But she got distracted with a T-shirt he'd left wadded up
on the mattress. As if he had cooties, she lifted it with her
fingertips, raising it so she could read the front. "I only look
sweet and innocent." She rolled her eyes. "Gawd, your
shirts are so lame."

"It's true." Wishing he could drop on the bed the same
way she just dropped that shirt, Lucius ran a hand through
his hair and sighed. "On the inside, I'm all bad boy."

"Tell me something I don't know."

Dead serious, he said, "You're every bit as hot as your
sister. Probably more so."

She froze.

"Given what you said earlier, I thought maybe you were
unaware— "

"Be quiet!"

He grinned. Would it be as easy to get her going in bed?

Marci poked her head into the bedroom. She looked
from one to the other, but settled on addressing Lucius. "I'm
running back to my place to get showered and dressed."

"Okay." He made a concerted effort to keep his gaze on Marci's face and off her bare legs—legs he knew looked identical to Bethany's.

"Then I'll take Hero to the vet for you. I'm wide awake now, and you look exhausted."

"I'm fine," he lied. SWAT guys did not go around whining about exhaustion. They sucked it up and toughed it out.

"He's pooped," Bethany said. "Look at the circles under his eyes."

He did not have circles. How dumb. "That's irritation, not weariness, smart-ass."

"Ha!"

"Is that your answer to everything? I thought school secretaries were more articulate."

Marci crossed her arms, which plumped up her breasts—not that he noticed. "I'm assuming that if Hero rescued a lady, you were in a high-risk situation?"

Lucius rolled one shoulder. "You could say that. But thanks to the dog, no one got hurt. He proved enough of a distraction that we saved a woman from having her throat sliced open."

Bethany gasped, reminding Lucius that bloody, brutal murders weren't everyday conversations in her world. After being a cop for fifteen years, ten of those years on the tactical unit, he'd grown accustomed to nerve-wracking experiences. The twins hadn't.

"She was kidnapped?"

"Not exactly. See, her son held her captive in her own home."

The women wore similar aghast expressions, putting Lucius at a loss for words. The dog came to his rescue by slinking in at that precise moment.

Again, Lucius crouched down. "Hey, boy. You feeling better now?"

Hero crept forward and butted his head into Lucius's side. Lucius stroked him, carefully because while the dog looked strong enough, he hadn't been treated well and Lucius didn't want to startle or alarm him. He'd rather take a beating himself than make Hero feel threatened.

Hero wallowed in the petting for about thirty seconds before leveling a cautious stare at the wide-open closet. He gave it a wide berth on his path toward . . . Lucius's bed.

Swallowing a groan, Lucius said softly, "No, he's not," with a touch of desperation. "He's not."

Marci said, "Shhh . . . He's finding his place."

"But please, not in my bed." Lucius pushed wearily to his feet. He needed sleep himself, damn it.

Both ladies frowned at him, making him feel like an ass. But he hadn't had a chance to bathe Hero yet and he sure as hell didn't want to sleep with fleas.

With one agile leap, the dog landed in the middle of the mattress.

Lucius didn't say a single word, and still, worry etched heavy wrinkles on the dog's black face. He peered at Lucius, waiting, and Lucius caved. "Good dog."

Relieved, Hero circled, dropped, and groaned out a long sigh of bone-melting pleasure.

Lucius's heart turned over. "Well, hell. I guess I can change the bedding after you leave with him."

Marci patted his arm. "You are such a good man, Sergeant Ryder."

Grinning, Lucius turned to her, and got the close-up view of her in that long T-shirt. Her eyes were shining, her mouth smiling, and she looked dead-on Bethany.

At least, he thought so until he actually looked at Bethany and caught her sour, pinched appearance of disapproval.

Just to push Bethany, he put his arm over Marci's shoulders. "You really won't mind taking him to the vet's for me? I want him checked out, any shots he needs, maybe a flea dip—"

Bethany started to say something, no doubt something mean and nasty, and Marci beat her to it. "Come to my place to sleep."

Tucking in his chin and quickly dropping his arm, Lucius stared at her. "Come again?"

"You really do look exhausted. I'll get my stuff and shower here so you can go to my bedroom and sleep."

"Ah, no." He glanced at Bethany, but she only glared back. No help from her. "I wouldn't feel right." That is, he'd be randy as a goat and it was tough to sleep with a boner.

"Don't be silly."

Bethany was right—her sister was oblivious to the sexuality of her suggestion.

But hell, Marci smelled enough like Bethany to put a spin on his libido. Lying on those scented sheets would put him right over the edge. "I'll wait."

Marci rolled her eyes. "Bethany, take him for me."

Color flooded Bethany's face, making her blue eyes brighter by contrast. That soft brown hair he'd touched a million times in his dreams whipped around her face as she shook her head. "No way."

"Bethany." Marci put a hand on her hip.

"But, but . . . " she sputtered, "I can't—"

"Take me?" Lucius offered.

She rounded on him, her face on fire. "Don't—"

"For Marci?" he coerced, and even as he prodded her, he thought he really should shut up. It wasn't that he liked to be tortured, but now he wanted to go to Marci's apartment.

Just because Bethany didn't want him there.

Marci huffed out a long breath. "Will you two quit acting like bumbling high-schoolers and just go? Bethany, after all your upset last night—"

"What upset?" Lucius asked, but both women soundly ignored him.

"—you need more sleep, too. You know, on second thought, you can take my bed, and Luscious can—"

"His name is *Lucius*."

"—take the couch, and I'll take Hero to the vet." Content with the arrangement, Marci smiled. "There. Everyone should be happy." She turned and strolled away. The hem of the T-shirt bunched up on her rounded rump, putting her panties, and a very fine ass, on display. Lucius stared.

Until Bethany popped him one on the shoulder.

"Ow. Damn." He gave up the view of Marci leaving his apartment to glare at Bethany.

Seething, she said, "You are such a perv."

"I'm a perv? Your sister is the one sashaying around in her undies." Giving me an idea of what you'd look like in your undies.

Arms crossed tight beneath her breasts, bare foot tapping, Bethany stared off at nothing in particular. Finally, she muttered, "You're a hypocrite, too."

"Oh, really?"

"You ridicule Marci's abilities, then come running the second you think she can help you."

"I don't ridicule her. I tease her. There's a difference."

"Whatever you call it, you've always discounted her ability."

What was he supposed to do? Should he say, Great, you're a pet physic. Just what we need in the complex? Lucius didn't like being put on the spot.

"Admit it," Bethany pressed.

He argued the point instead. "You're telling me that if a

woman came to you to rent a room, and she claimed to be a pet psychic who needed a place to hide out to avoid the media and unscrupulous scam artists hoping to use their pets for fame, you wouldn't bat an eye?"

"Not if it was my sister."

Lucius threw up his hands. "Now *that* makes a lot of sense," he said, with complete and utter facetiousness. "But news flash, honey. Marci isn't my sister."

"That shouldn't matter. What I meant was that Marci comes across as genuine."

"Genuinely loony." Never had Lucius known a woman more flighty, more prone to melodrama, more . . . ethereal. The twins might look alike, but they were night and day in disposition.

Marci floated through life.

Bethany stomped.

"She's also honest," Bethany insisted.

"You've got me there." Marci might be strange enough to chat with every squirrel in the trees, but she never caused trouble, and she paid her rent on time. Lucius could trust her. Hadn't he just agreed to trust her with his dog?

"And caring. About everyone and everything."

"No argument." What the hell were they talking about, anyway? With Bethany standing there, full of fire, he could barely think, much less chatter. How could a woman look so good first thing in the morning? Ratty hair and sleep creases around the eyes had never turned him on before.

Now they had him close to a full-blown lust-fest.

"So you know she's honest and caring." Bethany looked ready to rest her case.

"Sure." Lucius smiled to himself. "But she's still a ding-bat—and before you take aim on my poor arm again, I say that with affection."

"You can jam your affection where the sun don't shine, Sergeant."

"Doesn't shine," he corrected, and watched her eyes burn like blue flames. He tsked. "And you call yourself a school secretary. The fate of our young people is not in good hands."

She growled better than Hero. Spinning away from him, she started to stomp off, and Lucius caught the back of her shirt. Her legs almost came out from under her.

Fists raised, she reared around and he quickly backed up.

"Uncle, uncle. Don't batter me. I just wanted to apologize."

Suspicion kept her guarded. "For what?"

"For deliberately razzing you. Obviously, you're not a morning person. But the truth is, I like your sister. Always have."

If anything, his confession made her angrier. "Great," she said through her teeth. "Just great. Glad to hear it. So you two are cozy? Never mind. It's . . . great. News, that is. What a relief."

He couldn't hold back his grin. "Now Bethany, don't get jealous."

Her gasp nearly parted his hair.

"I like Marci as a friend," he soothed. "Granted, a female friend. But I'm not hot for her or anything."

She wore an expression of clear disbelief.

"It's true. As a rule, I avoid getting romantically involved with the women I rent to." He closed the space between them. "Which, come to think of it, is a damn good reason not to rent to you."

Bethany's mouth opened twice before anything came out. "You . . ."

He noticed that she didn't move away. "Yes?"

"Conceited . . ."

She seemed to flounder after that, so Lucius tried to help out. "Handsome?"

"Obnoxious . . ."

"You mean confident, right?"

"Egomaniac . . ."

"Now that's just not nice."

"Jerk!"

His blood sang through his veins. "If I kissed you right now, would you slug me?"

To his surprise, she pokered up and glared and—seemed to think about it.

Not that he'd kiss her, Lucius assured himself. The fantasies alone nearly killed him. To get the real thing would do him in, especially if she kissed him and then sent him packing, which, given her past and present attitude toward him, seemed a pretty good possibility.

Besides, she was the twin sister to a tenant. Too close for comfort if things went south. Bethany Churchill would be nothing but trouble. Tasty trouble, for sure. Just look at her mouth. So soft and damp . . .

"No."

"What's that?" The barely-there whisper sort of snuck by him while he'd considered licking her lips for her.

"I said no."

"I've forgotten my question." He needed clarification. He needed more oxygen. He needed her under him. "No, you don't want me to kiss you, or no, you wouldn't object?"

She blinked hard and fast. Somehow, that seemed like a come-on.

"Bethany?" He got so close, his feet touched hers— which meant her breasts brushed against him and he knew damn good and well she didn't wear a bra. He bent to touch his nose to her hair, taking in her scent . . .

Her hands flattened on his chest and in a small voice, she whispered, "Please, don't."

Well, shit. Disappointment cleared the fog. "Okay." But he didn't back off. He couldn't. Not just yet.

The dog started to snore, making Lucius smile. But Hero didn't count against their privacy. They were alone. In his bedroom. "Wanna tell me why?"

Her shuddering, indrawn breath moved her breasts against him, and he felt her stiffened nipples. He swallowed a groan. "Bethany?"

"I have . . . enough guy trouble already."

Those words landed like lead in his gut. "I see." He didn't want to hear about her with other guys. He knew she dated. How could she not? She was gorgeous, sexy, funny, and smart. But the last he'd heard from Marci, she didn't have anything serious going on. "And you assume I'd be more trouble?"

"You're a bad boy, remember." She chanced a quick look up at him, and Lucius snagged her gaze.

Unable to stop himself, he slid one hand into her hair. "You telling me you don't like bad boys?"

Her smile trembled. "You're not really bad and you know it."

"Now, how'd you get that impression?"

"For one thing, you're a cop."

"Yeah." His thumb touched just below her ear. "I get to shoot at people."

She smiled, seeing through his humor. "For another, you help women."

His heart missed a beat. "Come again?"

"Lucius. You rent only to women, and those women were all in dire straits and in need of housing. You can't tell me that happened by accident."

"Sure, I can." But she might be onto something there.

She gestured at the bed. "You also rescue dogs."

Throwing her words back at her, he said, "It's an attitude thing."

"What is?"

"Being bad. It's not what you do, but how you do it. When it comes to relationships, I'm as bad as can be."

"Oh, I have no trouble believing that. Any woman with a brain knows you'd be disastrous to her heart."

"I don't want your heart, Bethany." Liar, liar. His gaze slid over her. His voice dropped. "I want the rest of you, though."

Regret filled her eyes—and she took that fatal step away. "Sorry, Lucius. I'm off the market for a while. If the past week—the past month hadn't happened . . ." She dropped that train of thought with a shrug. "Right now, I'm just looking to relocate, not get involved."

Protestations arose—until the last of what she'd said finally sank in. "Relocate?" He strangled on the word.

Brassiness returning, she grinned and patted his jaw. "Yup. I quit my job, dumped a guy, and canceled the lease on my apartment. I'm moving into your neck of the woods."

Lucius clutched his heart. He pretended dread, when really all he cared about was that she'd rid herself of his competition. She didn't need any old flames—not when he intended to be her new love.

Yeah, she claimed to be uninterested. But he'd change her mind about that. How, he didn't know, but he'd make it happen. He had to.

Because deep down, he knew he'd fallen in love with her from day one. Now he had to work on keeping her around . . . forever.

Twenty minutes later, Lucius should have been dead asleep. Exhaustion dragged at him, but instead of nodding off, he thought about Bethany sleeping in the bedroom just a few feet away.

Had she skinned off those jeans again, so that she wore only the shirt and sexy panties? Was she thinking about him? His stomach tightened at the thought.

She'd be warm. And soft.

And probably grouchy, but he could live with that. Hell, after so many fawning women, her grouchiness turned him on.

Frustrated on several levels, he put an arm over his eyes and groaned raggedly. He might be tired, but the old John Henry was wide awake.

A moment later, the bedroom door opened, startling him. He dropped his arm and rose to one elbow to stare at Bethany.

For endless seconds, they watched each other.

Finally, she asked, "What are you groaning about?"

Not bothering to censor his thoughts, he said, "I'm horny."

Her gaze dipped down his body to where a boner tented the sheet. She did some serious staring.

He got a little harder.

"Oh," she finally said.

He groaned again. "Your sister must be a sadist. She had to know how I'd react to all this."

"This?"

"You. The proximity of you. My thoughts of you. My lusting for you."

She touched her mouth with one hand and shook her head. "No, she's not real clued in to guys."

"But you are?"

She laughed, but with hurt, not humor. "No, I'm worse than she is."

"Because some idiot boyfriend did you wrong?"

One shoulder lifted.

"The guy you dumped to come here?"

"He wasn't even really a boyfriend, just someone I dated a few times. He wanted to use me to get to Marci. I was dumb enough to think he was interested in me. Luckily I figured out the truth early on." Her gaze remained south of his face.

"It's not going to do tricks, ya know."

"What's that?"

"My dick." Her gaze shot up to meet his. "Sorry to disappoint you, but that's as big as it gets, and without some action from you, not much more is going to happen, no matter how long you stare."

She sucked in a furious, embarrassed breath while turning bright red-hot. "You're . . ."

"Really turned on. And sort of pissed at this jerk who misled you. And a little worried about Hero. But yeah, mostly turned on."

She looked around, probably for something to throw at him.

Lucius took pity on her. "Go back to bed, Bethany. I'll try to suffer in silence."

"Good idea."

What, his suffering? Before she could shut the door, Lucius said, "But Bethany?"

She kept her back to him. "What?"

"I won't ever lie to you. You'll always know exactly what I'm thinking—"

"Which is part of the problem!"

"—and exactly who I'm interested in."

She hesitated, her back rigid, her breathing deep. Then she gave one quick nod and muttered, "Thanks."

"My pleasure, and yours if you ever decide you're interested."

This time, Bethany groaned. She started to walk away, but hesitated. "Lucius?"

"Yeah?"

"I'm far from disappointed."

"Is that right?"

She cleared her throat. "If you were any bigger, well . . . Never mind." She dashed inside the bedroom and closed the door with a firm click.

A few seconds later, smiling from ear to ear, Lucius settled back down on the couch. He'd only been teasing her
about being disappointed. Hell, he knew he wasn't lacking
in that area—but it was cute that she wanted to reassure
him.

He chuckled, and despite his state of unrelieved arousal,
fell into a deep sleep that led to erotic dreams. Of Bethany.

Three

Lucius awoke with a pounding head and a lot of disorientation. His legs were cramped, his right arm numb from hanging over the edge of a cushion, and the silence in the apartment sounded louder than a gun blast.

A squinty-eyed glimpse at the clock showed it to be dinnertime, which maybe explained why his stomach rumbled in demand for nourishment.

Where had Bethany gotten off to?

How was Hero?

Did Marci have any pants on yet?

Funny that the image of a beautiful woman in her panties was his last thought and not his first.

He sat up, listened, but the apartment was definitely empty. To be on the safe side, he stood, stretched, then retrieved his pager and phone from the pockets of his jeans.

Normally he slept in the nude, but given the circumstances, he'd left on loose shorts, so he clipped both devices to the waistband. SWAT could get a call-out at any time, so he went nowhere, not even on his off days, without the phone, pager, and everything else that might be needed.

His pickup truck had a lockable hardtop tonneau cover

on it. In the bed of his truck, he stored several thousand dollars worth of equipment that included anything he might need on a run, from camouflage BDU uniforms to two large bags of tactical and sniper gear, and a variety of ammunitions.

Being the cautious sort, Lucius wanted to make sure he was alone. He snuck toward the bedroom and peeked inside. The neatly made bed proved that Bethany was long gone, and that he'd slept like the dead. How the hell had she tiptoed out around him, without him hearing her?

Had she paused to look at him? Had he snored? Had he enticed or repelled her?

He ran a hand over his rumpled hair and laughed. God, he was worse than a woman with all his fretting. Enough, already.

Still groggy, he made use of the bathroom, then splashed his face and rinsed his mouth. He'd kill for coffee, but the carafe sat cold and empty, and he wanted to find Bethany more than he needed the caffeine kick.

Wearing only the loose drawstring shorts with his phone and pager, he opened the door to head for his apartment—and faltered.

What the hell? Even through the closed door, he could hear music and laughter. Were they having a party without him? At his place?

Annoyance rose, until he remembered that Marci, who worked as an aerobics instructor, gave free classes to the other tenants once a week.

Usually they gathered in her living room, but since he'd sacked out on her couch, he supposed he should be grateful that they'd chosen his living room instead.

Regardless of Bethany's accusations, he hadn't deliberately rented only to women. At least, not consciously. But he was a sucker for a woman with a hard-luck story, and in his line of work, he saw a lot of women burdened with the shittiest luck imaginable.

Fifty-year-old Esther owned a boutique. Now. But when he'd met her, she'd just left a long-term abusive marriage that ended with a threat deadly enough to warrant SWAT. It had taken almost a year of adjustment before Esther really started to live it up. Then she dyed her graying hair black to match her dark eyes and she started dancing again. The boutique she bought afforded her just enough cash flow to handle Lucius's cheap rent in the less-than-quality neighborhood.

Amanda, with her red hair and rhinestone-studded glasses, epitomized his vision of a forty-year-old barmaid. He'd met her during a holdup.

Devine was a beautiful brunette dancer in her early thirties who'd been taken hostage by a stalker who claimed to "love" her.

And twenty-three-year-old, ebony-skinned Tyra was a student/waitress who'd been in class when an escaped fugitive tried to use the college as a negotiating point.

Through tragic circumstances, he'd met all the women and learned of their financial, personal, and professional troubles. Naturally, he did what he could.

They all lived on very fixed or limited incomes. They were all without family support. They each worked hard just to stay afloat.

Originally, he'd planned to rent out all six units in the building. But then the women grew on him. He liked their quirky personalities and respected their gumption. Since he enjoyed doing repairs on the old building himself, and because he figured they could use a man around to keep an eye on things, he took up the sixth unit himself.

The arrangement worked.

The ladies paid their rent, sometimes cooked him dinner, and all in all, added joy to his life.

Well, except that they liked to play games with his name, calling him Luscious and making cracks about what type of "rider" he'd be.

From Tyra to Esther, they came on to him in a teasing, hope-to-make-him-blush way. But he just wasn't the blushing sort. He couldn't recall the last time he'd gotten honestly embarrassed about anything. He adored women and their antics. Anything they dished out, he took with glee, and he always gave back as good as he got.

Curious, Lucius stuck his head inside the entry door. With the loud music and physical gyrations of the aerobics, no one noticed him. Women of all ages and wardrobe preferences littered his home. Marci, dressed in a white leotard, faced the rest of them, dancing this way and that while smiling about something. Esther stood up front and center in a flowing caftan, with Amanda and Devine close behind her, wearing colorful sweats. They were all chuckling. Tyra, in shorts and a crop top, was bent double in laughter.

Hero took up half his couch, napping during the confusion.

Where was Bethany?

Marci said, "You see, Bethany?" proving that she was somewhere in the room, just out of sight. "Men aren't all jerks. They do have their uses." The women raucously agreed.

Lucius leaned on the wall and prepared to be educated.

"Sex without them is just not the same."

Sex?

Esther said, "My favorite part is kisses on the neck." She ran her fingers up the side of her throat with a lusty sigh. "What about you, Tyra?"

Lucius blanched. They were talking about their favorite parts of lovemaking? Oh, hell. He wasn't at all sure he wanted to hear this.

"Let me tell you, honey," Tyra said, "far as I'm concerned, sex is overrated."

From somewhere on the other side of the room, Bethany said, "Hear, hear."

Lucius forgot about fleeing. Bethany didn't like sex? Why the hell not?

"But I enjoy the cuddling," Tyra continued. "Men are just so big and warm."

"And deceiving," Bethany grumbled.

"Not all of them," Marci insisted.

"I like to be swept away." Amanda threw out her arms while navigating a step. "Passion, passion, passion!"

"Passion's nice," Marci agreed. She took everyone through a few vigorous steps. "But love is better. You can tell he's in love by the way he looks at you." She paused to shiver. "That's my favorite part. Right before you're actually intimate, and he looks so possessive and hot and in love."

"And horny," Devine said, starting another round of female hilarity. "My favorite part is when they get so hot, they'll agree to anything. That's when the real fun begins."

Interesting, Lucius thought. Was he really more agreeable when turned on?

Probably.

Suddenly Hero lifted his head from the couch and stared right at Lucius. Excitement brightened the dark brown eyes, and the dog gave a bark of greeting, jumped to the floor, and trotted over to sit on Lucius's foot. Lucius put a hand to the dog's head.

Startled females turned. Arched eyebrows rose at the intrusion of a man. They all stared at him.

Marci said, "Lucius?"

And feeling like a devil among angels, he shrugged. "Blow jobs."

He heard a gasp, a giggle. Amanda adjusted her flashy glasses. "What'd he say?"

"My favorite part." Lucius laughed when a towel hit him in the face. "You weren't asking me? I thought it was my turn."

Esther cackled out a laugh. "You are so naughty, Luscious."

"But it's interesting to know," Marci said, and she sent a

sly grin in the direction from where Bethany's voice had emerged. "Don't you think, Bethany?"

Tyra giggled again. "Actually, it was Bethany's turn to share, not yours." And they all turned to peer in the same direction . . . at Bethany.

Lucius stepped farther inside so he could see around the wall. Sure enough, Bethany sat stock-still on his ottoman, her back ramrod straight, her face pinched and pink.

Unlike the others, she hadn't been working out. She was fully dressed and very displeased to be the center of attention.

"C'mon, Bethany," he teased softly. "Inquiring minds want to know. What's your favorite part?"

As he spoke, her attention drifted to his naked chest and thighs. Her interest was so hot, catastrophe almost struck. The last thing Lucius needed was a flagpole with a bunch of gaping women taking notes.

Don't get hard, Lucius thought with desperation. Do *not* get hard. Chanting that instruction to himself, he made a point of looking at Esther and Amanda and the utterly wicked way they anticipated his reaction. He patted Hero, noted that the dog's fur was now clean and soft, and finally, when he was sure he had control of himself, he leaned against the wall, a man at his leisure.

He could actually see Bethany gathering her gumption. She stood, and her smile was mean. "I agree with Tyra—it's all overrated."

"All of it, huh? Even the cuddling?" he asked.

"What cuddling?" She snorted as if such a thing was unheard of. "Groping, yeah. Slobbering, sure. But not cuddling."

Teasing slipped away, replaced by honest concern and indignation on her behalf. "I'd say you've been with the wrong guys."

Her look of disdain would have flattened a lesser man. "Too bad there aren't any right guys around."

Such a blatant challenge. Lucius took a hard step toward her. "Maybe you've been looking in the wrong places."

Her eyes narrowed. "Doesn't matter now, since I'm done looking." Raising her nose, she started forward and as she reached him, she said, "If you'll excuse me, I have other things to do," and, as if she lost her nerve, she sped up to dash past him.

Lucius turned his head to watch her race into his kitchen. Her clothes were . . . hideous. A short-sleeved white blouse that surely belonged on someone's aunt and super-funky, dirt-brown trousers that hid everything but her waist.

It was one of those outfits that piqued a man's interest, making him wonder just what it might hide. But after seeing her in her panties, he knew exactly what Bethany hid—and he almost did some of that slobbering she mentioned.

How difficult would it be to get her out of those ridiculous mannish trousers? And how long would it take him to prove to her that sex with the right guy—him—would be as much fun as she could handle?

"Earth to Lucius? Hello?"

Drawn from his ruminations, Lucius looked around the room and realized that the music was off and the aerobics ended. Hero and all five women watched him, waiting for his next move.

He couldn't really disappoint them by appearing disconcerted, now could he?

"Hero looks great." He patted the dog some more.

Marci nodded agreement. "The vet says other than being a little malnourished, he's fit. I purchased the special food and vitamins he recommended."

"Great." Lucius didn't care if she purchased T-bones if it'd make the poor dog happy. "Let me know how much I owe you."

"It cost you a lot more than it would at the market," she warned.

"He's earned it."

"The vet had a tech dip him and shave off some of the matted fur so we could check out his skin. He's got a few bald patches now, but he's fine. Mostly he'd just had a few allergic reactions to the fleas."

"And now the fleas are gone?"

"Yes. I bought you a brush so you can keep up on his grooming."

"I'll make it a nightly routine." Right behind seducing Bethany.

Marci watched him petting Hero with a lot of interest. "You know, Bethany is probably in the kitchen stewing."

"I am not!" Bethany shouted.

Pretending she hadn't heard her sister, Marci said, "We tried to convince her that some guys are worth the trouble, but the more time you give her, the more stubborn she'll be."

Lucius looked toward the kitchen, anxious to be on his way. "You think?"

"I know my sister." And taking pity on him, she called the dog back to her. Hero trotted over, jumped up on the couch, and curled into a circle. "Don't mind us," Marci told him. "We can entertain ourselves."

"Oh God," they all heard Bethany groan.

Lucius saluted Marci and headed out of the room.

The second he turned his back toward the women, Divine said, "Nice drawers, Luscious."

The seat of his shorts read: *Small piece of heaven.* Lucius just laughed. "Glad you like them."

Standing at the counter, doing not much of anything while trying to look busy, Bethany felt her heart begin to race. It wasn't exactly dread, was in fact more like anticipation. Damn it, when would she learn?

The second Lucius stepped into the kitchen, the air crackled around her. Good God, the man brought a lot of sexual tension into a room.

She felt his presence a few feet behind her, unmoving, silent, probably waiting for her to do or say something. But she couldn't dredge up a single clear thought or any type of polite conversation.

"What the hell are you wearing?"

Somehow, he always knew exactly what to say to provoke her out of her stupor.

Bethany spun around to face him. It wasn't easy, but she kept her attention off his super-fine and blatantly exposed body and on his mocking expression instead. "Clothes?"

"Those pants don't fit you. They look like something my grandpa would wear." He tipped his head and put his hands on his hips. "Is this some sort of warped Annie Hall thing? Or man-aping?" He shook his head. "Whatever it is, I don't like it."

"Oh, my goodness." Bethany clasped her hands together beneath her chin. "Well then, let me just rush home and change as fast as I possibly can." She dropped her hands with a scowl. "Not."

Lucius chuckled. "They look two sizes too big."

"They're just comfortably loose through the seat and legs." She hooked her thumbs in the waistband, which hugged her middle. "See? And speaking of pants . . . where are yours?"

He glanced down, pretending he only then realized how little he wore. "I slept in shorts—which is more than what you slept in. I think I left my jeans on your floor."

She nodded at his waist. "You left the pants but took the phone and the pager? Are you expecting a call? Perhaps from your girlfriend?" The words no sooner left her mouth than she bit her lip in regret.

"I'm SWAT, honey, which means if I'm in town, I'm available." He patted the Nextel. "Neither rain nor shine nor sexy broad—and that'd be you, by the way—can keep me from answering the call of duty."

"Lovely." Did he really consider her sexy?

His teasing expression sobered. "In case it matters, I don't have a girlfriend."

"It doesn't." Liar, liar. "Why should it?"

Voice dropping low and intimate, he said, "You know why. You keep fighting it, honey, but it's still there."

What would happen if she stopped fighting?

Dangerous thoughts. To keep herself from landing in a verbal or emotional quagmire, Bethany sidled around him. "Why don't I just go get those jeans for you?" And while she did that, she could grab a little time to collect herself.

After a sleepless morning spent imagining Lucius on the couch, knowing he was so close and that he was aroused, and that he wanted her—or so he kept saying—her resistance level had sunk pretty low. Seeing him dressed in nothing but shorts, with a lot of bare skin and firm muscle and sexy hair showing, made it nigh on impossible to keep her attention on his face.

'Course, she'd already taken her time looking at him before leaving the apartment that morning. Luckily, he'd slept through her thorough and intense scrutiny of his body.

Only Lucius could look as powerful and imposing in sleep as he did awake. Sure, the lines of his face had relaxed in slumber, but his muscles remained defined, as did his strength and capability.

He'd sprawled out on his back, stretching his big body along the length of the couch. One arm rested above his head, the other hung off the side. His right leg was bent at the knee, and the sheet had barely draped his lap to preserve his near-nonexistent modesty.

His tousled blond hair contrasted with darker body hair; he was just hairy enough to make her mouth go dry. His relaxed hands, deep breathing, and unconscious state hadn't lessened his impact on her system, but at least he hadn't stared at her with those intense green eyes—as he did now.

Bethany shivered and dashed from his apartment, paying no mind to the catcalls and bawdy suggestions from the other women as she flew through the living room. She crossed the hall, stepped over the threshold into Marci's place, and turned to shut the door.

Lucius's hand flattened against it, keeping it open.

Heart shooting into her throat, Bethany yelped in surprise.

He stood right there, in the way, hulking over her, his expression hot and suggestive and determined.

He stared down at her.

She could do no more than stare back.

Taking one step in, he murmured, "I figured I might as well follow along and collect my things."

The words were innocuous enough, but oh, the way he said them, and the way he looked at her while saying them.

He hadn't even touched her yet, and she felt overwhelmed. "Oh boy."

"Deep breaths, honey." He didn't change expressions, except that something bright and hot lit his eyes. "It'll help."

She doubted that.

Releasing the door, he put his hands on her shoulders and eased her back so he could fully enter the apartment.

"Take your time," her sister called, and then she shut the door to Lucius's place, giving them a modicum of privacy that Bethany hadn't requested.

Did Marci hope to play matchmaker? Did she approve of Lucius? Of course she did. Hadn't she been singing his praises for months?

Bethany had feared that, despite her protestations, Marci liked him for herself. But would she throw them together if that was the case? And what about Lucius? Did he hope to use her for a substitute because of Marci's disinterest?

Bethany didn't know what to do. Flee back across the hall—or brazen it out?

Lucius quietly shut the door while keeping all the bone-melting force of his attention on her. "There's definitely something between us."

"Space." She couldn't pull her gaze away from his. "Let's leave it there."

"All right." His agreement surprised her, until he added, "You have to know I won't ever push you."

What a joke. He pushed her all the time. His mere presence pushed her—almost over the edge—but he verbally baited her, too, and taunted her and harassed her. She couldn't help but laugh, and said, "Ha!" with as much sarcasm as she could muster.

His hand lifted, brushed against her cheek. "I admit, I enjoy teasing you, but if you ever flat-out tell me to get lost, I will. I won't want to. And it won't be easy, because I care about you. But no is no in my book."

He waited, but damn it, she couldn't quite squeeze the denial out of her throat.

"You're not making this any easier, Bethany. Right now, I'm dying to kiss you. And I'm hard again."

She started to look but he caught her chin and kept her gaze on his.

His brows came down in seriousness. "My job is really tough."

What did his job have to do with this particular moment? "I'm sure it is."

"It's one of the reasons I have trouble with relationships." His shoulder rolled. "Not many women can handle it."

She said, "Wimps," before she thought better of it. Then, looking for some errant humor, she added, "You want tough, you should try being secretary of a middle school. You know, most detentions, suspensions, and expulsions happen during the early teen years. Boys sprout hair and horns at about the same time. The girls all become drama queens. The teachers start going crazy, and the parents—"

"I need to kiss you, Bethany." Lucius turned her so that her back touched the door. Destroying that small bit of space that had meant less than nothing anyway, he leaned down while keeping her chin up with his fingertips. "Tell me you want me to kiss you."

She started to shake her head, but she did want his kiss, and she ended up sort of waggling her head around in a nonsensical way.

Lucius laughed. "Yeah, that's real clear." His mouth brushed hers. Barely there. His hands flattened on the door at either side of her head, his wrists resting on her shoulders. His hips angled in—and she felt all of him.

Her eyes sank shut on a long sigh.

In a rough whisper, he warned, "If you don't kiss me back, I'm stopping."

And then his mouth pressed to hers, warm and firm, and her head spun and she had no choice but to clutch at his broad, hard shoulders. His bare skin was sleek and taut, and so hot.

And holy cow, she'd had no idea a kiss could be so awesome.

If anyone asked her now, she'd happily say that this was her favorite part. Kissing. Tongues and lips, and humid breath . . .

Enthused by her response, Lucius stroked his right hand over her shoulder, spread his fingers wide on her collarbone, and slid down onto her breast with a bold, possessive but gentle hold.

His thumb circled her nipple, once, twice, and her insides did a thrilling flip. Oh yeah. That was her favorite part, by far. Her fingers dug into his back while she went on tiptoe, trying to get closer to him.

"Damn," Lucius muttered, "that's definitely a yes," and he turned his head for a better fit, taking the kiss from seducing to devouring. His tongue sank in, withdrew, moved over her teeth and twined with her tongue.

His hand left her breast and she started to moan a complaint, until both hands cuddled her behind, lifting her, and then his thigh pressed between hers. Somehow her feet all but left the floor and she ended up straddling his leg and the friction was . . . her favorite part.

"Ohmigod."

"Shhh. Let me lock the door."

He fumbled behind her, and she heard the click of the lock falling into place. Cupping his face in trembling hands, she whispered, "This is incredible."

"Not yet—but it will be." He took her mouth again, hard and deep and hungry, all the while keeping her snug against him, nudging her back and forth in a mind-blowing rhythm.

The most amazing pressure began to build, so sharp and sweet she almost couldn't bear it. Freeing her mouth, she tipped her head back and gulped air. Lucius used the moment to taste her throat, licking, sucking lightly, probably leaving a hickey or two, not that she minded at that particular moment.

"Tell me you want me, Bethany, before I explode."

"Oh yeah, you betcha."

He set her back on her feet and attacked the button on her slacks. The long zipper required both his hands, and he groused a complaint. "Damn it, these stupid pants are . . ." They came undone, and because of the generous fit, promptly fell all the way to the floor to bunch up around her ankles.

Lucius stared. "Great pants. Love the pants."

Bethany grinned even as she felt horribly exposed. Lucius never failed to amuse her, to turn her on, to provoke her many senses and emotions.

He put a hand beneath her blouse and opened it over her belly. In gravelly tones, he said, "Have I told you lately how drop-dead gorgeous you are?"

That struck a nerve, upsetting her state of arousal. "I look just like my sister."

"Naw." He angled his fingers downward, and without warning, slid inside her panties.

She squeezed her eyes shut at the shock and thrill of it.

His mouth touched her temple. "On the outside maybe, yeah, you two look alike. But where it counts, you're plenty different."

His fingers cupped her, just that, nothing more, and she wanted to scream with frustration. She couldn't think. His hand felt hot. Hard. So very enticing.

Holding still required great concentration. She wanted to move against him. She wanted him to explore her. "We're . . . identical twins."

"True." She felt his smile against her skin. "But like you said, it's an attitude thing. And honey, I love your attitude." He pressed the heel of his hand against her, right above her mound.

"God, Lucius."

Slow and gentle, using only his fingertips, he parted her lips and pressed one finger between. "Damn, you're wet."

She stuck her face in his shoulder and held on tight. "This is awful."

"It's sexy as hell." He stroked back and forth, spreading her moisture, then up and over her swollen clitoris.

Her whole body trembled and she clenched her fingers on his shoulders. "I . . . I don't believe this."

"Told you so." Urgent and hot, intent on devastation, he

nudged her face up so he could kiss her again, all the while his fingers played with her, circling her, making the pressure build and build.

Something buzzed against her hip, jolting her, and she jumped. Her mind couldn't assimilate the new sensation, but she had no problem understanding Lucius's curse.

Other than the wild thumping of his heart and his fast breaths, he went utterly still.

"Lucius?" she said, and his name sounded like a moan. "What's wrong?" She lifted heavy eyelids and encountered a pained expression on his face. "Lucius?"

His forehead touched hers. "Jesus, I hate to do this."

She gulped. That didn't sound good at all. "This?"

"I have to go."

What? He still had one hand squeezing her butt. He still had his other hand in her panties! She was hot and ready . . . Very ready.

A little desperate, she said, "Please be kidding."

"I am so damn sorry."

All she needed was another minute or two at the most. She'd never had a climax with a man. By herself, yes. But it wasn't the same, not by a long shot. "You can't wait just a few more—"

"I'm sorry. More sorry than you can know." He removed his hand, smoothed her hair back, and stepped away. "Duty calls."

Her panties had dropped down to her knees, her pants around her ankles, her shirt displaced and twisted. She'd all but begged him to stay.

Mortification rippled through her. She stared at him, dumbfounded, lost. "I was so close."

He drew in a breath and every muscle in his body looked painfully taut. Two seconds ticked by, then he growled, "Hold that thought, okay? And trust me—I swear I'll make it up to you." He looked her over, groaned, and turned away in a rush.

Just that easily, he dismissed her from his mind and went into battle mode.

Flummoxed, Bethany watched as he removed the phone and pager from his shorts. He retrieved his jeans and shirt and jerked them on, then made a call. Holding the phone with his shoulder, he sat on the couch to pull on his socks and tie up his boots.

She heard him speaking, something about the "Incident Commander" and the "Command Post"; she even heard the word "barricade," but he didn't say enough for her to piece it all together, not with her brain still sluggish.

He didn't look at her.

She couldn't stop staring at him.

He disconnected the phone and clipped it, and the pager, back to his waistband. As if they hadn't just been very intimately involved, as if he didn't even see her, he nudged her away from the door and walked out without a word, leaving her to untangle her clothes and her emotions before she literally got caught with her pants down.

Through the jumble of confusion and embarrassment, Bethany heard his apartment door open. He said to Marci, "I'm in a situation here. Could you watch Hero until I get home? Eventually he'll be all right by himself, I'm assuming, but right now—"

Marci said, "Wait. Slow down. Where are you going?"

"I have to work. Can you stay with him?"

"Of course I can. It's my pleasure. But what about my sister?"

"She threw me out. Said she had some things to do. Gotta run. Thanks, Marci."

Bethany heard a smooching kiss that had better have been on a forehead or cheek, and then the trotting footsteps as he left the apartment complex.

Threw him out? Well, at least he hadn't told Marci that he'd left her shaking with need. She appreciated his consideration.

Before Marci could catch her in the lie, Bethany pulled up her pants and rushed into the bathroom. She turned on the shower. Cold. She doubted it would help, but what choice did she have? She stripped off her clothes and stepped under the spray, gasping with the shock of it even as it cleared her head.

And then it hit her.

Lucius was on a call, which meant danger with a capital D. Despite the icy water, a rush of heat left her head spinning and her knees weak. Someone might shoot at him. He could be gone for hours. Even days.

She could lose him forever—when she'd yet to really have him.

Suddenly, she understood what he meant about his job being tough. Before kissing him, she'd been able to keep the danger inherent in his work in the peripheral of her mind.

Now everything had changed. Now she had to accept that she cared about him. She would most definitely worry about him. Counting the minutes until he returned would be excruciating.

This was just what she didn't need—more complications.

Four

Lucius returned around midnight, and this time he wasn't in the least sleepy. Hungry, yes. But for Bethany, not food.

He started to go straight to his apartment, but he couldn't make himself do it. Regardless of the time, he wanted to see her. The way he'd left her, on the verge of satisfaction, had plagued him.

After the cracks she'd made about men and disappointing sex, he'd expected some resistance.

He'd expected to have to really work on her.

Instead, she'd all but melted the second he touched her. And remembering that had him ready to melt.

As soon as he'd finished the job, which had been a clusterfuck of the first order, thoughts of her had taken over his brain. The scent of her skin and hair; the scent of her excitement. Her hair was silky, her flesh more so. When his fingers found her sleek and wet . . . Lucius groaned.

No way could he just go to his place and sleep.

Besides, he needed to collect his dog. A good enough reason to disturb women so late at night.

He tapped lightly on the twin's door.

It opened almost immediately. Big blue eyes stared up at

him with concern and caring. A tremulous smile. Tangled brown hair. A very cute housecoat that covered a killer body.

Disappointment washed over him. "Hey, Marci." Why couldn't Bethany have opened the door? Wasn't she concerned and caring, too? "Sorry it's so late." He looked around behind her, but didn't see Bethany anywhere.

While holding the door open for him to enter, Marci asked, "How do you do it?"

"Do what?"

"Tell us apart."

He had no idea. But from jump, he'd always known which woman was which. One set him on fire, and one he just considered cute. "You're different from your sister."

Where the hell was she? And where was his dog?

"But how? Even our parents have had trouble keeping us separate."

He rolled stiff shoulders in a halfhearted shrug. "You're each unique."

"In what way?"

Marci wasn't going to let it go, so he admitted, "I feel different around Bethany."

"Hotter?" Her mouth quirked.

"That's about it." He tweaked her chin. "I see you, and enjoy your company. I see her, and I want to jump her bones."

Marci laughed. "Delighted to hear it."

So he had her on his side? Good to know. "Where is she, by the way?"

"She's at your place. With Hero. She was . . . worried about you and didn't want to go to bed until she knew you were safe. And I see you are." She tipped her head. "But you look wired. Want a cup of coffee or something?"

He'd love one. "I don't want to put you to any bother."

"It's already made. I waited up for you, too. Come on in." She headed for the minuscule kitchen.

"Why'd you wait up?"

"I wanted to talk to you about Bethany."

Hopefully not a lecture on relationships and all that crap. But since he had her alone for a minute, Lucius thought it might be the perfect time to find out more about her irresistible sister, so he agreed.

"All right." He followed her into the kitchen and leaned on the counter that separated the kitchen from the living room. "We can chat over the coffee. But just one cup. No reason to keep Bethany fretting."

"Don't worry about it. She's asleep."

That amused Lucius. "Yeah, sounds like she was pretty frantic with worry." In truth, it relieved him that Bethany wasn't up pacing the floor, wringing her hands the way some of the women he'd dated had done. It only added to his pressure with the job. Knowing Bethany could nod off put his mind at ease on at least one issue.

Marci frowned at him. "She was plenty worried. But it's been a horrendous time for her lately and she's exhausted."

"Do tell." He wanted to know about this bozo who had upset her.

But Marci waved that away. "I went over twenty minutes ago to check on her, and she and Hero are sacked out in that big lounge chair you have." Marci poured fragrant coffee into a mug and set it on the counter in front of him. "You two have a penchant for sleeping on the furniture. I'm beginning to wonder if you'll ever both be in a bed at the same time."

"Count on it." In fact, he planned to have her in his bed, with him, just as soon as he finished his coffee and got the lowdown from Marci.

A smile curled her mouth. "Somehow I knew you'd say

that." The smile vanished. "I think you might be just what she needs."

He knew he needed her, so he hoped she needed him, too. "I'm all ears on this one."

Marci wasted no time diving into her subject. "You're hard-nosed, Lucius. And you're too good-looking, too confident for your own good."

He cocked a brow. "Is that an insult or a compliment?"

"Neither. It's a simple fact that you're a very competent man. Strong. Intelligent. Gorgeous. And very sexy."

Did Bethany feel the same? He hoped so. "Now, Marci, don't make me blush."

"As if that's even possible." She grinned. "The thing is, Bethany hasn't had much experience with guys, and she's had no experience with a guy like you. We're twenty-six. I know why I don't date much. It's too risky when so many people want to expose me for a nutcase. Having a special talent hasn't made it easy."

"People really do get on you about it?" He still thought it a little nutty, too, but he didn't doubt her ability.

For once, her gaze wasn't direct. She toyed with the edge of her coffee cup and her voice dropped. "I don't really blame others. I denied it myself for a long time."

Seeing her uncertainty, Lucius regretted his past teasing remarks. "It's a talent, hon. You should be proud of it."

Her laugh sounded bitter. "At times it feels more like a curse." Her breath shuddered out, and she looked up at him. "When I was a kid, I couldn't bear to walk down the street. I felt the emotional pain of so many animals. A dog chained out to a tree. A cat ignored. A bird locked in a cage. It made me so furious. People take in pets, and many of them make the pet a member of the family. But a lot don't."

Lucius reached for her hand. "People are sometimes idiots."

"And often cruel." She squeezed her eyes shut. "At first,

it was impossible to deal with it. I went into a depression and I cried a lot and my folks got fed up with me." Her eyes opened again. "But not Bethany. She's always been there for me."

Yeah, he figured Bethany for the loyal sort. It was one of the things he adored most about her. "Have you thought about marketing your talent?"

"Right. Like on Jerry Springer? No, thanks. I prefer to help quietly. When I sense that an animal has a problem, I contact the owners and try to help. That way, they can either take my advice or not. I'm not exposing myself. I'm not opening myself to ridicule. Only the believers listen. The others sometimes hang up. I don't want to be a spectacle ever again."

"If I can ever help . . ."

She straightened with determination. "Now there's my perfect lead-in." She gave his hand a squeeze, then released him. "Bethany has been put through hell because of me. All through school she got teased about having a loony sister."

Lucius winced, remembering how he'd said similar things—and Bethany's immediate defense.

"Don't do that, Lucius. Never, not even once, has your teasing felt malicious or mean-spirited. Support—that's all I've ever gotten from you, and I appreciate it. I told Bethany that, so she knows it, too."

"Still . . ."

"There's a man. I knew him as Mitch Tracer, but he told Bethany his name was Michael. He's making her life hell."

Lucius straightened. An alias? He didn't like the sound of that. "This is the ass she used to date before coming here?" No way in hell would he let anyone hurt Bethany.

"He started out by pretending an interest in her, and she liked him enough that she went out on several dates with him. But when she mentioned him to me, I recognized the description. Blond, glasses, nice clothes, and a not-so-nice smile. See, he'd wanted to date me months before. I refused him. He asked too many questions about my work, about animals. I avoid intrusions into my personal life, and he made me uneasy."

"He tried to use Bethany to get close to you?"

She rubbed her forehead. "Unfortunately, it's not the first time it's happened."

"But that doesn't make any sense. No insult intended toward you, hon, but hell, you're twins. What makes you more appealing than her?"

"Nothing. It's just that Bethany is more . . . independent, and that can put some men off. But they see me as an airhead, somehow sweeter and easier than Bethany, and so they come after me."

"That's just idiotic."

She laughed. "Yeah, I know it, but . . . Bethany doesn't. Sometimes, too, they're just trying to get to me because of my ability. They want to expose me, interview me, maybe use my talent for something, but I'm not dumb. I can see through them. So, I don't date much."

Lucius could understand her way of thinking, but he didn't like it. If he ever caught anyone giving Marci a hard time, he'd handle it for her, with or without her permission. "Those are your reasons. What are Bethany's?"

She drew a deep breath, then admitted, "More than once, men have gone to her after I've rejected them."

Damn. That'd be a tough pill for a woman to swallow.

"They act as though we're interchangeable. Can't have first pick? Well, then, they'll take second."

"Shit."

"Exactly."

It felt like the right time to make something perfectly clear, so Lucius leaned forward over the bar and took her hand again. "Far as I'm concerned, Bethany would never be second best. Like I said, you two are different. One isn't better than the other, but one sure as hell affects me differently."

"I believe you, but Bethany has taken to distrusting any guy who knew me first."

Which included him? Smiling, he released her and leaned on the bar. "She wasn't exactly slapping my face earlier today."

"I hoped not. But she hasn't said much about it, and you said she threw you out . . ."

"I got called in for a barricade. Let's just say, the timing sucked."

Appearing delighted, Marci asked, "Interrupted some interesting things, did it?"

Not even for her sister would Lucius kiss and tell. Bethany could share the details as much or as little as she wanted. "Some dip-shit sped his pickup through a residential area, and when a deputy tried to pull him over, he fired a shotgun at the patrol car's window. The deputy wasn't hurt, but soon as he ran the plates, he found some outstanding warrants for possession and trafficking. The truck pulled into a house and the driver disappeared inside."

"He broke into someone's home?"

"Nope. It was his own place. The officer called for backup, and they tried to establish contact with him, but he wouldn't respond. That's when we got called in."

"Does that happen a lot?"

"Often enough that it can make relationships difficult. If I'm in town, then a day off is never guaranteed."

Marci seemed to consider that. "So what happened?"

"We tried the loudspeaker, the phone, we even lobbed some tear gas in there, and still, for over four hours, the guy wouldn't come out or make contact. So we stormed the place."

"Oh my God. Was anyone hurt?"

Lucius rubbed the back of his neck, remembering. He

had a well-trained team, and they always wore the appropriate protective gear, but that only offered so much security.

"As soon as we hit the door, we encountered gunfire. One of my men got shot in the knee, another in the hip."

Her hand covered her mouth. "You got the man responsible?"

He nodded, pissed off all over again. "I shot the idiot in the hand, and we were finally able to subdue and arrest him."

"The others will be okay?"

"Last I saw them at the hospital, they were patched up and flirting with the nurses." Thank God, SWAT knew how to keep a cool head in chaotic situations.

Marci worried her bottom lip with her teeth. "You could have been shot, too."

"I wasn't." He finished off his coffee. With Marci now distracted from the intimate details of his time with Bethany, he put her back on track.

"Tell me everything you know about Michael Tracer."

"There isn't that much to tell." She sipped her coffee, thinking for a moment. "I met him shortly before I left the area where Bethany still lived, right before I moved in here. I didn't like Mitch or Michael or whatever his name is, so even though he continued to call and ask me out, I didn't tell him I was leaving, and I sure didn't tell him where I'd be going."

"He knew about Bethany?"

"Most everyone in town knew us both, so it wouldn't be a stretch to think he'd quickly piece it together. Twins stand out, especially when one of the twins is known as a fruitcake."

It angered him to think of anyone calling Marci names. "This was the town where you grew up?"

"Yes, and I shouldn't sound so bitter. I had friends there. It wasn't all bad. But after Mom and Dad retired to Arizona . . . well, there didn't seem to be enough reason to stay." She closed her eyes, looking pained. "But I should have stayed for Bethany."

It sounded selfish, even to his own ears, but Lucius said, "I'm glad you didn't. If you hadn't moved here, I never would have met her."

Her lashes lifted and she smiled. "That's a nice way to look at it." Then she nibbled on her lip some more. "Michael wasn't local. He just showed up one day. He told me he was in real estate, but he's probably a reporter or some whack job hoping to write the next great exposé. That's the only reason I can think of to explain why he'd be stalking Bethany now."

A dangerous tide of rage rolled through Lucius. "Define stalking."

"Now Lucius, don't look like that. He hasn't done anything threatening. Nothing dangerous. It's just that he won't leave her alone, even now that she knows he was lying. He kept calling her, and he started showing up at her house. Once he even peeked in the windows, like he knew she was home and refusing to answer the door."

"Son of a bitch."

"At first, Bethany tried ignoring him, but . . . he makes her as nervous as he made me, and that's enough for me to worry."

It was enough for him to worry, too. "Police?"

"When Bethany called them, a very nice officer offered to talk to Michael, but they can't find him. The address Bethany had was bogus. Maybe both the names we have are bogus, too. Who knows?"

"When did she last hear from him?"

"The first night she came here, he kept calling her cell

phone until she turned it off. When she checked in the morning, he'd filled her mailbox. I don't think she's turned it back on since then."

"I want to hear the calls."

"I think they were personal—you know, sort of embarrassing stuff. She might not be keen on sharing them with you. But talk to her about it. She's not unreasonable where her and my safety is concerned."

Lucius left the stool with a purpose. "Thanks. I think I'll do that right now." The sooner he got a handle on the jerk harassing Bethany, the better he'd feel.

Marci stopped him by coming around the bar and taking his arm.

"Just so you know . . . Bethany's looking for the whole package, not just a good time."

That gave Lucius pause. He stared down at Marci—and wondered how anyone could consider her a better catch than Bethany. "By the whole package, you mean what? Marriage and kids and all that?" The idea didn't seem too bad to him. "I have to tell you, marriage to a cop isn't easy, and SWAT is especially—"

"I mean love."

"Oh." His heart beat a little too fast, mostly because he already knew he loved her, but he had no idea how Bethany really felt. She'd softened a lot, and now that he understood her reserve, he intended to get past it.

"I'm not going to lecture you on relationships, Lucius, so relax. Bethany's a big girl and she can take care of herself where men are concerned."

"Stalkers aside."

"Stalkers aside, yes. But as a friend, I want you to know that she's vulnerable right now. Because of Michael, she's turned her life upside down, mostly to protect me. Just as I feel guilty that Michael contacted her to get to me, she worries that she might have said or done something to encourage him in that regard. She's given up her job, her home—"

Lucius caught her shoulders in a gentle squeeze. "I plan to look out for both of you, so don't worry about it, okay?" He had plenty of contacts who would help him find Michael or Mitch or whatever name he used. He'd see to it that the man got out of their lives, pronto.

Marci sighed. "That's all well and good, but I don't want to see her deliberately hurt. If you hurt her, I'd have to move out of here, and that'd just suck."

Lucius laughed. "Well, I certainly don't want to start looking for a new tenant, either." On impulse, he cupped Marci's face. "Thanks for everything, hon. The relationship advice, the insight on your maddening sister, and the info on Michael. I appreciate it."

He pulled Marci into his arms for a tight hug—and the apartment door opened behind them.

With Marci still snagged up close, Lucius turned and found Bethany standing there, Hero at her side. She looked sleepy and rumpled and . . . devastated. But only for a second or two.

Then she looked enraged.

Five

Bethany wanted to shout from the hurt exploding inside her. Seeing Lucius wrapped around her sister destroyed her composure, but pride kept her tone calm and icily polite.

She found a smirking, sarcastic smile. "Come on, Hero. It looks like we've interrupted . . . something."

With that parting shot, she walked off. She started to go back into Lucius's apartment, but hey, it was his apartment, which meant he'd surely just walk in behind her. In mid-step, she switched course and headed for the front door. With his dog. Which only served him right.

Where she'd go, she had no idea, but she sure as heck didn't intend to stay. She didn't blame her sister; Marci couldn't help it that men preferred her. And Marci didn't know how Bethany felt about him; she hadn't even admitted it to herself until that day. He was a great catch. No woman could resist him.

The bastard.

Marci and Lucius both came into the hall at the same time. They were both fast explaining. She turned to her sister. "It's all right, Marci," she said, all magnanimous and forgiving. A saint, even. She didn't look at Lucius. "I understand."

"The hell you do," Lucius shouted.

Upstairs, Devine's door opened, and a second later, so did Tyra's. "What's going on?" Devine yelled down.

"Bethany's being an ass," Lucius replied.

That stopped Bethany in her tracks. She pivoted around and stomped back to him. Hero trotted along beside her.

When she reached him, she opened her mouth to blast him with invective—and he squashed her up tight against his chest and planted a hard, wet one on her.

Naturally, she resisted . . . for about three seconds. Then her knees went weak.

"There you go," Marci said with satisfaction. And while Lucius continued to rape her mouth in a most delicious and convincing way, in front of God and tenants alike, Marci added, "He has no interest in me, Bethany. Trust me on this. I wouldn't lie to you. He's a good man, so I hope you don't blow it."

Lucius lifted away a scant millimeter. "I want you. Not her. Not anyone else." He kissed her again before she could think of anything to say to that.

Amanda stepped into the hall. "Oh my. Well, why didn't anyone tell me this was happening?"

Only Esther slept on, but then, it was well known that very little could rouse Esther out of her bed.

"Come to my place," Lucius whispered against her lips. "I've missed you, and we have unfinished business to see to."

Little sparks ignited deep in her belly. "You're not interested in Marci?"

His forehead touched hers and he smiled. "How could I be, when there's you?"

"Oh." That sounded pretty sincere.

Hands cupping her face, he held her gaze. "My only interest in Marci is that she's your sister, so a part of your life. She's important to you, so that makes her important to me. But other than a brotherly peck or friendly hug, I have no desire to touch her. Ever."

Now that she thought about it, what she'd seen had been rather perfunctory. Sort of a friendly snuggle, not a heated embrace. "I see." She was starting to feel a little foolish for overreacting.

"You, on the other hand, are impossible to resist."

Her heart soared. "Okay."

In the next instant, he had her hustling along and she said, "Wait."

Vibrating with frustration and sexual energy, he halted. "What?"

"Hero . . ."

"Is coming with us. He's mine, too, and I haven't spent enough time with him."

He's mine, too. Some indefinable emotion expanded within Bethany, making her heart feel full, her limbs weak. Her lips curled into a vague smile. "He needs to make a trip outside first. That's what I was doing when I walked in on you two."

Lucius smiled back at her. "We'll walk him out together." He looked around at their audience, then dismissed them all with a friendly, "Good night."

Women of varying ages grinned. "Good night, Luscious," they said in near unison, making Bethany laugh.

Arm in arm, they stepped out front. Lucius held Hero's leash while the dog sniffed several bushes, a telephone pole, and a scraggly patch of grass until he found just the right spot.

"It's a beautiful night," Bethany said, staring up at the stars.

"It's hot and humid and perfect," Lucius agreed. He kissed her forehead, the bridge of her nose, and she could feel his anticipation, which made her feel it, too. When the dog came over and sat on his foot, Lucius patted his neck. "What more could a man want?"

Feeling wicked, Bethany said, "Well, I don't know about man, but a woman could want a continuance of that little business from the afternoon."

"Little business?"

She grinned, knowing she'd never been so happy before. "Incomplete business? Is that better?"

"Not really." He grew serious, tipping up her chin and kissing her gently. "I'll make it perfect. I promise."

God, she loved him. "It already is."

That seemed to set him off, and once again, he hustled her along. Once inside, he left her standing there while he locked the doors and fetched a fluffy blanket for Hero, which he spread out on the couch.

The dog stretched, looked at them both, then bounded up to circle the bedding before dropping with a lusty sigh.

"He's a good dog, isn't he?" Lucius remarked, giving Hero a few strokes along his back.

"He's a wonderful dog. Very easy and well-mannered and gentle."

That made Lucius smile. He sat at the edge of the couch by the dog's feet and continued to stroke him. "He wasn't gentle when he attacked Steve Seeder. Somehow, he knew things weren't right. He knew Steve's mother was in danger and he took care of it." Lucius glanced up at Bethany. "It still amazes me. He went from being timid to ferocious, then back to timid. He would have just crept away if I hadn't stopped him, like he figured his job was done and no one needed him anymore."

Bethany wondered at his patience now, when moments before he'd been so anxious. "Animals have some psychic powers—did you know that?"

He grinned, looking so handsome that she felt like dragging him off to the bedroom right then. "Like your sister, you mean?"

Bethany shrugged. "I'm not quite sure how they do it, but it's been proven that animals respond to us, just as we respond to them. They sense things. You've made Hero feel welcome, so he's relaxed a lot. He still gets jumpy at times, whenever he's uncertain, but that'll fade with time."

Sitting at the head of the couch, she, too, stroked the dog. "It's been proven that animals help people with high blood pressure to lower their systolic and diastolic levels. They bring a calming effect. Cardiac patients usually live longer when they own pets, the elderly stay less depressed, handicapped children, and children of abuse, will respond to animals when humans can't reach them."

He seemed fascinated. Using that low, melodic voice that never failed to give her shivers, he whispered, "Makes you wonder how anyone could ever mistreat them, doesn't it?"

Half asleep, Hero nuzzled his nose into Bethany's hand, telling her how much he enjoyed the attention. "It destroys Marci when she knows an animal has been mistreated. She's helped so many, but it's never enough."

"It leaves her vulnerable, doesn't it?"

His insight didn't surprise her; Lucius was a very astute man. "I remember the most recent incident. A woman was about to marry a man without knowing that he was mean and nasty to her dog when she wasn't around. The dog, poor thing, was losing weight and sort of . . . fading away."

"He felt betrayed."

"Yes." She bent to hug Hero, wishing all dogs could find a good home. "Marci picked up on it, and she contacted the woman."

"I hoped she kicked the sorry son of a bitch to the curb."

"She did. From the very beginning, she believed Marci. Especially when the dog, a mid-sized mutt, took to her. She called Marci the very next day, saying she'd confronted the guy, and although he denied it, she could see her dog was terrified of him. The wedding was called off, and now the dog is doing great."

Lucius pushed to his feet and reached for Bethany's hand. "Both you and your sister are pretty remarkable, you know that?"

"I know Marci is." She allowed him to pull her up and into his arms. "But I'm just me." As a child, she'd been almost jealous of Marci's abilities because, even though much of the attention was negative, it was still a lot more than she received. She'd outgrown that, and accepted her mediocrity.

"I think you're the most amazing, caring, loyal, and gentle woman I know."

"Marci is—"

"A very nice person with an awesome talent, but she doesn't have your gumption and fire." He started for the bedroom, towing her along. "Like you said, it's an attitude thing."

"Are you going to keep teasing me about that?"

He tugged her past the bedroom door, then closed it and caged her there, angling his body in so that his arms framed her shoulders and his hips nestled against hers. "When you're right, you're right. I love your attitude."

Love. Hearing that particular word nearly sent her heart through her rib cage. "Show me."

"Yes, ma'am. Now where were we? No—wait. I remember. We were right about—" His hand slid past the waistband of her shorts, then inside her shorts and inside her panties. Very softly, he whispered, "Here."

Head back against the door, Bethany breathed, "Yeah, that seems about right."

Lucius kissed her, and then kept on kissing her while he worked her T-shirt up to her chin. He lifted his head and stared down at her breasts. "Damn."

Bethany held her breath, but let it out in a groan when he bent to her, closed his mouth around one nipple, and suckled softly. She waited for him to move on to the next step, to take her to the bed, but he didn't. He seemed content to keep her pinned against the door while he drove her a little crazy with lust.

"Lucius . . ."

He switched to her other breast, circling her nipple with his tongue, gently closing his teeth over the very tip, tugging.

"Oh God."

One long finger pushed inside her. Bethany couldn't keep still. She felt her hips moving, grinding against his hand, blindly seeking the pleasure. He brought his thumb into play, lifted his eyes to watch her face, and she came with a wrenching moan, her eyes squeezed shut, her teeth clenched, her fingers gripping tight onto his shoulders.

It seemed an eternity before she collected herself and realized that his hands were now repositioned, one on her bottom to support her, another on her breast. She got her eyes open, and when she did, it was to see Lucius eyeing her with a slight smile.

She flushed.

His grin widened. "You're beautiful."

"I'm a little embarrassed. That is, I've never . . . well, climaxed like that."

"S'that right? Well, honey, plan on being real embarrassed tonight, okay?" He lifted her and moved her to the bed, laying her crosswise over the mattress, so that her legs hung over the side. He came down beside her instead of atop her. "Now, let's get these clothes off you."

"Okay." She lifted her hips and pushed her shorts and panties down to her knees. Lucius skimmed them the rest of the way off, then tossed them onto a chair in his room. He whisked her T-shirt up and over her head. With the fingers of one hand spread wide, he stroked her from her shoulders to her hip and everywhere in between.

Shyly, a little uncertain, Bethany told him, "I'm ready."

"I'm not."

She raised herself up and stared down at the erection pressing hard against his jeans. "Yes, you are."

"Not yet."

Understanding, she said, "You don't have to do this."

One brow lifted. Rather than look at her face, he caught her knee and opened her legs a little. "This?"

"Pay so much attention to me."

The side of his mouth quirked. "I love looking at you and touching you."

"But . . ." She regretted her earlier jibes against men and lovemaking because now he felt obliged to spend extra time on her. "I know you want to . . . well, you know."

"Fuck you? Get inside you? Get my rocks off?" Finally, he looked at her face, but only for a brief glimpse. "Yeah, I do. And I will. But let me enjoy myself first, okay? I've been thinking about this for a really long time."

"You aren't . . . anxious?" Every guy she'd ever known had been anxious. A kiss, a fondle, and they were ready to get it over with.

As if he'd known her thoughts, he said, "Don't compare me to other men, babe, okay?" While saying that, he pushed up and off the bed. Reaching back, he caught a fistful of his shirt and jerked it over his head. Next, he removed his phone and pager and placed them on the dresser behind him, then shucked off his jeans and underwear.

Bethany stared. "Wow."

He stood there, giving her a chance to look while he parted her knees farther. His chest expanded on deep breaths. "Trust me, I'm anxious."

Her voice almost deserted her. "Then . . ."

He knelt down—between her now widespread legs.

"Oh, uh . . ."

"Shhh." Hot lips and a hotter tongue trailed up the inside of her right thigh. "Damn, you smell good."

Bethany's head dropped back on the mattress. She stared at the ceiling, so rigid with anticipation that when his mouth touched between her legs, she almost jumped out of her skin.

"Easy," he whispered, and with his big hands caging her pelvis, he used his thumbs to part her, leaving her fully exposed. His tongue licked over her, in her. She felt his breath, the rub of his whiskery jaw on her tender inner thighs. She felt so much, all of it incredible and mind-blowing.

Never had she imagined anything like it. "Lucius," she practically yelled.

"Yeah?" He drew on her clitoris, flicked with his tongue, and she knew she would climax again.

"This is my favorite part."

Did she hear him chuckle? She wasn't certain, not with the blood rushing through her veins and her heartbeat sounding in her ears. Her whole body throbbed with her orgasm, leaving her utterly spent.

She was still buzzing when Lucius put a light kiss on her mouth. That got her eyes opened.

"Hey," he whispered. And then he slid into her. "I already put on a condom," he told her. "All you have to do is relax."

Relax? She couldn't feel her bones, she was so relaxed. But the full, delicious sensation of having him inside her quickly changed that.

Propped on his forearms, watching her intently, Lucius thrust slow and deep, in and out. He was patience personified, although dark color showed on his cheekbones and his eyes glittered brightly. "You wanna come again? Maybe with me, this time?"

Could a man be more amazing? "Oh, Lucius."

He smiled that amazing smile. "Is that a yes?"

"I don't think I can."

He adjusted, moving one hand beneath her derriere, tilting her hips up, sinking deeper.

She gasped.

Satisfied, he rumbled, "I think you can."

He lowered his head and kissed her, stealing what little breath she had so that her head buzzed and her body quivered with sensation. The tension built, tighter this time, almost painfully. He began thrusting faster, harder, rocking the bed and groaning. His mouth ate at hers, voracious, his tongue thrusting in and out—and everything exploded.

Just as she felt herself coming, he stiffened, lifting his mouth away to growl out his release while keeping himself buried deep inside her.

As the pleasure faded, he collapsed against her, breathing hard, his body damp with sweat.

Despite her state of euphoria, Bethany grinned. "Lucius?" she asked breathlessly.

"Yeah?"

"I'm changing my mind."

He pushed up to look at her, his expression dark. "About what?"

"My favorite part." She touched his beloved face. "I think that last one has to be it."

Six

Hero's wet nose, poking over the side of the bed, woke Bethany the following morning. "Hey, you," she said to the dog while stretching awake. "Where's your lord and master?"

The dog barked and wagged his tail, urging her to leave the bed. She pulled on Lucius's oversized T-shirt and padded barefoot and bare-bottomed out of the bedroom.

Lucius was nowhere to be found, but she located a note on the kitchen counter.

"Gone for donuts. The dog's been out and the coffee is fresh. Stay in bed. I won't be long."

She covered her mouth and giggled, then hugged herself. Last night had been . . . incredible. The stuff of dreams.

Hopefully, the start of forever.

Lucius hadn't said anything about that, but he'd been so tender, so sweet, she couldn't help but start planning.

The dog whined and scratched at the front door.

"So Lucius took you out, but once wasn't enough? Okay, then. Let me throw on some shorts and get your leash."

The dog scratched again, more anxious, making Bethany

curious. "What is it? Is someone out there?" Was Lucius back already?

She put her eye to the peephole. A man stood in front of her sister's door, checking a notepad and the address of the apartment.

Even from the back, she recognized Michael Tracer.

Her stomach bottomed out and her skin went clammy. How had he found her? Hero leaned against her side, offering silent comfort. Marci would be alone, but she wasn't. The dog would protect her.

Before her sister could be disturbed, Bethany jerked Lucius's door open. Trying for a gentle smile that wouldn't look too false, she said, "Mitch. What are you doing here?"

He turned, looked her over, and deep satisfaction settled into his features. "Marci. At last, I've found you."

Hero lurched out past her, snarling, bunching for an attack. Bethany was ready to let the dog attack, until Michael pulled out a gun.

Staring at the dog, he said, "Restrain that beast or he's dead."

"No!" Bethany quickly caught Hero's collar. "Easy, Hero. It's okay."

Glancing around in nervousness, Michael hissed, "Get back inside, right now, before someone hears us."

Having no choice, Bethany held onto Hero's collar, kept her gaze on Michael, and backed into Lucius's apartment. As long as Michael thought she was her sister, she might be able to juggle things to her advantage.

A hand on her shoulder shoved her the rest of the way inside and the door shut behind her. Going to her knees, Bethany hugged Hero close, but the dog refused to be placated. She could barely restrain him.

"Shut him up, Marci, or I will. I mean it."

What to do, what to do?

Maintaining a tight grip on the dog's collar, Bethany surged back to her feet and snatched up the keys from the wall hook. "Let me put him next door. My sister, Bethany, lives there. She watches the dog sometimes, so she won't think anything of it if he's there."

His expression brightened. "I'd love to get the two of you together." A slick, smarmy smile appeared. "It's a favorite fantasy of mine."

Bethany shuddered in revulsion. "She's not home right now." *Please, Marci, don't make a liar out of me. Stay in bed just a little longer.*

"I could shut up the dog for good."

Stark fear squeezed her lungs. "But someone might hear you. There's no reason to do that. You want to talk to me, right? Why else would you have come looking for me?"

"Yeah, I'm going to talk to you." His grin promised awful things, further rattling her composure.

Bethany concentrated on breathing. "Listen to me, Mitch. I can put the dog next door. He'll be out of the way—and we'll be alone. Please." *And when Lucius returned, he'd take care of everything. He'd know what to do.*

Michael chewed over her suggestion, waffling between agreement and his hatred of animals, but finally, to her relief, nodded. "Fine. Get rid of him. But don't you dare try to run away from me. If you do, I swear I'll make you sorry—starting with killing the damn dog."

"I promise." With the gun trained on her and Hero fighting her, Bethany went across the hall and unlocked the door. Hero resisted, but she managed to get him inside without too much noise. Thank God, Marci didn't appear in the doorway.

Tight fingers clamped around her arm and Michael yanked her back into Lucius's apartment. He spun her around and smacked her up against the wall, the gun aimed at her chest. "Now, bitch, you'll pay."

Bethany was so terrified that nausea crawled up her

throat, and she almost barfed on him. She swallowed several times until she could get her voice to work. "For . . . for what?"

"Like you don't know."

She shook her head. "I don't."

"Then let me clue you in." He stepped back, and she sucked in a much-needed breath. "I had things all planned out. I had a well-to-do wife lined up who would have given me everything I ever wanted. But you went and made up some damn story about me mistreating her stupid mutt."

Good God. Bethany blinked hard and fast. "You . . ." She couldn't get any other words out.

"That's right. I'm the one you tattled on. Like that stupid mutt meant anything. It was just a damned dog, and not even a purebred."

Her own surge of anger gave her voice strength. "Dogs are living, breathing creatures! They have feelings and—"

His raised fist halted her tirade. Gasping, Bethany cowered back, but no strike came.

"Oh, no," he said, his tone singsong-gentle as he lowered his arm. "It won't be that easy. You won't get me to lose control."

Far as she could tell, he'd lost control a long time ago. Cautiously, she lowered her arms. "What are you going to do?"

"First I'm going to ruin your life the way you ruined mine. I'm going to expose you for the fraud you are. Then . . ." He laughed. "I'm going to get rid of you. But don't worry. It'll be painless. I promise."

Yep, that'd definitely ruin her life. The cruel idiot. The only thing Bethany could think to do was keep him talking until Lucius returned. "How . . . how are you going to expose me?"

"You're going to tell me how you do it, how you get people to believe you're a psychic. You're going to tell me about some of the others you've duped. As your last boyfriend—"

"You were never my boyfriend."

"No one else knows that."

"Bethany does."

"She knows that I wanted you first. That's all. What can she say? That she was second choice?" He laughed. "You'll tell me everything, and in my grief over your death, I'll let it leak to the press. You'll be confirmed as a fraud, in life and in death." He grabbed a bar stool and pulled it around to face her, then seated himself, legs crossed, arms propped loosely with the gun barrel toward her. "Spill it, Marci. I want to know everything."

"Right." A trained SWAT member would know how to handle a lunatic like Michael. She had to believe that. Because if anything happened to Lucius, she'd never forgive herself. "Should I start by sharing a few stories?"

Lucius had spent the time walking to and from the bakery in blissful euphoria. He was in love. And unless Bethany was damn good at deception, she cared a lot about him, too. Soon as he woke her up with coffee and sweets, he'd tell her how he felt.

Then he'd propose.

He felt so good, he almost wanted to whistle.

But the second he turned the block and could see the apartment complex, he sensed a problem. He didn't understand it, but alarm bells started going off in his head, and without another thought, he broke into a trot.

He was still several yards away when he saw Marci on the narrow balcony outside her apartment. She had Hero with her.

Her gaze met his and she lifted one finger to her mouth, warning him to silence while frantically signaling him close.

The urge to go straight to his place, to skip the subterfuge and assure himself of Bethany's safety, burned throughout him. But he had to trust Marci, because he knew she loved her sister.

As he neared, he saw the tears in Marci's eyes.

"Lucius," she whispered, "thank God you're here."

He dropped the stupid donuts, grasped the balcony railing, and vaulted himself up the few feet to join her. "What's happened? Where's Bethany?"

She shook her head. "I heard some noise and woke up and Hero was here. He's really upset, something about there being a man with Bethany at your place. She had to have shoved Hero over here for a reason, so I didn't want to knock on the door. Instead, I called your apartment. The first time she didn't pick up. But I called back and she answered . . . as me."

Lucius tangled a hand in his hair. "She's impersonating you?"

Marci nodded. "Which probably means—"

"Michael Tracer has found her, and she hopes to protect you."

"She wouldn't talk to me. She only said that you weren't home and she was busy. Then she hung up." Marci hugged herself, trying to contain her tremors. "I'm so afraid."

Lucius jerked the phone from his waistband and put in a call. Backup would arrive in less than ten minutes, but he couldn't wait that long. "Listen to me, Marci. Do not get hysterical. I need you with me. Do you understand?"

She swallowed hard, and straightened her back. In a calmer voice, she said, "What can I do?"

"I'm going to go around back and climb in the bedroom window." Lucius paced as he formulated the plan. "I need you to make a ruckus in the hallway—you know, cause a distraction. Maybe take Hero out or something, but make sure he's on his leash. And if the door to my apartment

starts to open, get the hell out of there. I don't want the bastard to have two hostages, understand?"

"Yes."

"I'm going to come up behind him. Try not to worry. I
won't let him hurt her."

She grabbed his hands, and the strength of her grip
stunned him. "Promise me, Lucius."

"I promise. Wait two minutes. That'll give me time to
grab some gear from my truck."

"What gear?"

"My sniper rifle, for one thing."

Her eyes rounded. "You keep a sniper rifle in—"

"I keep all my gear locked in my truck." He cupped her
cheek. "You're okay?"

"Yes."

"Be careful, Marci. Bethany will never forgive me if anything happens to you."

"And vice versa." She gave him a shove. "Now go. Show
me what a badass SWAT guy can do."

Lucius didn't grin, but he did go back over the balcony
railing and hit the ground running. Thank God his truck
was in the back lot rather than out front, where someone
might see him. Still, he used caution as he unlocked the
truck and took out what he'd need.

Getting in the back window of his apartment might have
been tricky except that he'd done it before, when he'd accidentally locked himself out when he'd first bought the place.

The building sat on a slight incline, so while they had
balconies out front, at the side, the windows could be
reached with a little stretch.

With the Blaser LRS2 slung over his shoulder, he hefted
himself up, pried the window open, and after one quick
glance inside, slithered silently over the sill. Crouching down,
he crept across the floor to the open bedroom door.

He could barely see Bethany as she plastered herself against the door, speaking in a trembling monotone about dogs and psychic ability. He couldn't see Tracer, but judging by the direction of Bethany's gaze, Lucius knew he had to be positioned in front of her, probably with a weapon trained on her.

More than anything, Lucius wanted to take him apart. It wasn't easy, but he utilized patience, waiting for Marci's part.

Then it happened. From one second to the next, Hero barked furiously in the hallway, no doubt wanting in to protect Bethany. Marci called to him loudly, causing all the racket Lucius asked for.

A man's voice said, "What the fuck?" and then he was there, in plain sight, shoving Bethany aside and putting his eye to the peephole.

Lucius saw the gun gripped in his hand. He saw Michael stiffen and spin around to face Bethany. "You little lying bitch! You're Bethany, aren't you?"

Michael started to raise his gun hand—and Lucius put a bullet clean through his shoulder.

With a scream, Michael fell back against the door, splattering blood. His arm went limp from the wound.

In a few long strides, Lucius reached him. He retrieved the weapon, spared a quick glance for Bethany, who looked shaken but fine, and then he secured the scene—just as he'd always been taught to do.

"You're sure you're okay?" Lucius asked her for the umpteenth time.

Bethany curled in closer to his right side. She wore a pair of his shorts with his tee. The shorts read: *Monkeys steal my underwear while I sleep*. He wasn't sure Bethany had noticed.

Everyone else had.

"I'm okay." But she continued to tremble, so he tightened his hold, kissed her hair, and allowed others to handle everything.

On his left side, Marci leaned into him, too. Like her sister, she was still pretty shook up, so Lucius hugged her.

Hero sat before them, keeping them all three in his sights while paramedics worked over Michael, and officers helped themselves to coffee.

Lucius's team members kept looking at him—and grinning. But hell, with two gorgeous twins plastered to him, he could have been in a porn video. What red-blooded male wouldn't stare?

He kissed Bethany again, making sure everyone knew she was more than a mere conquest. Then, to seal the deal, he asked, "Will you marry me?"

Her head shot off his shoulder and she stared at him. "What?"

"I love you. I want to marry you."

His men hooted and raised their coffee cups in a salute.

Marci chuckled and finally freed herself from his hold. "This is wonderful." Then, to her wide-eyed sister, "Just say yes, Bethany."

Bethany looked ready to hyperventilate, but she nodded. "I do love you."

"I know. I love you, too. And unless I stake a claim right now, one of my guys is going to start getting ideas and I'll have to set him straight and there'll be more damage to my apartment."

One man laughed. Two snorted in challenge. Another said, "I just got the blood off your door. You make another mess and you can damn well clean it yourself."

Marci glanced at the other men, all of whom watched her from across the room. She chuckled. "They're a cute bunch. All single?"

"Yeah." And then, loud enough for them to hear, Lucius

said, "Of course they're single. What woman in her right mind would have them?"

There was more good-natured ribbing back and forth as the men touted their dubious qualities and flexed some outrageous muscle until finally, almost an hour later, everyone left the apartment and Lucius was alone with Bethany, Marci, and his dog.

Holding Bethany close, Lucius said, "I'd suggest we go out to dinner to celebrate, but I don't want to leave Hero alone."

Marci hugged the dog and sighed. "You are the most perfect man, Sergeant Lucius Ryder. I'm so glad you love my sister."

"I'm so glad she loves me back."

Bethany grinned. "You know, sis, if you'd give a guy a chance, we could both settle into marital bliss together."

"A double wedding would be nice," Lucius added.

Marci shook her head and backed up three steps. "No way. I'm happy single. Besides, what guy would want to hook up with a fruitcake like me?"

Both Bethany and Lucius quickly objected to that description.

"I appreciate the support, guys, I really do. But let's face it—I'm an oddity."

Lucius thought about it, then winked. "Well, like I said about the guys on my team, no woman in her right mind would want any of them. But a woman with an exceptional mind like yours . . ."

Marci balked. "Oh no, you don't. You will not play matchmaker, Lucius." She backed up until she reached the door. "I mean it. Now I'm sure you two have things to talk about, so I'll leave you to it."

The second she left, Bethany turned her face up to Lucius. "She's not happy, no matter what she says."

"Don't worry about it, hon. Given the way my guys were

eyeing her, I won't have to play matchmaker. I'm betting they'll be calling on her tonight at the latest."

"You really think so?"

"Absolutely. SWAT guys are astute. We know a good thing when we see it." He pulled her onto his lap, then stood with her held in his arms.

"Where are we going?"

On his way out of the room, he said, "To see if I can find another favorite part for you." He kissed her, a tickling kiss because he smiled. "I'm thinking there might be dozens you aren't even aware of yet."

Giving in to her own grin, Bethany said, "You know, you could be right."

Hero sighed, turned a circle, and plopped down to sleep, secure that he now had a very happy home.

It's About
Time

Erin McCarthy

One

It was a good thing Trish never intended to get married, because from what she could tell of the male population as a whole, they were mostly idiots and not worth the reception expense.

She'd been stood up again.

How hard could it have been for Brad to call her midday when he had known she was at work and leave a wimpy cancellation on her home voice mail?

A lot less difficult than sitting by himself in a restaurant for an hour waiting for a date who never came, which was what she had just done.

Sighing, she pushed the door open and stepped into Ryan's Pub, wondering what it was about her that made men smile and promise things they never intended to deliver. While she had no desire to wade into matrimony despite her friends' recent success with it, she would still enjoy a little companionship. Someone to take to the Christmas party at work, a dinner partner, a man to fulfill her very real and getting slightly urgent sexual needs.

"Hey, Trish. What's up?" Joe called from the bar as he deftly shook a martini shaker.

Wiping the seat with her hand first, Trish dropped down onto a stool in front of Joe. She slid her outrageously uncomfortable shoes forward on her feet, until they were dangling, held on only by the grip of her toes. "The usual. I got stood up by my date."

Joe looked properly outraged on her behalf, jaw dropping and shaker hitting the counter with all the force of his meaty arms. "No way! Well, the jackass obviously doesn't know what he's missing."

"Is there something wrong with me? Do I have a sign on my behind that says 'Lie To Me'?" she asked in exasperation.

Trish pushed the ashtray in front of her to the side and marveled at how morose she was being. This kind of thing didn't usually bother her. Life went on, with or without men, and thankfully, she'd never actually been emotionally hurt before, just annoyed. But lately she was getting lonely, and while good for many things, a computer couldn't carry a conversation or sexually satisfy her. Okay, if you wanted to get technical, it probably could do both in a roundabout sort of way, but it just wasn't the same. She wanted to hear someone breathing next to her when she had a conversation, and she didn't think that was too much to ask, damn it.

"You just intimidate men, that's all." Joe turned to deliver the drinks to customers, leaving Trish to ponder that. Intimidation was all about power, something she appreciated.

Intimidation was good in the courtroom, but not the bedroom. She'd never thought her sex life—if she could remember that far back—was lacking in anything. But put in those terms, she wondered if she had ever really had a relationship with a man where they weren't both scrambling for control.

It was not an uplifting thought for a lonely Friday night

in September when her good friend Kindra was three weeks away from her wedding to Mack, and Ashley was flashing a mammoth engagement ring from Lucas. Even Violet, who shied away from men, had managed to snag a pro baseball player, and Trish figured it wouldn't be too long before they went down the aisle. Dylan was already chomping at the bit to marry Violet since she was having his baby.

On nights like tonight, when Trish was alone and her friends were all cuddled up with their men, she couldn't help but feel a little tinge of something.

God, she was actually jealous. How small.

Joe bustled back and offered her a glass of wine but she shook her head. "Just a water, please." She didn't want an innocent glass of wine. Nor was she certain she could stop at one or two drinks of the hard stuff, not when her defenses were feeling as weak as they were tonight. And getting drunk alone was the adult equivalent of being the last kid picked for the dodgeball team in grade school. Sad. Better to stick to water.

"Shake it off, babe—you know you're hot stuff."

The drinks were so-so at Ryan's Pub, but it was nice to see a familiar face, nice to hear Joe's staunch support. Trish had been wandering into this pub off and on for five years, and hung out with her girlfriends there twice a month after their bowling night. "You know what, Joe? I don't feel like shaking it off. I want to feel sorry for myself tonight."

Maybe she wasn't justified. After all, she had a budding career as county prosecutor of domestic violence, a great apartment, and good hair. But men didn't seem to appreciate any of those things. She didn't think she was asking too much. It wasn't like she expected comfortable pantyhose to be invented. She just wanted a nice guy, loyal, honest, friendly.

She supposed she could get a dog.

But Kindra and Mack's yappy poodle annoyed the hell out of her. A lizard was more her style.

"If you're going to feel sorry for yourself, slide on down the bar and join my buddy Caleb there. He's having a hell of a pity party tonight."

Without much interest, she glanced over. A guy was propping his head up with a massive, muscular arm, and trying to sip his beer without lifting his head. Moisture from the bottle dribbled onto the bar and his arm, and he made a halfhearted swipe at it. A quick count showed six empty bottles in front of him.

Now there was a winner. Hold her back.

"Do you know him?" she asked Joe, hoping she didn't look that pathetic. This guy looked like he'd set down some serious roots in Loserville.

"Yeah, I've known him for more than fifteen years. We played ball in high school together and he's a good friend." Joe leaned on the counter, moving closer to her, and kept his voice low. "He never drinks."

The six bottles hadn't emptied themselves. "Could've fooled me."

"I'm serious. But tomorrow his ex-wife is getting married. He's celebrating by getting shit-faced."

Trish forgot to clench her toes, and her shoe fell to the floor. "That does not look like a man who is celebrating."

Joe stood back up. "I know. Looks to me like he's feeling sorry for himself. But that's what he said—that he's celebrating."

This was not a man who was about a blow a party horn and throw some ticker tape. If he called this celebrating she'd hate to see sulking. "Did you know his wife? Was she a bitch or something?"

Trish would lay down five bucks she was. The ex was probably a busty blonde who had henpecked her mild-mannered husband while weeding the flower bed in her bikini. And clearly this guy was still passionately in love with her, devastated by the divorce. Sitting in a bar plotting the new fiancé's murder. Or worse, planning to dash into the wedding ceremony in one of those cringe-inspiring moments and yell, *Bambi, no one loves you like I do! Don't marry him!*

It was definitely a court case waiting to happen. Public intoxication, disturbing the peace, stalking, assault and battery—one of those was probably in his future. Trish's whole career revolved around that kind of idiotic behavior.

Joe paused and scratched his light brown goatee. "No, she wasn't a bitch at all. She was one of those people who's always smiling, always something nice to say, always dressed like she was on her way to church."

Well, that didn't fit Trish's image of his wife at all. No wonder he'd gotten divorced—he'd been married to the wrong woman.

"He said he has a plan," Joe said.

Here it was. Poisoning the fiancé, slashing the tires on the limo, kidnapping the bride. Trish leaned closer to Joe. "What is it?" If he was planning something illegal, it was her duty to warn him of the ramifications.

"He said he's not leaving until he finds a woman to sleep with. Tonight."

What? Well, that wasn't worth the buildup. She'd at least been hoping for a midnight serenade of the ex or something. But it was not news for a man to bury his problems between a woman's thighs. This guy had probably slept with a dozen women in the past two years in his quest to forget or get over his wife. The world revolved around sex, not love, as she had seen over and over again as a prosecutor.

"That just sounds like another Friday night man on the make to me."

"Except he hasn't been with a woman since he left his wife."

Trish didn't know which was more curious—that an able-bodied man in his twenties had willingly gone two years without sex, or that he had shared that fact with Joe.

"How do you know?"

"By beer number five, he was starting to get loose-lipped." Joe shuddered. "Look, it was a really embarrassing conversation for me. I think I'm permanently scarred."

Trish bent over to retrieve her shoe and tried really hard not to brush her hair against the sticky black lip of the bar counter. "Then why the hell are you telling me? I don't want to know about his sex life any more than you do." In fact, less. The only person's sex life she cared about was her own, and how she could actually get one.

"So maybe if you go down there and talk to him, you'll distract him and he'll forget about it. He's not in any shape to be picking up a woman. He'll probably wind up married to a stripper by the morning if he doesn't chill out on the beer."

Why was it her job to save him? He was a big boy. Really big boy. He could take care of himself. Trish sipped her water, thinking. She blew her hair out of her eyes. She studied the guy, his arms as wide as porch pillars. He looked like he could pick up a building, all muscular and brawny.

She wanted to be alone in her sulk.

He looked over then. Sexy, deep-green eyes stared at her blankly, glazed with alcohol. Damn, he was cute.

She groaned, knowing she was going to regret this. "Dammit. Fine, I'll talk to him."

"You're such a good person, Trish." Joe clapped her on the shoulder, almost knocking her off her stool.

It wasn't a compliment people usually paid her. She was reliable, efficient, and ruthless with criminals in her job, but no one had ever attributed inherent goodness to her before. She wasn't even sure that's why she acted now. But there was just something about a guy with six bottles of beer and a broken heart that had her standing up.

"Drinks are on me, Trish."

"Then get me two bottled waters."

Under the pretense of grabbing a book of matches, Trish sat in the chair next to Caleb. "What are you watching?" she asked, looking up at the TV. Baseball, of course. It was September.

He didn't look at her. "The game."

"Who's winning?" She squinted through the dim light at the TV, seeing little men standing idly around a baseball diamond. In baseball, it always looked to her like the players were waiting for something good to happen, and that given the choice, they'd rather be eating barbeque.

There was silence. Trish discreetly shifted her bra strap under her black clingy dress and marveled at how huge this guy next to her was. Joe was big in a fleshy sort of way. But this guy was massive, his T-shirt straining against rippling muscle—and he towered over her, even sitting down. It was fascinating for a woman who spent all her time with professional men, who tended to be a little pale and thin, though with impeccable suits. She'd never dated a man who could snap her in half with his bare hands. Maybe that had been a mistake.

His rudeness didn't bother her. She wasn't even sure he'd heard her. He seemed to be floating in an alcohol haze, and when Joe put the waters in front of her, she gestured for him to clear away the empty beer bottles.

"Get me another one, Joe." The giant tilted the bottle in his hand and drained it.

Joe nodded. "Sure, Caleb."

Trish glared at Joe. Hadn't he been the one to say this

guy needed to go easy on the beer? Watching Caleb, she had to agree, and apparently it was up to her to be his salvation, savior, Saint Trish. That was her. Sure thing. Not.

But she did feel significantly less sorry for herself than she had when she'd walked in the door, and she owed it to Joe's friend to save him from himself. Especially if he had truly loved his wife, the prospect of which she found strangely compelling. For some weird reason, she wanted to believe a man could love a woman enough to be upset when she got remarried, and Trish didn't want this guy to cheapen that by having a one-night stand, his judgment impaired by alcohol.

Nor did she want to see his name come across her desk as the defendant in a crime of passion. Those were always such a waste of taxpayer dollars.

Leaning over the counter, she grabbed the beer out of Joe's hand when he returned with it. Using her best courtroom voice, she pushed it out of Caleb's reach. "Take this back and don't bring any more. I've cut him off."

Caleb Vancouver had a good little beer buzz going, but he wasn't drunk yet. Not the way he wanted to be, at any rate. Snapped out of his stupor by a stubborn woman's voice, he glanced over at her.

"What?" he said, taking her in with one swift glance.

Woman wearing a scowl, looking at him like he was a pathetic lush, that's what he saw. Caleb wondered if she was right. He was feeling pretty damn pathetic.

She was very attractive. But definitely not his type. Not what he was looking for. He had come to the bar to find a woman, true, but the smiling, laughing, big-hair kind who thought nothing of going home with a guy she'd just met, and didn't expect or want a phone call after the fact.

So far he hadn't seen any likely candidates, which was

starting to piss him off. A guy goes two whole friggin' years without sex and then he can't even find one chick to sleep with? It didn't seem right. Not that he was looking all that hard, if he were totally honest. Somehow his plan to celebrate April's wedding with a drunken night of sexual revelry had disintegrated into him sucking down beers by himself in a sulk.

And he suspected, despite the physical urges and the emotional need to stick another woman in his bed, if only for one night, that he wouldn't actually go through with picking anyone up. Hell, he'd been there for three hours already and hadn't spoken to anyone besides Joe.

He'd never had a one-night stand in his life. Of course, maybe that was because he'd married April right out of high school. But regardless, he wasn't a sex-with-a-stranger kind of guy. He liked to know a woman, liked to learn how to please her, share an intimacy in bed and out, before and after.

"I said you can't have any more beer," came the persistent voice.

Caleb shifted on his stool and took another gander at the bossy broad next to him. Who the hell did she think she was?

If he wanted a beer, he'd have a beer, and some woman with nice shoulders and a scowl couldn't stop him. No one could stop him, especially not when he was determined to drink enough beer to forget how annoyed he was, and he wasn't nearly there yet. It was going to take a lot of beer to get over his confusion that his ex-wife was marrying a guy old enough to be her grandfather. And was so happy she was beaming. Glowing. She'd never glowed with Caleb, and it bothered him.

"Get me another beer," he told Joe.

"No," the woman next to him said quite clearly.

Was this the morality committee? Annoyed, he turned to

her. "I don't mean to be rude, but would you mind your own damn business?"

He blinked hard, trying to focus a little better. Damn room was dark and the cigarette smoke hanging like a factory cloud always made his eyes water.

She switched tactics. Her hand rested on his arm. Her tone became conciliatory. "Just take a break," she said. "I hate to be the only one not drinking."

But Caleb wasn't fooled. She looked and sounded too wily and calculating to be genuine. Women with short hair were like that. They existed in a world of hair products, where everything could be sculpted and molded and tamed to their liking, and he thought she probably viewed him as an unruly cowlick.

Unsure what to say, and wanting to ask why she was in a bar if she didn't want to be around drinkers, he gave a grunt that could be interpreted any way she liked and turned back to the TV.

"Can you pass me a nut?"

She smiled at him, her hand held out expectantly. Caleb felt prickly annoyance as he passed the bowl of peanuts to her. Was she bored or was she flirting with him?

His brain was a little addled from the beer, so he decided if he were uninteresting, she'd move on to someone else. Because she really wasn't what he had in mind.

Oh, she was pretty enough if you were into perfection. Long cheekbones, artful makeup, stylish dark-brown hair with lighter highlights. Great shoulders, tanned and toned, making him wonder just briefly if the rest of her would be the same before he stopped himself. Only the message didn't quite reach his bottom half in time and he felt a hard-on rising in his jeans.

Thanks, pal, he told his unruly appendage.

Despite his body's reaction, he knew he wouldn't know quite what to do with a woman like this. Self-assured, bossy, clipped and manicured, wearing a sleeveless dress that screamed classy businesswoman, she was from a different world. One of cappuccinos, Audis, and business trips to New York—nothing like his life managing his small construction business, and living in a dingy little duplex.

"You know, I've never met a huge man who grunts before," she said, popping a nut into her mouth and pouching it in her cheek. "I mean, I've seen guys like you on TV and checking purses at the airport, but I've never actually talked to anyone like you. Are you a cop, a welder, or a mechanic?"

He gave her a hard stare, hoping to scare her into leaving. He did not want to be her blue-collar novelty of the night.

Instead she shivered and gave him a smile. "Oh, do that again. And growl this time."

She was making fun of him. Caleb frowned deeper.

"Here." She took a peanut and shoved it between his lips. "I think the alcohol is dulling your reflexes. You're just staring at me."

With good reason. The woman was friggin' crazy. But he couldn't protest, not when her warm finger was still resting on his lips, the salty, fleshy taste of the tip still lingering on his tongue. If he sucked, he could draw her into his mouth.

It was nothing, a little gesture that meant nothing, but his long-neglected body stood up and took notice. *Hey,* it said. *I remember this. This is foreplay.*

It could be, but it wasn't.

He hated to disappoint his gonads, but this woman was only amusing herself. At his expense.

"Chew the nut," she said. "Food will help absorb the alcohol before it hits your bloodstream."

"One peanut?" he asked.

"Good point." She grabbed a whole handful and started toward him.

Caleb clamped his mouth shut and shook his head.

She grinned. "No? Well, Joe can get a sandwich for you. They make club sandwiches and really greasy fries here."

"I'll have one if you do. I don't like to eat alone." He smiled smugly, throwing her words back at her.

A snort of laughter flew out of her mouth, and she covered it with a soft, golden hand, her short, rounded fingernails painted white at the ends.

Diamonds flashed in her ears, and dark, intelligent eyes gave him another once-over. "I might as well, I guess, since I missed out on dinner when my date stood me up."

Caleb figured his brain was firing a little slow, but he couldn't believe this woman had been stood up. Personally, he would have been scared to. She was intimidating as hell.

"Some idiot stood you up?"

"Sad, but true." She popped a nut into her own mouth, then offered him another one by hovering her hand over his.

He opened his fist and let her drop the peanut into his palm. "So you came here instead?"

She nodded. "Even more sad, isn't it? That when lonely and pissed off, I came to a bar."

If it was sad, then he was doubly so. "I can understand that." More than he even wanted to admit to himself.

Gesturing for Joe to come back over, he chewed the nut. And looked down at the woman beside him, all straight-backed and confident, one leg crossed over the other, a hint of cleavage popping out of her little black dress. "What's your name?"

"Trish," she said, and stuck her hand out like they were in a business meeting. "Trish Jones."

He took her hand, small and soft in his, but possessing a firm, bold grip. "I'm Caleb Vancouver."

She pumped his hand up and down twice, then let go, a

mischievous smile on her perfectly painted, caramel-brown-lipstick lips.

Those lips were very distracting. Very luscious, very arousing. Caleb had a sudden image of what exactly she could do with those perfectly pretty lips on what part of him. He shifted on the stool.

And when Joe came over to see what he wanted, Caleb completely forgot to order another beer.

Two

Trish watched Caleb pack away his second club sandwich in awe. The guy was huge, granted, and probably needed a lot of fuel to drive that big old muscled body of his, but Jesus. Come up for air once in a while.

"Don't you feel better now?" Trish asked, not sure how she felt. He was really damn cute, in a pathetic, kissable, lumberjack sort of way.

He nodded. "I didn't realize I was so hungry. You're a smart woman, Trish, but I bet you hear that all the time."

Damn good at her job. Dedicated. A bitch. She'd heard all of those lately, but not *smart*. Sometimes it seemed like a woman was only allowed to be intellectual, academic, with her intelligence—not sharp, driven.

The compliment meant more to her than it should. "I'm a prosecuting attorney. I handle all the sex-crime cases."

Caleb licked mayo off his lip, and carefully set his sandwich down. "No kidding? Are you sure you're in the right joint? Me, I'm a construction worker, and not your usual type, I would guess."

Of course he was a construction worker, and of course she had to have an arousing vision of him shirtless in the summer heat pop into her head. Carrying a two-by-two, or whatever those pieces of wood were called, jeans sinking down low. Sun lightening that short brown hair until it was the color of milk-doused coffee. Tan. Hard.

And of course she was wearing a dress that revealed that her nipples had suddenly gone leaping out toward the bar like they wanted to join that sandwich being palmed by his fingers.

Waving her hand, Trish gave a scoff, striving for cool and sarcastic. No need for him to see that she was tilted a little off her axis. "My type for what? Besides, I've adopted you for the night."

Snatching one of the bottled waters off the bar, he glared at her. "Adopted me? I don't need you to baby-sit me, Miss Prosecuting Attorney."

"You were drunk when I sat down."

"So? And not nearly enough, in my opinion."

Trish nibbled on a French fry, then tossed it down as her stomach recoiled. It was like licking bacon grease. "But you feel better now that you've stopped drinking, don't you?"

He didn't answer.

Irritation rose in her, and she wasn't even sure why. "And what were you getting drunk for, anyway? To talk yourself into dragging some woman home with you tonight?"

Caleb shifted on his stool, pinning her with another one of those hard stares. "What does it matter? Why do you care?"

She rolled her eyes. "I don't!" Stupid lug. Here she was, being friendly, reaching out, something she did *not* normally do. Let him wallow. "Order yourself another beer, for all I care. Get blitzed and pick up some giggling, brain-dead bimbo who might be impressed by all that muscle you're hauling around."

"Maybe I will."

"And maybe I'll just leave you here to do that."

"Fine."

"Fine." Yet Trish didn't move. She just switched legs and wondered why she wasn't walking away.

Because she didn't want to. Caleb was drunk, totally not her type, and he drank domestic beer. Yet she just didn't want to go home alone. Again. So she'd stay with Caleb for a little while longer, another minute or two, before she headed back to her empty apartment. He needed the company.

She needed the company.

Caleb picked his sandwich back up. "Aren't you leaving?"

"No." She shrugged. Let him think what he wanted.

But he shot her a quick glance out the side of his eye. "Good."

Trish laughed. "You are drunk, aren't you?" And she nudged his brawny arm with her side.

He grinned. "Maybe just a little." And his finger reached out and moved past her face to touch her earring. "These are pretty."

"Thanks." She reflexively ran her own finger over the spot where his had been. "They were a present from my parents when I graduated from law school."

"Are you a good lawyer?"

"The best," she said, never doubting it for a minute. She'd been born to argue, and she was good at it.

"I believe you. You look like you could run circles around those guys downtown. I bet you won every staring contest when you were a kid."

"Of course." Trish pushed the plate of fries away from her and went back to the nuts. It had been too much to expect that Joe could produce a salad for her. But instead of leaving and finding a grocery store or deli, or just scrounging something up in her fridge at home, she was still sitting there on a stool so hard her backside had gone numb.

It was stupid.

Caleb took another swallow of water and some of it sloshed down the front of him. "Damn. Got a hole in my lip."

Trish reached for a napkin. The guy clearly needed a keeper. He couldn't even drink water without slobbering all over himself. There would be no telling how he'd find his way home if she didn't stick around.

"Here." With less-than-gentle fingers, she swiped at his chest. His solid, football stadium-wide chest.

His hand grabbed hers, stilled it. A big, scratchy hand that swallowed hers whole like a shark with a tuna. He was strong, holding her immobile even when she tugged a little, and she was annoyed, yet simultaneously fascinated.

"Trish?"

"What?" Damn if she wasn't actually leaning toward him, gazing up into his murky green eyes like some soulful Juliet wannabe.

Only she didn't have a romantic bone in her practical body. The dating game and her job had only confirmed that romance was dead in the twenty-first century, if it had ever existed.

"I think you're a lot nicer than you pretend to be."

Giving up on retrieving her trapped hand, she let him cup it like a baby bird, while she sat back and snorted. "Don't bet your tool belt on it, buddy."

But she was secretly pleased.

Caleb had figured out that his beer buzz was still racing, and that the room was pulsing in bright, fuzzy, undulating waves. Which had to be why Trish looked so deliciously tanned and perfect, perching on her stool with posture that would make a chiropractor proud, and why he suddenly wanted to taste her. Every polished and smooth inch of her attorney ass, from that tidy hair down to her rounded breasts.

Past her firm belly, skimming over her dark, wispy curls, down her toned and tan thighs to satin toes, capped off with a dash of red toenail polish.

Two years was a long time to go without sex.

At the moment he couldn't even remember why he'd been celibate. It had something to do with his ex-wife, and how he'd vowed not to make the same mistake twice. April had been about the neediest woman he'd ever met, lacking in confidence and unwilling to give him any independence. He had loved April in the beginning, loved that she was a generous, caring woman, but in the end he'd realized he wanted to be friends with her, not married to her.

And if he ever got involved with a woman again, he wanted passion this time. Not just friendship. Not just companionship. But passion, and deep, lasting love.

He'd been holding out on the sex. Waiting for the right moment, the right woman, when he was so turned on, so intrigued by a woman that the thought of waiting was downright painful.

He was thinking he was just about there.

Enough so that his jeans were straining at the crotch and he was shocked at himself. He'd just met Trish—what the hell?

He let go of her hand. "I was married for eight years." Flicking the crusty rye bread on his sandwich, he stared at the bare spot on his left hand where his wedding ring had been. He had felt a tremendous relief when he'd taken that ring off. He'd been more than ready to move on, to a new life, to a new woman. Yet it was April getting a second chance, not him.

"Was married?"

"Yep. I'm divorced. Been two years, and my ex is getting remarried tomorrow."

"Yeah? So I guess you're heartbroken? Jealous of the new hubby?"

That startled him. Jealous? Definitely not in the way Trish meant. "Nah, I actually feel kind of sorry for the guy. Everybody loves April, but not everybody's had to live with her." It had been exhausting to always ease April's insecurities.

"So it was a mutual breakup?"

"Nope. I left her. She dragged out the divorce as long as she could."

"So you're here getting drunk . . . why?" Trish wrinkled her nose. "I'd think you'd be happy to get her out of your hair."

"I'm celebrating, that's why I'm getting drunk." Caleb frowned. "Was getting drunk."

"Yeah, you look like a barrel of laughs to me. Party on, Caleb." She made a funny face and stuck her fingers out in some frat-boy gesture.

It made him want to laugh. "Okay, so it's kind of hard to celebrate by myself."

Trish played with a French fry on her plate. "Why'd you leave her?"

"I left her because I wanted something more, you know what I'm saying? And here she's moved on, getting married."

Trish leaned over the bar counter, propping her arm up as she watched him. Caleb wasn't sure how the conversation had turned to his life story or why he was telling her anything about his ex-wife. He'd have to blame it on the beer, because he was not the kind of guy who talked about his friggin' feelings on a regular basis.

After studying him for a second, Trish nodded. "Aah. I get it. You're feeling bad because she's over you. Found someone else. She's got a lot of nerve picking up the pieces of her life after you broke them."

Wait a minute. "What's that supposed to mean?" It didn't sound flattering.

"That you're just such a typical guy. You don't want her, but you don't want anyone else to have her." Trish made a face at him. "What was she supposed to do? Sit around crying for the rest of her life because you decided the marriage wasn't working? You should be happy for her."

Trish had it all completely wrong. "I am happy. Very happy. Happy that Harry fell on my grenade. If you don't press down April's pin at all times, she'll explode."

"I have no idea what that means except that it sounds vaguely sexual. If it is, do *not* explain any further. If it's not, enlighten those of us who can't follow military metaphors."

Caleb grinned at the look on Trish's face. He hadn't meant to sound sexual, but now that she mentioned it . . . he wondered where Trish's pin would be. What would set her off? Before he could stop himself, he glanced at her cleavage again. Trish had a fabulous body that he'd love to see more of.

"I mean April's really insecure. She can't make any decisions on her own, and she gets whacked-out upset if you don't do everything exactly the way she thinks it's supposed to be. For eight years I walked on eggshells, until I got tired of it."

"But everybody loves April?"

"Yes. Because she's so damn generous and sweet and unselfish."

"Tricky bitch." Trish's mouth quirked up.

"Exactly." Caleb fingered the lettuce on his plate, feeling a little better about the whole thing. "Harry's sixty years old," he added.

That was a little embarrassing, though he wasn't sure why. Maybe it made his masculinity feel a little threatened, if he wanted to get all talk-show about it.

Trish's lip twitched again. "Now we're getting to the bottom of it. How old is April?"

"Twenty-eight."

"Huh. And loved by all."

"Yep. My mother is acting as mother of the bride in the wedding tomorrow. My sister is one of her bridesmaids."

Trish burst out laughing. "Are you kidding me? Now that's pretty damn funny."

Caleb fingered the water bottle and found himself grinning. It was kind of funny. "And we still all go over to April's house for holidays. Sometimes I think April wanted to marry my family more than she wanted me."

Trish lifted her water bottle. "Here's to Harry and April—may they live long and prosper."

He lifted his own water. "Alright, I'll drink to that." He guessed he really was happy for April. Even if she was having sex and he wasn't.

They clunked their plastic bottles together.

"You ever been married?" he asked.

She shook her head. "I've never been convinced that it's worth it in the end. That people can be selfless enough to stay together and in love forever."

Caleb thought that was a cynical view. He still believed in marriage, despite his first mistake. "Who says you have to worry about forever? Can't you enjoy one day at a time?"

"I don't know. Have you ever been in love, Caleb?"

"I loved April way back when. I wouldn't have married her if I hadn't. But there are different kinds of love, and ours was based on friendship. What about you? Ever been in love?"

"No," Trish said, her head shaking. "And I don't think I ever will be, and that scares me. I don't want to spend my whole life alone."

Trish couldn't believe she'd just said that. Neither could Caleb, given that his eyes had dilated and his jaw had slackened, hovering above the still-damp water spot on his T-shirt.

Afraid of what might come out of his mouth, and mortified that she'd acted so pathetic, she bit her lip hard and got her shit together. She was a successful career woman. It was what she'd always wanted and she was damn proud of herself. She wasn't lonely, she was just horny. Big difference.

"So enough of Trish's Deep Thoughts. Tell me about your ex." Trish used a brisk, nonchalant voice that had Caleb narrowing his eyes in confusion.

She added to prod him along, "Short? Tall? Good at sports, what?"

Caleb didn't say anything for a minute. When he did, he sounded distracted. "April's small, delicate, sweet. Quiet voice, polite, loves to cook, to can preserves, to sew. She has honey-blond hair and wears those sweatshirts with things stuck on them. You know, cats and stuff."

Oh, yikes. Caleb's ex-wife sounded like Holly Hobbie sprung to life. Virtuous, demure, bad fashion sense.

The exact opposite of Trish.

She wasn't the type who could get his engines revving. Pressing flowers and whipping up biscuits and gravy were not scheduled in her PDA for the near future. Not that she cared. She didn't *want* him to be attracted to her.

Which did not explain why fantasies of climbing onto his broad lap were flitting through her head.

"She sounds perfect for a sixty-year-old guy."

He shrugged, like he didn't care one way or the other. "Yeah." Then he turned, and reflected in his green eyes was something that resembled interest. Lust, even.

It had to be her imagination, a result of being stood up, a need to feel desired.

"I don't want to talk about . . . that anymore," Caleb said, and there was no mistaking where his gaze dropped. Right into her cleavage. "Tell me about you, Trish Jones."

She'd tell him about Trish Jones, but that's as far as the whole thing was going. No way was she going to be stupid enough to fall for the wounded animal act, and take this guy home and lick his wounds, also known as his ego. Nope, she wasn't going to lick anything of his. She did not need that kind of entanglement in her life. Besides, she felt concern for him, that's all. She did not have any interest in seeing if he was that huge everywhere.

Light. Fun. Witty. That's all. "The quick breakdown of the facts is as follows. Trish Jones, prosecuting attorney, age twenty-eight. Raised in Rocky River, currently residing in the Clifton Boulevard area, with no pets, though considering a lizard. I bowl with my friends twice a month, work shockingly long hours, and have been credited with always being direct in both my personal and professional lives."

She smiled at him, what she hoped was a confident, flirtatious smile. "How about you?"

"Caleb Vancouver." He spoke slower than she did, which could be his temperament or the alcohol dulling his reflexes. "Thirty last June. Grew up in Lakewood, still live there, in a double on Cordova. My two brothers and I run our own construction business, but we focus mostly on concrete. And I already have a lizard, Spanky, who only moves at three A.M. when I'm trying to sleep and he's screwing around with the rocks in his tank."

"So I should rethink the lizard thing? I prefer to sleep at three A.M., not listen to an amorous lizard."

Caleb laughed. "I didn't say he was screwing the rocks, I said he's screwing *around* with the rocks."

"So you think."

"I don't want to know."

Trish switched her legs and took a sip of water, taking some weird pleasure in making Caleb laugh. This do-gooder shit wasn't all that hard.

And her interest had nothing to do with the fact that he was damn cute, with the hottest body she'd ever seen off the WWF circuit.

"We grew up practically neighbors then. When I wanted

to be daring and pretend I was hip, I used to go to Lakewood."

"Let me guess—you grew up in one of those lakefront houses with private beach privileges. And went to private high school."

Damn. "Maybe." It was fine for her to make assumptions about him, but having it turned back on her was annoying. Especially since he was right.

"You like to come here and slum after a day out sailing or dinner at some trendy restaurant?"

If he only knew how little she had fit in at her all-girls high school, how often she'd been reprimanded for breaking dress code with striped black-and-white socks, and how the administration had not appreciated her turning the school newspaper into a hotbed of debate on crime and punishment in America. No one was extending her an invitation to the yacht club, and her parents indulgently referred to her as their "driven" daughter.

"Sure, I get a cheap thrill from eating greasy food and gawking at the commoners." Trish swatted him on the arm. "Come off it! I work with criminals all day long. I have no pretensions. I grew up in comfortable surroundings, but so what? I drive a crappy, ten-year-old Toyota, my favorite hangout is the bowling alley, and while I've never dated a guy who was technically blue collar, that was never intentional. It was more a convenience factor, but I'm rethinking that. The guys I know are all schleps, so a welder has to be a step up."

Caleb had stopped brooding long enough to look amused. "You know any welders?"

"No, but maybe you could hook me up. You know, I may be on to something here. You realize that we all date in a very narrow circle, usually people we work with or through mutual friends. There are probably a thousand single guys I've never even come into contact with, all right here in like a ten-mile radius."

"You going to date all thousand?"

"Maybe," she said airily. It would keep her busy for the next ten years or so, while her friends all settled into domesticity and diapers and had increasingly less time to spend with her.

He laughed. "You should probably just start with one, Trish."

For some insane reason, she smiled up at him and moistened her lips with her tongue. "Know anyone who might volunteer?"

The grin faded off Caleb's face. "Maybe I do."

Three

"Hey, Caleb, Trish." Joe leaned over the bar in front of them and Caleb was annoyed at the interruption.

"What's up, man?" In other words, leave so he could go back to talking to Trish, who after two hours of conversation, had shed her shoes and her reserve. She had a cute little spot of pink on each cheek as she dissected her favorite movie for him.

"Last call, buddy. You want anything?"

Jesus, make that four hours. Caleb looked at Joe in surprise. "It's one-thirty?"

"Yep. Time flies when you're sitting on your ass gabbing. But when you're a working stiff like me, you feel it. It is most definitely one-thirty."

Trish laughed. "And we haven't even gotten started on the second *Lord of the Rings* movie yet."

Joe groaned. "Oh, God, spare me. Caleb's always boring the shit out of me with that fantasy elf crap, trying to drag me to those movies. I'm glad he's found another geek to talk about it with."

And talk they had. About everything. He'd confessed to Trish he liked bowling, too, but riding his bike better. They liked the same books, movies, sports, and thought getting on the back of a horse was just nuts.

"Geek at your service," Trish said wryly, bending over to pick up her shoes.

She obviously had no idea he could see right down her dress to the tops of her breasts, pushed up with a black satin bra. Caleb's mouth went dry and he felt a surge of lust so powerful he almost shot off the damn stool.

"Gorgeous geek," he murmured.

"What?" she murmured, breathless as she stayed bent over, fooling with the straps on her heels.

"Nothing. I said you're not a geek."

But Joe had heard him and gave him a questioning glance. "You want some coffee or something Caleb, before you head out? You were pounding 'em pretty hard earlier."

Joe must think it was the alcohol talking. And maybe it was, though Caleb didn't feel drunk anymore. He just felt a heightened awareness of the room around him, sound louder than normal, color vibrant. And he felt interest in something, someone, for the first time in a hell of a long time.

"No, thanks, man, I'm fine. I guess I'll head out soon." Not that he wanted to leave, go home to his empty house, listen to the silence, and Spanky getting it on with his rocks.

Trish sat up, all remnants of a smile gone. "You're not going to drive home, are you?" She nodded to Joe, commanding and prissy and somehow damn sexy. "Joe, call him a cab."

Joe, the idiot, nodded. "Sure thing, babe."

"Wait a minute! I can't take a cab. I rode my bike here and I'm not leaving it in the parking lot overnight."

Trish fiddled with her bra strap, giving him another flash of flesh. He took a deep breath and shifted, his cock caught in an uncomfortable position as it swelled enthusiastically.

"So what? Just throw it in the trunk of the cab." Trish rolled her eyes. "I'm not letting you drive."

There was something she was missing here, and it struck him as funny. "I don't think a Harley will fit in the cab's trunk."

Joe laughed. "I'll let you two work this out. Let me know if you want the cab company's number."

Trish gave him a blank look, then raised her eyebrows in understanding. "Oh, I get it. Here I was picturing you, this huge guy, pedaling a bicycle, and the thought was killing me, I'm telling you. But on a hog, okay, that makes more sense."

"Thanks for your approval."

"But you still can't drive."

And she stood up and leaned over him, hands sliding down past his waist, groping and feeling all over his thighs, her breasts brushing against his chest.

"What the hell are you doing?" He wasn't sure whether to move out of her reach or grab her, throw her on the bar, and kiss her. Odds were two to one on kissing her.

"Whoa!" He jerked when her hand dipped into his jeans pocket and fished around. Christ almighty, if she shifted to the right a little she'd be stroking his johnson.

"I'm looking for your keys." Her voice was a little breathy, and her eyes had darkened as she looked up at him, fingers stilling in both of his front pockets.

"You're going to find more than my keys." He tried to maneuver back, but all he managed to do was force Trish to lose her balance. With her hands still trapped in his jeans, she fell forward against him.

"Umph," she said, her chin colliding with his chest, breasts giving softly against his lower ribs.

He put his hand on her back to steady her and forced himself to speak, even though every inch of him was aching with desire. "Trish, I can drive. I'm fine."

"That's what everyone says—then they plow into a utility pole."

Maybe she had a point. Better to be safe than sorry. And he was having fun letting her fish around for his keys. He moved his hands to the bar, off of Trish, as she stood back up. "Alright, fine. You're right. But it's a moot point if neither of us can get the keys out."

"I walk away for two minutes and she's got her hands in your pants?" Joe cleared the empty water bottles from in front of them. "I've known her for four years and she's never felt me up."

Trish was on the move again, tickling his thigh as she pushed herself off him slowly.

"Shut up, Joe," Caleb said, thinking the whole scene would be a hell of a lot more interesting if they were in private.

Then Trish moved like lightning, holding his keys up before dancing out of his reach. "Got them!"

While he knew she was right, and he no longer had any intention of driving, he still made a grab for her just for the fun of it. She shrieked and slipped out of his hold before he had more than a fistful of her silky dress.

"Damn, Trish, you're like a greased pig."

"That's the sweetest thing anyone's ever said to me." She taunted him with the keys, dangling them in front of her, laughing.

Caleb hadn't laughed with a woman in a long time. It felt good now, right, easy. He stood up to stalk her, back her against the bar, maybe accidentally stick his hands on various spots of her body until he came up with the keys.

She looked up at him, her grin disappearing in astonishment. "God, you're huge. Even bigger than I thought when you were sitting down."

Caleb was used to that reaction from women. He was a little broad and on the tall side, and while he was comfortable in his own skin, it had always made him a little nervous around women. Like he might knock them down by accident. He took a tentative step toward her, holding his hand out. "Give me the keys. I'll ask Joe to drive my bike home for me."

"What kind of prenatal vitamin was your mother on? You're like a freak of nature," Trish said, cocking her head a little.

That stopped him short. He grunted, though he was amused. "That's the sweetest thing anyone's ever said to me."

Trish laughed, not a girlish giggle or an obnoxious snort but a beautiful, rich sound, her teeth gleaming in the dark room, her hair framing a heart-shaped face. "You like reading fantasy novels, have a lizard and a Harley, are in touch with your emotions, and have a sense of humor, too. Very interesting."

Not really, but his heart started a goddamn tap dance in his chest. She looked delicious standing there, rolling her ankles off her shoes, smelling like warm flesh and a subtle layer of sweet perfume.

"Keys, Trish."

"I'll drive the Harley and you can ride on the back."

Clearly she thought he was shit-faced enough to agree to that, but there was no way in hell, drunk or sober, he was going to agree to let a woman drive his chopper.

No way.

Trish knew Caleb was nervous, given that gasping, choking sound he was making in the back of his throat, but she was confident as she straddled the motorcycle.

"You sure you know how to drive this?"

"I told you, I passed the test and everything. I'm a fully licensed motorcycle driver." That had been in her early twenties when she had been in a retro-seventies phase, wearing mirrored sunglasses and listening to CDs by angry women. But she was sure she could handle the thing. And as an added bonus she wouldn't need to use her Thighmaster the next day after squeezing her legs around the wide bike.

"We're only going two blocks to my place. It will be fine." If she could just find the ignition.

"Your place? What are we going to do when we get to your place? Call me a cab? I know I'm not drunk, and I'm missing the logic in your cunning plan."

When Caleb shifted, the whole bike tilted. He towered behind her, six-foot-four or so and about two hundred and forty pounds of muscle. If she were faint of heart, it could very well be intimidating. But Trish had been subjected to curse-laden tirades from psychotic criminals and had even had a rapist spit on her after his conviction. No, fear was not the reaction Caleb was wresting from her.

More like screaming desire.

Somehow over the past few hours, he'd morphed into just about the sexiest man she'd had the horny pleasure to meet.

"No, we're not calling a cab, because then you'll be stuck without your bike. We'll leave my car here, drive the bike to my place, you'll spend the night, then in the morning you can drive us back here on the bike to get my car." Trish was glad he was behind her as she delivered this little speech.

She honestly wasn't implying anything sexual, but if he expressed an interest, she wasn't at all sure she would say no.

"Spend the night? With you?"

Since she hadn't started the engine yet—an impossibility, since she couldn't figure out where to put the key—the summer air was still and quiet around them. He had spoken in a low, rough voice that sent shivers racing across her shoulders.

"Well, not *with* me. You can crash on my couch."

"I don't think this is such a good idea."

She chanced a glance over her shoulder. He looked . . . alarmed. Like she might lure him to her couch and have her wicked way with him. It was an embarrassing reminder that he hadn't slept with a woman in two years and that he was used to his ex-wife, who surely never would have straddled a motorcycle in a short black dress.

For a minute, she'd allowed herself to get carried away, which was so not her. Never once had a guy swept her off her feet. Most couldn't even get her big toe to lift. And she sure in the hell wasn't going to do the sweeping herself.

"Oh, come on. I've adopted you, remember? If you go home, I'll just spend the whole night worried that you're dead in a ditch, and then tomorrow I'll have bags under my eyes for my friend Kindra's bridal shower."

And she *would* worry about him. He had compelled her, intrigued her, from the first moment they had locked eyes, and she couldn't just walk away from him without knowing he was safe and sober. Besides, it didn't seem right to send him home alone tonight, when his whole family was off celebrating with his ex. Trish knew what it was like to be alone, and sometimes it just wasn't all that much fun.

"Is it safe to leave my Harley at your place overnight?"

"I rent the second and third floor of a house and it has a garage."

"Alright then." He leaned over and whispered in her ear, making her shiver when his hot breath touched her cool cheek. "I'm trusting you with my life and a really expensive piece of metal. Are you sure you can handle it?"

Trish turned her head so that her lips were an inch or two away from his chin. She couldn't see his eyes but she could feel him everywhere, surrounding her with his powerful, masculine body, coarse caramel whiskers dusting below his lips. "I can handle it."

"I thought so." Then he moved out of her personal space, and Trish was disappointed.

But he came right back and shoved a helmet onto her head, jerking her forward with the force, and sending her hair straight down over her eyes. Her ears bent painfully in half.

"Caleb!" She parted her bangs to either side of her eyes so she could see, and lifted the helmet to adjust it.

"Keep it on," he ordered. "If we wreck, I'll probably land on you. At least this way I won't squash your head. And the key goes in there." He pointed to the ignition.

No wonder she hadn't been able to find it—it was in a stupid spot, nowhere near the handlebars. "Of course it does." She started the bike with a loud roar. "And I'm not going to wreck," she yelled over her shoulder indignantly, but she kept the helmet on.

Caleb's hands went around her waist.

Then lower, to her thighs.

Controlling the rumbling bike meant her skirt had inched up.

So that his rough hands were on her bare skin.

And by the time they crossed West 117th and turned onto her side street, his hands had somehow traveled under her bunched skirt, a healthy distance above her knee.

She concentrated on driving. Not on the way her legs were vibrating wildly from the engine of the bike. Not on that delightful little jolt of awareness that was rolling through her body. Or that things had suddenly gotten warm, and maybe even a little damp, not so very far from where he was touching.

Then his hands slid higher. Resting on the outside of her thighs, thumbs dangerously close to her black seamless panties.

Trish nearly took out the telephone pole turning into her drive. That would have been ironic. But did he know what he was doing? Or was he so immune to her sex appeal he could pat her crotch like he might the head of a nice, friendly Lab?

Maybe he was falling asleep.

Because men always fondle women's thighs when they're dozing off.

Crap.

This whole idea of having him over to her place obviously fell under the heading of extremely bad judgment.

"You know," she said, as she turned the motorcycle off in front of her garage. "You probably don't realize it, but you have your hand up my dress."

"Do I?" he said in a voice that left no doubt he knew exactly what he was doing.

Thank God.

"Sorry. Your driving scared me, so I just grabbed and held on."

"Uh-huh. Okay. Well, we've stopped, so you can let go now. I need to open the garage."

The retreat of those big hands was gratifyingly slow.

Caleb stayed on the bike while she bent a little, twisted the door handle, and lifted the garage door up. Before she could say anything, he had pulled the bike inside with a roar of the engine and a squeal of the brakes, and was standing up. Way, way up.

Dang, he was gorgeous, in a really cute, big sort of way. And he was walking toward her, sticking his bike keys back into his pocket. Trish still had her hands up in the air, holding on to the garage door, ready to pull it back down once he was out.

But instead of heading toward the house, he walked right up to her and put his hands over hers. "I'll get it."

"It's okay, I've got it," she said, even as he dropped the door with a casual flick of his wrist. "Or not. Thanks." She took a step away from him.

But he stopped her, with a tug on her fingers, his face dark in the shadow of the house, the streetlight's feeble glow not penetrating the backyard where the garage was.

"I need to thank you, Trish. For watching out for me. I was drinking myself under the table when you . . . introduced yourself."

She laughed. "You mean interrupted you like the bossy bitch that I am."

He grinned, but shook his head. "No, that's not how I see you at all."

Crossing her arms over her chest, she shivered a little as a breeze kicked up. She wanted to get inside, take her heels and her bra off, and relax, far away from him, but Caleb seemed inclined to linger in the driveway. "How do you see me?"

He glanced up into the sky, and Trish followed his gaze. The stars were out, dim but straining to be seen against the lights of the city and the dark backdrop of the sky. Crickets were chirping wildly like they'd never get another chance, and voices from the next street could be heard as a car door slammed. When Caleb touched her lower back, shifting her clingy dress as his finger rubbed back and forth, she turned to him.

"You're beautiful, Trish. That's how I see you. Absolutely gorgeous."

Before her frozen brain could formulate any adequate response, he was bending and brushing his lips across hers, a soft, light touch that almost wasn't even there, and sent a rush of longing through her body. She could have sworn her soul sighed—which was such a ridiculous, girly thought that she was momentarily too stunned to kiss him back.

Then he was gone, standing full height, and she recovered herself. But when she reached to return the gesture, maybe expand on it, she couldn't quite manage more than the bottom of his chin, even on tiptoe.

Gripping his steel biceps, she gave up straining. "Shit, I can't even reach you. Come here by the side door so I can stand on the step."

Rushing on her heels, she about broke her ankle, but wasn't in the mood to care. Stepping onto the stoop that led through the side door of the house and up to the second floor where her apartment was, she turned back to Caleb. It still wasn't an even match, but he bent his head a little, she reached up, and she was there.

On his mouth, tasting him, dragging her lips across his while her hands clung to his shirt and every part of her exploded in electrifying lust. He groaned, she moaned, and the kiss went deeper, harder, rougher, his hands pressing against her back while she opened up for the thrust of his tongue.

Trish molded against that hard body, wrapped her leg around his, ignored the fact that her dress had bunched up a hell of a lot more than was appropriate for her driveway. Then his tongue touched hers, and she sank into ecstasy for a split second before jerking herself back out.

He tasted like beer.

What the hell was she doing? He was drunk, which generally didn't make for rational behavior.

Trish fell back against the screen door, scratching her bare shoulder on the metal frame, breathing hard. Caleb was also sporting an incredible erection in his jeans. But that didn't matter.

She eyed that burgeoning denim and flattened herself further against the door. Okay, it did matter, but it shouldn't.

What mattered was that she not take advantage of him. The last thing in the world she wanted was to sleep with him, then have him wake up with a throbbing head and regret, mortification, or horror at what he had done.

He was lonely, embarrassed that his ex was marrying an old guy, and Trish could not be selfish about this and give in to the lusty urge to just rip her dress off and hop on him right now.

He reached for her. She turned around, hugging the door, digging in her purse for her key. "Sorry. Sorry, Caleb. God, I didn't mean for that to happen. Not to worry, though. I won't lay another finger on you for the rest of the night— you have my word."

Oh, yippee. Caleb stared at Trish's cute little backside wiggling as she fiddled around in her purse, and wondered why she was apologizing for kissing him exactly like he'd wanted her to.

And wanted her to again.

He enjoyed her company, liked the way she was so confident and direct, and he was rapidly developing intense interest in her body. She was compact, firm, with a little curve to the hips and a luscious swell of breasts. He was afraid to touch, yet at the same time itched to slide his hands everywhere.

It was the last lingering effects of the alcohol that had emboldened him to rest his hands on her thighs, and when he'd felt that toned and satin-smooth flesh, he had about fallen off his bike. Two years was too damn long to go without touching a woman.

Now as Trish climbed the stairs in front of him, he swallowed hard. "It's okay, Trish. I enjoyed it."

She paused, but didn't turn around. "Caleb. I lost my head for a second there, but let's be up-front here."

He followed her into a small living room with hardwood floors and a vibrant red couch. "Up-front about what?"

Trish kicked her shoes off under the coffee table. "Look, I'm not embarrassed to admit that I'm attracted to you. But you're sleeping on the couch tonight. That's all there is to it."

"Okay." No matter how hard he was, he didn't want her to have any doubts at all. But that didn't mean he wasn't going to ask her out for tomorrow night. He had every intention of seeing Trish again.

"Okay then. Great." She put her hands on her hips. "Let me get you a sheet and a pillow. And I can get you something to eat if you're hungry. Or coffee—do you need coffee?"

"I'm fine." Caleb sat on the couch and fought a grimace. It was like a pine board. Stiff and smelling chemical, like she'd had it sprayed with stain repellent. It was a look-good-but-shit-for-comfort couch.

He lay down as she came back into the room with a bright red pillow. "You like red, huh?"

It seemed to be jumping at him from every direction, including by his feet. He nearly clipped six red candles on metal sticks on the end table when he lay down. Shifting, he tried to bring his feet back onto the couch. His head, shoulders, and chest shot off the other end and almost collided with a lamp. Red, of course.

"It's my signature color. I've gone with a monochromatic decorating scheme."

Okay. He took the pillow but there was nowhere to put it since his head was dangling three feet above the couch arm. He tried to adjust his feet so part of his lower half and part of his upper half were both off the couch, and he wound up feeling uncomfortable everywhere, muscles tense and bunched.

Trish laughed. "You look like a foot-long hot dog in a regular-size bun."

He searched for a compliment in there, but couldn't find one. "This is a small-ass couch."

She rested her finger above her lip. "Well, I'm not cruel, so you can sleep in my bed and I'll sleep out here."

"You don't want to sleep on this couch. It's like laying on a brick."

"I guess we could share the bed."

Oh, yeah, baby. She didn't need to ask him twice. "I guess we could."

Four

Trish was left with one burning question.

What the hell had she been thinking?

She was lying in her bed, staring at the ceiling, inches from Caleb, and she couldn't do anything about it.

Damn her parents for teaching her ethics. If she hadn't felt sorry for him, she would have left him tortured on the too-short couch. Or for that matter, she would just do what she really wanted and have hot and sweaty sex with him. Or if she hadn't been a total softie, taken in by the big lug's pathetic solo drinking, she never would have talked to him in the first place.

Being nice and responsible was a bitch.

Because she was wearing shorty pajamas that clung to her body, no bra, within smelling distance from the sweetest, most interesting guy she had met in about *ever*, and she was just going to fall asleep.

After having told him that she didn't mind in the least if he took his T-shirt and jeans off.

It had taken incredible discipline not to look when he'd climbed on the bed with her.

"Trish?" he asked as he turned toward her.

She grabbed the edge of the mattress so she wouldn't roll toward him. Every time he shifted, the bed sank on his side and she started to skid downhill, right toward him.

"Yes?"

"How long does my adoption last?"

He was using that voice again, the one that had traipsed past her ear while his hands had managed to fall up her skirt.

She clung tighter to the mattress. "Until I've decided you're grown up and don't need me anymore."

"That's nice of you."

Oh, yeah. She was nice all right.

Nice and horny.

And wide awake. Inches from him.

It all came back to that.

Caleb watched Trish staring at the ceiling, covers up to her chin. He was under those covers with her, in nothing but his underwear. She was wearing tight little black shorts and a clinging red top that had revealed her nipples to him before she'd gotten into bed while he was stripping off his jeans.

If he shifted, he would be on her side and could pull her into his arms.

And she would probably knee him in the nuts.

"I'm not usually as pathetic as I was tonight, Trish. I'm not sure what that was all about."

She finally turned and looked at him, eyes softening. "Hey, you spent a lot of years with your ex. We all have some baggage."

"Thanks." It made him feel less like a loser, knowing she understood.

"When I walked in there tonight, I was sure that all men are selfish bastards who wouldn't know love if it bit them on the ass. You reminded me there really are good guys out there. I enjoyed talking to you."

"There are probably more of us than you think." He followed his urge to brush her bangs off her forehead.

She didn't even seem to notice. Her expression was wistful. "Maybe someday I'll actually find the one that's right for me."

I'm right here, he thought, then was shocked at himself. He was attracted to Trish, he thought she was funny and sexy, and he'd love nothing more than to see what was under that red shirt, but that was it. He wasn't looking for anything that resembled a relationship in any way. Wait—yes, he was.

This thing with Trish, it had definite possibilities. Possiblities that could stand exploring. Now he just needed to convince her to let him do a little exploring come tomorrow when she didn't have his blood alcohol level to use as an excuse.

"I'm sure we'll both find the right person for us." Maybe even sooner than she thought.

She shrugged and pulled the covers down a little. "Good night, Caleb."

"Good night, Trish." And he reached over and pressed his lips to her forehead, wishing it were tomorrow already.

"Want to crash the wedding?" she asked, her voice mischievous.

He laughed and lay back. "That would be really damn inappropriate." But really friggin' funny.

"But funny," she said.

Man, he could not wait for tomorrow.

Trish was wet, slick, and swollen, giving little moans of encouragement as Caleb swirled his tongue over her aching nipple, and her hands roamed across his broad steel chest. His licking wasn't enough—her clitoris was tight, desperate for his touch, and she arched against his hard thighs, trying to entice him to slip a finger inside her hot vulva.

Instead he pulled back and with a wicked grin, flipped her onto her stomach and gave her something much bigger than a finger. And Trish came, jerking on the bed, and straight out of sleep.

She blinked her eyes, shuddered, and flopped back down onto her pillow. Now that was just embarrassing. She had just had an *orgasm* while sleeping, and a lousy one at that. There was nothing worse than coming with nothing touching her but her own moist panties.

Sucking in air, she squirmed on the sheets, unfulfilled, her inner thighs still throbbing, and hoped like hell Caleb was still asleep. And that while fantasizing herself to a blistering O, she hadn't squealed out his name between moans.

She chanced a look at him.

Green eyes met hers. Open. Curious.

"You okay?"

No, she wasn't okay, she was so desperate she was getting off in her sleep while she had a half-naked man in her bed with her. There was something inherently wrong with that.

He rolled on his side toward her. "Did you have a nightmare? You whimpered a little bit."

No kidding. And she wanted to again.

The sheet only came to his waist, and the sight of all that man skin so close to her, that solid golden chest, that sprinkling of masculine hair, undid her. There was only enough space between her chest and his for a book. A thin, paperback book. His eyes looked clear and sober, his soft brown hair sticking up a little.

Nothing ventured, nothing gained. It was like prosecuting a case with circumstantial evidence. You could lose, but if you were lucky, you might just force a plea.

"It wasn't a nightmare. I was having a sex dream."

His eyebrows rose under his disheveled hair. "You were *what*?"

Surreptitiously, she kicked the bottom of the sheet with her feet, dragging it down so her tank top was visible. "Having a sex dream. About you."

Caleb looked frozen in fascination. "You were?"

"Yes, and it's your fault for looking so cute and for being too big for my couch. I told you last night I wanted you. I wasn't lying."

His look of shock had smoothed away—his hand reached out and touched her cheek, thumb rubbing along her bottom lip. "I wanted you, too, more than anything. So why did you tell me to stop?"

"Because I wasn't sure how drunk you were, and I didn't want to take advantage of you when you were feeling down." Trish brushed his hair off his forehead in a gesture that was totally foreign to her.

She nearly laughed. Good God, next she'd be offering to do his laundry. But this wasn't about a relationship. Caleb wasn't ready for that, and she didn't want one. But they could have one time together, here, while he was in her bed. She could satisfy this driving need for him. Or at least try to, really hard, while they were both naked.

"I'm not drunk now. And I'm feeling more up than down." Caleb's hand dropped to her bare shoulder, his eyes dark, his voice low and coaxing. "Want to tell me about your dream?"

She'd rather act it out. "Well . . . you were inside me. And I whimpered because I was having an orgasm in my sleep."

"No shit?" He looked thoroughly intrigued by that.

Trish nodded, going up on one elbow, her tank top pulling taut. "And, well, it hurts, you know, to come with nothing touching me."

Caleb cupped her breast, brushing across her nipple, and she bit her lip.

"Poor thing," he said. "It sounds awful."

"It was. I'm very unsatisfied." Her breath was hitching and her thighs were throbbing and his hand was teasing and torturing, and her sleep-relaxed muscles tensed up.

"Let me fix that, Trish."

She thought he'd never ask.

"Okay." And she closed her eyes when his mouth covered hers and he gave her a deep whoa-baby kind of kiss that had her losing her grip and falling back against the pillow.

With one arm and very little effort, he pulled her up on him, so her body was snug along his everywhere that mattered and she clung to him like dog hair to black pants. His thick arms surrounded her, while his mouth tasted her, and Trish knew never again could she entertain sexual thoughts about a man shorter than her. Not after Caleb. Not after feeling his hard strength and being flush against so much masculinity. Paired with his very appealing compassion, he was damn near irresistible.

Not that she was resisting.

When he broke off their kiss, she actually went and whimpered again.

Caleb stroked Trish's back, sliding down past the bottom of her tank top, feeling her bare flesh in the dip of her body before it reached the firm curve of her smooth backside. She was nibbling his ear, running her fingers through his hair, and he loved the way she took what she wanted. He had her on him, part for the press and grind of her luscious body along the length of him, but also because he knew he was big and strong, and didn't want to overpower her or trap her or hurt her.

But he should have stripped her naked first. He wanted to see, feel, and taste her bare breasts. He tugged on her tank top, trying to work it up awkwardly. Trish caught the hint. She sat up with her legs around his thighs in an enticing straddle and raised her shirt over her head.

It went flying across the room, hit the wall and slid to the floor. Trish ran her fingers through her hair and arched her breasts toward him.

Caleb forgot to breathe.

He didn't know what was sexier—the curve of her breasts, the tips of her dusky nipples, or the sexy I-know-you-like-them smile on her face.

His air came back on a desperate groan.

"In my dream, you were sucking my nipples, refusing to touch me anywhere else," she said.

"I wouldn't be that cruel," he managed to say, though he was feeling something like a two-by-four had been taken to his head.

He should have known Trish would be different from his ex, but he hadn't really had time to follow the thought through. April would never have sat on him, baring her breasts so enticingly. Nor would she ever have spoken out loud what had happened in a sexual dream, though Caleb doubted she'd ever even had any. April had been inhibited sexually.

And hot damn, it looked like Trish wasn't at all.

"Then touch me," she said, leaning forward and clasping one of his hands in her own. "I'm still wet from my dream," she added, like this was a selling point.

He'd been sold the minute she'd dug in his jeans for the bike keys.

With a groan, he reached for her breast with the hand she wasn't holding, took the fullness and squeezed. Trish gasped, her eyes drifting closed. He dragged his thumb across her nipple, felt the tight plumpness of it, felt the tremor that stole over her as he whispered her name.

Her eyes snapped open. "Caleb, oh, I want you so much."

His briefs were too tight, his cock strangled alongside her inner thigh as she rocked over him, her breast heaving in his hand. Heat from her sweet spread reached him even through her tight shorts and his underwear.

Still holding her small, soft hand in his rough one, he sat up and swiped his tongue across her nipple. "I want you, too."

His intent was to settle her firmly in his lap and suck her nipple into his mouth for a good long taste. But Trish had other ideas. She pushed on his chest.

"Lay back down. I need to take my shorts off."

He did as he was told, and she collapsed on his chest, hot, perky breasts fitting over him. Caleb stroked her back, kissed her chin, while Trish wiggled around, pulling on her waistband.

"Dammit, I can't get these off. Help me."

"I'm just going to enjoy what you're doing for a minute or two." All that moving around felt pretty good, in a painful, torturous kind of way.

"It will feel better with my shorts off." She buried her head in his shoulder as she lifted her hips and shoved.

He felt the fabric of both shorts and panties go down, felt her hot skin hit his, right above his briefs, felt the soft, feathery touch of her pubic hair on his midriff, and he swallowed a bucketful of saliva.

Then when he cupped her tight ass he swore at the pleasure of it. "You feel so incredibly good."

Caleb stroked her in delicious exploration, rolling his thumbs across the swell, slipping into the dip between her cheeks with his middle finger as he palmed over her. He breathed hard, so primed just from touching her that he was afraid he would embarrass himself. Damn, he had waited so long, and she felt so fucking right.

"Your hands are huge." She gave him a glassy-eyed stare. "How big are your fingers?"

"Not too big," he assured her, not wanting to scare her.

Shuddering, he lay still, battling his need into submission. "Look, Trish, anything that you're not comfortable with, just say so. If I'm hurting you in any way, yell or slap me or whatever to let me know."

He'd castrate himself if he hurt her.

But Trish shook her head and licked his bottom lip. "I wasn't concerned. I was actually hoping your fingers would be big."

Damn.

And she rolled off of him and onto her back, slipping her shorts the rest of the way down her legs, kicking them off with a little flip of her toes. Her hands lifted over her head and one knee elevated. Her stomach dipped in, her breasts rose and fell, and her mouth turned up in a wicked smile.

"Hurt me, baby."

Caleb watched her for a second, all laid out for him to touch and taste and fuck, and he felt something akin to awe.

"Now that's a beautiful thing, Trish."

Then he reached for her.

When one of those rough hands of Caleb's cupped her between the legs, Trish gasped, rising up into his touch. His mouth played with her nipple, sucking lightly first one, then the other, while his hand just sat there and she squirmed in agony.

Trying to encourage him to do something besides letting his hand lie like a crotch-potato, she squeezed the solid muscles right above his waist. Then promptly did it again, enjoying the tight, wide feel of him.

He pulled away from her breasts. "Am I hurting you? Should I stop?"

Not in the way he meant. Trish wiggled again and his hand started to retreat.

No, no, no. Wrong answer.

"You're not hurting me at all. I want you to show me how big your fingers are."

Her voice must have driven her meaning home because he nodded his head. "Aah, I see." Then with a grin, he lifted his hand off her completely and held it in the air. "This is what my fingers look like." He wiggled them.

Never having entered into a study of finger-size comparison, Trish could draw no immediate conclusions. Caleb's fingers certainly looked bigger than average, and his hand looked like he could palm a watermelon, but there was only one way to really tell.

"I don't want to see them, I want to feel them." She took his hand and guided it to her, sliding his index finger across her slick folds.

She rolled her eyes back in her head.

Caleb moaned. "Oh, shit, Trish, you feel so damn good."

Look who was talking. His finger pushed inside her, filling her, and sending her muscles into little jerks and spasms of pleasure. He retreated, came back, went deeper, pulled out to swirl moisture around the swollen button her clitoris had become.

Her hand still rested on his wrist, his movements dragging her with him, and Trish decided this was indisputable proof of a much-argued maxim.

Bigger was definitely better.

"Like that? Not too big?"

"Absolutely not," she managed, the thought of him withdrawing striking terror in her sex-crazed heart.

"Try adding another one," she suggested.

His green eyes darkened to the color of a dense forest. His mouth covered hers with a moist, demanding kiss at the same time another finger plunged into her, stretching her and setting off a climax that she couldn't stop.

Holding on to his arm with both hands, Trish let his tongue take her while she came with tight, shattering pulses. She yanked her head away from his to suck in air and let the pleasure take her under.

For a long, quiet second after she stopped shuddering, he held his fingers inside of her until she finally gave him a shrug and a smile. "Oops."

Caleb pulled back and laughed. "Don't give me *oops*. You knew what you were doing."

"What are *you* doing?" It appeared he was taking his underwear off, which left one thought in her head. *Yes, yes, yes.*

Struggling to sit up for a better view as he bared his skin, she asked curiously, "Are you . . . proportionate?"

His briefs were off and he rolled back toward her on his side.

Her question was answered. Oh, God, that thing was astonishing. Trish gulped.

"Yes, I'm proportionate."

"I see."

"I know you claimed I'm a freak of nature, but honestly, Trish, I'm not that big."

She'd be the judge of that. "You look like you take your vitamins to me." Ripping her eyes off of his fully engorged penis, she slid closer to him, licking her tongue across his chest. "I'm impressed."

"I won't hurt you."

Closing her mouth around his nipple, she sucked, her fingers digging in his chest hair. "Put a condom on, Caleb. Before I throw a temper tantrum."

He went still. "I don't have any condoms. I . . . I just don't."

A thousand angry no's went screaming through her head. Then she picked her head up off his chest and dragged her thigh off of his as hope restored itself. She resisted the urge to grind herself against him and sat up. "Don't panic. I think I might have some."

Crawling off the bed, she rushed across the room to her dresser. "My friend Ashley decided to become a Pleasure Party consultant a few months ago."

"What's a Pleasure Party consultant?"

"Someone who sells sex toys. Officially, they call them romance-enhancing products, but they're really sex toys." Trish dug through the drawer. "Come on, they've got to be in here. I was trying to support her, you know, so I bought some lingerie and stuff and condoms."

Her hand closed over them. The condoms had been a joke. Because they were glow-in-the-dark pink.

But they were fully functional.

She ripped a row out of the box.

And turned and collided with him. "Oh! I didn't know you were so close."

Hitting that much immobile man sent her bouncing back into her dresser, and she nearly took a handle in the butt before Caleb steadied her. With hands that were now sliding across her backside and making interesting little crossroads into her inner thighs.

All while that impressive erection nudged her in the belly.

"Condom," she said, holding the packets up in front of his chin before he distracted her with his talented tongue, currently running along her neck.

He took them and moved out of her space. Dammit.

Caleb ripped the pack open and got one out. And dropped it.

"Holy shit. It's pink, Trish!"

"Novelty condoms." She shrugged.

"I can't slap a pink rubber on my dick." The look of horror on his face made her laugh.

"It's not like I'm going to doubt your masculinity." Unable to stop herself, she wrapped a hand around him and stroked. No, no question there. "Come on, it's this or it's nothing. I don't have any other ones."

He was tense, grinding his teeth together. But it didn't take him long to decide. He bent over and retrieved the pack, knocking her hand off him with the motion.

"Don't laugh."

"Of course not." Hilarity was not the overriding reaction his presence brought on.

Turning slightly from her, Caleb rolled on the condom.

"Need some help?" Trish asked, fingers itching to lend assistance. She should be shocked at herself. She'd never been quite so voracious about sleeping with a guy before.

But analyzing her rioting emotions wasn't top on her to-do list right now.

"I got it, thanks." Caleb turned back, an endearing and adorable stain on his cheeks—Trish glanced down—that matched the hue of the condom sheathing him.

Five

He was wearing a pink condom and Trish was laughing. Somehow this wasn't the way Caleb had pictured events playing out.

Hands on his hips, he grimaced and fought the urge to cover himself with one of Trish's red pillows. "You said you wouldn't laugh."

She covered her mouth. "I didn't mean to." She struggled to wipe the grin from her face. "Sorry. Okay, I've got it."

Then she glanced down and nearly suffocated herself trying to hold in a laugh, fingers pinching her nose.

Granted, he was a little embarrassed. The thing was pink. Shocking pink, not-found-in-nature pink. But he was still turned on, and watching Trish was a joy. She was so direct, honest, so up-front about what she was thinking and feeling, and he liked seeing her laugh, especially since she was doing it naked.

"It's not really your color."

What would be, he wondered. "I can take it off," he said, brushing his thumb over her nipple.

Her laugh cut off on a thin moan. "No, you can't do

that. Don't worry about its color, pretend it's just normal."
Fingers clung to his arms. "Better yet, just—hide it."

When her breath hitched like that and she got that excited, aroused look of anticipation on her face, he thought
he could wear a spotted or floral condom and not give a
crap. At least, the spotted. Floral would probably be too
much to handle with a straight face.

"Where should I hide it?" Caleb pressed against her
body, before giving in to impulse and lifting her into his
arms.

"Whoa!" she shrieked, grabbing at him. "I wasn't expecting that."

"I'm hiding the condom from your view." Caleb bounced
her a little, adjusting her in his grip, her bottom nestled
against his abdomen, her breasts brushing over his chest in
a torturous tease.

"Really? Well, I had a better way to hide it than this."

He just bet she did. "I'm taking you to the bed, so you
can show me."

"Perfect."

She was. When he laid her down on her crisp white
sheets, the red bedcover piled on the floor, he forgot about
pink condoms, and without any thought or plan or warning, pushed inside her moist opening.

Caleb held still, pleasure pulsing through him. Her hot
little body writhed under him and tight, moist walls
clamped down on him, making him grit his teeth. *Holy shit.*
He'd forgotten how good it felt to be in a woman, how
much he'd missed it.

But he didn't want to finish before he started. And he didn't
want to crush her with the weight of his body, so he held
himself over her and pulled back for a nice, long, slow
stroke, savoring the snap of acute ecstasy in his nerve end-
ings.

"More."

Another thrust. Another demanding "more" from Trish. Pausing, Caleb stared down at her, thrown off his game, not sure what she was really asking for.

"What . . ." he trailed off when she pushed on his chest.

"You're holding back," she accused, giving another little shove.

"I don't want to hurt you." Neither did he want to be talking. He stared at her in confusion.

"You won't. Now get on your back."

For a second he just lingered there, half in her, half out, feeling like a gigantic goofball who didn't know how to please a woman. Then because he wasn't sure what else to do, he rolled onto his back, Trish gripping his arms and following him, until she wound up on top of him.

A bolt of lust shot through him.

It had possibilities.

Trish splayed her hands on his chest and arched her back. "You've got to understand something about me. I'm not a nice girl. I send men to prison every day and I enjoy it. And when I want something, I really want it."

She moved, lifting off and on him, with sure, confident strokes, and Caleb couldn't keep his eyes off her. She was gorgeous—mouth open, eyes glazed with pleasure as she rode his cock slowly at first, then increasing in speed.

"And I . . . want . . . you."

Her carefully painted nails dug into her mussed, but still stylish, hair as she went up and down with frantic thrusts.

Caleb held the small of her back, fought to keep his eyes open. "You've got me, gorgeous."

She was smooth, slick over him, pushing herself down so hard that he went deep inside her, and the little bud of her clitoris pressed into his pelvis. It was almost too much, too fast, sensation winging through him, and he knew he couldn't stand that hot, wet friction much longer.

But without warning, Trish dropped her hands onto his

chest, eyes wide, and convulsed against him in an urgent orgasm, so damn sexy that Caleb gave up holding off and
joined her.

He heard his own moan rushing past his ears, forced
himself not to maul her too hard as his body jerked in its release, hard and satisfying. It went on for a good, long, hot
minute, and when he finally relaxed back against the pillow,
exhausted and satisfied, Trish gave a throaty laugh.

"My sentiments exactly." And she draped herself across
his chest with a sultry sigh.

While he liked having her there, he knew he was sweat-
ing, and probably smelled rank. He gave her a gentle nudge.
"You don't want to lay on me, I'm all sweaty."

"So?" Trish played with the ends of his hair and yawned.
"After we take a nap we can hop in the shower together."

With an enticing little lift of her hips she moved off of
him, then resettled on his thigh. "But first, I have to sleep.
It's hard to settle into good REM sleep when you're orgasm-
ing."

Caleb laughed and wrapped his arm loosely around her.
But instead of sleeping, he tugged off the pink condom and
listened as Trish's breathing evened out. Wonder stole over
him at how amazing she was, and how right she felt in his
arms.

Trish was fascinating. She didn't care that he was sweaty,
she talked casually about her sex dream, and already had a
shared shower planned.

He liked it.

Sleeping across a hard, naked man was therapeutic.
Trish woke up rested and satisfied, more relaxed than she'd
felt in months. She stretched her legs and snuggled back
into his chest, glancing up to check him out. Caleb, the little cutie, was still asleep, a small snore emitting from his
mouth.

Trish really thought he was just absolutely adorable, which struck her as funny. The man was huge, and yet she was constantly pulling out adjectives like *cute*, *sweet*, and *adorable* to describe him. But he was.

He was probably one of the nicest guys she'd ever met, which maybe didn't say much for the company she'd been keeping. But Caleb was just a good, solid, loyal kind of guy who worried that he might hurt her, and she might be interested in exploring where the whole thing could go beyond her bedroom.

Except that she didn't cook, didn't own anything appliqué, was ambivalent about children at this point, and worked relationship-killing hours. Not exactly marriage-making material.

So that left her this morning to enjoy Caleb.

She tickled his ribs.

He jerked in his sleep, making an "unnnn" sound of protest, but didn't open his eyes.

Trish shifted a little, found his penis, and stroked it.

This jerk was enough to almost knock her off his chest. Green eyes locked with hers. "What are you doing?"

"Giving you a hand job." That hadn't been her original intent, but he felt pretty dang good beneath her fingers. "But I've been going for like ten minutes now and my hand's tired," she teased. "So I'd better stop."

He groaned. "Next time, wake me up first so I can enjoy it."

Next time. The fact that it pleased her to think there would be one had her sitting up, annoyed with herself. She'd just given herself the *Get A Grip* lecture and here she was, already fantasizing about waking up like this with Caleb every day.

Yet she couldn't quite make herself pull her hand off of him, not since he'd grown gratifyingly hard. Then Caleb sat up next to her. "Can you hold that thought, gorgeous?"

He shifted out of her touch. She was momentarily miffed until he yawned and rubbed his hand over his stubbly chin. "I really want to revisit what you're doing in like two minutes, but first . . . where's your bathroom?"

"To the right. Want me to make some coffee?"

He smiled and cupped her cheek. "That would be great, thanks."

Then he stood and walked across her bedroom toward the door, gloriously naked, muscles rippling. Was it her imagination or had her ceilings shrunk? He filled her apartment and made it seem small, poky. She'd lived there two years and was really happy with the place. She had two bedrooms and an office, lots of windows and extensive woodwork and molding, which had all been painted white, setting off her red furniture to advantage. But the minimalist decorating and the sharp edges screamed *single woman* to her, for some reason, and Caleb looked odd surrounded by her things. He needed sturdier furnishings. Pine, cedar.

Trish dug a pair of red boy-short panties from her burgeoning lingerie drawer and pulled them on, along with a tight white T-shirt that claimed *ANGEL* across the front. She had ordered it at Ashley's Pleasure Party and had meant to check the box "Princess," but somehow had checked the one below it and had wound up "Angel." Which wasn't exactly something she aspired to. But Ashley had given her crap when she'd asked to exchange it, so she'd have to be an Angel.

She rescued the condoms from the floor where they had dropped and set them on the nightstand. Just in case. Easy access. Then at the last minute tucked another one in the waistband of her panties. She liked to be prepared.

Caleb appeared in the door. He glanced at her chest. "Angel?" he asked dubiously.

Trish tried to move around him, but he blocked the whole damn door. "Yes. I'm an Angel, through and through.

Pure as the driven snow. Now move your big body so I can make the coffee."

"Give me a kiss first, Angel," he said, and lifted her up, straight off the floor.

Trish dangled in the air like a slutty puppet. Her T-shirt rode up, panties likewise. Her hands were pinned against his chest, and even though she felt ridiculous, she had to admit she was impressed with his strength. He wasn't even straining to hold her.

She laughed. "Put me down, you oaf."

"Kiss me first," he ordered, nuzzling in her neck.

"I can't with your mouth down there."

"Got an answer for everything, don't you?"

"Never doubt it."

He lifted his head, stared at her, his mouth inches from hers, waiting. Trish forgot about the coffee.

Dragging her tongue across his bottom lip, she maneuvered her arms around his neck. Then slowly, slowly nibbled her way across his hot mouth while her legs drew up and locked around his waist.

Over and over she licked, tasted, touched across his mouth, while his breathing grew hitched and his grip on her hard and tense. Trish rocked forward, bumping his erection with the apex of her spread thighs, drawing a shaky groan from both of them.

Still she didn't give him the kiss, just rubbed and sucked and tormented until her nipples ached and her clitoris throbbed and she wanted him so very, very bad. Then she kissed him, her tongue pressing hot and hard into his mouth, demanding, claiming, ordering him to respond.

He did, matching her tongue thrust, gripping her ass, grinding her against him.

Drowning in desire, Trish fumbled for the condom in her panties. She held it up as he bent over her, shoved her shirt up, and pulled her nipple into his mouth. Hard. Rougher than anything she'd seen from Caleb yet. And it turned her on, to see him let go, forget to hold back.

"I bet you're strong enough," she murmured into his ear, "that we could do it just like this, standing up."

"I bet I am," he said, starting to stroke between her thighs, running along her damp panties.

With her teeth, Trish opened the condom. "Hold on to me."

"Trust me, I've got you."

She did trust him. Letting go, she let Caleb hold her up by her waist as she reached below to unroll the condom onto him. She fumbled, her hands slipping around, but eventually she got it in place over his erection.

It never even occurred to her to laugh at the pink color this time. She was in agony, aching with want, arching to rub her nipples across his chest. "It's on."

Caleb kissed her—deep, penetrating and possessive— before urgently walking her backwards and slamming her into the wall. Her shoulders made contact with enough force to rattle the pictures hanging there.

It forced the air out of her lungs in a startled, "Oh!" Trish grabbed Caleb's arms, and held on as he shoved her panties to the side, and when his finger ran across her, sinking in, her exclamation drew out in a shaky sob of pleasure.

"Oh, God, yes."

Then Caleb replaced his finger with his cock in one out-of-control thrust that sent Trish's head snapping back into the wall, and her body into ecstasy.

Caleb held Trish around the waist with one hand, the other on the wall for leverage and he sank inside her over and over, lost to anything but the incredible reception of her body gripping around his. She was digging her nails into his flesh, making loud, encouraging sounds that drove him into her harder.

It felt incredible, raw, everything between them stripped down to the basics of lust and want, cushioned by trust. He knew she trusted him not to take it too far, and that was just as arousing as anything else.

Trish wrapped her ankles tighter around his ass, dropping her thighs wider to him, and when he gave another rhythmic push, he heard the sound of fabric giving way as her panties tore. She gave an excited little laugh, her eyes wide, lips shiny from his kisses, skin flushed, head tilted against the white wall.

Damn, damn, double damn, she was hot.

"Oooh, just like that." And her eyes closed as she came, arching forward into his arms, forehead falling on his chest in a sexy little shudder.

He was okay until she gave a vulnerable little whimper. "Caleb."

The way she spoke his name, so soft, so sweet, stole his last bit of control and sent him over into a pounding orgasm, as he let out a groan Joe probably heard back at the bar. A groan that strung out long and hard as his body pulsed with pleasure like he'd never felt before.

They stood together, holding each other, panting, his muscles straining and tired, for a drawn-out minute, as Caleb tried to rein his control back in, and figure out what in the hell had just happened to him. And how he could convince Trish that something powerful was stirring between them, something fun and fascinating, and damn well worth pursuing.

"Am I heavy?" she asked drowsily.

"Not at all." He liked holding her there, tucked around his waist, his hands on the sexy rise of her backside. But after a minute her panties were starting to cut off his circulation so he pulled back. Trish gave a sigh of disappointment, her inner muscles squeezing him a little.

"Sorry, Angel."

Her breath tickled his skin as she laughed. "You're not going to start calling me Angel, are you?"

"Maybe." She'd certainly popped into his life right when he'd needed one. Right when he'd been feeling sorry for himself, Trish had sat down next to him and had ordered him to stop being an ass. To take responsibility for his own happiness. If he wanted a relationship, wanted passion and love in his life, he had to go out and get it.

He wanted it with Trish.

He was about to open his mouth and tell her when the doorbell rang.

Sliding her down to the floor, he jumped when she yelled, "Go away! I don't want any."

Trish had a voice that carried when she wanted it to.

An astonished female voice yelled back. "Trish, it's Ashley and Violet. Let us in."

"Oh, crap." Trish let go of him and padded toward her room, shimmying out of the destroyed panties. "Caleb, it's my friends. You jump in the shower and I'll get rid of them, okay?"

Caleb took a full ten seconds to process the second half of her sentence. Once she'd started wiggling out of that red lace, he'd gone stupid. "Huh?"

His jeans hit him in the face as she reappeared, wearing a bulky nightshirt. "The shower. Get in the shower."

"Right."

"Trish, are you sick? Open the door!"

"Coming!" she called, then gave him a shove.

Caleb did as he was told and stepped into the bathroom, distracted with visions of pulling that nightshirt up and tasting between her thighs with his tongue.

Trish hoped Ashley had a damn good reason for pounding on her door on a Saturday morning.

"What?" she said as she opened the door, running her fingers through her hair. "Is the building on fire?"

Ashley and Violet gaped back at her. They were both wearing dresses, Violet pushing up her glasses, while Ashley twisted her engagement ring around and around her finger.

Why did Trish have the feeling she was forgetting something here?

"You're not even dressed! We're supposed to be at the restaurant an hour early to set out the party favors."

That's what it was. "Damn it! I forgot all about the shower." Trish craned her neck to see her platinum clock.

"How could you forget?" Ashley pushed past her and looked around the room, obviously seeking an explanation for Trish's sudden amnesia. "We spent all afternoon yesterday shooting e-mails back and forth with Kindra until I thought I would scream. Kindra has totally entered the frantic-bride phase."

"She's just nervous," Violet protested. "She wants everything to be perfect."

"You can say that because she left you alone since you were puking your guts out with morning sickness for four weeks straight. I work with Kindra, have no excuses, and trust me, this has been a painful process."

All the more reason not to be late and aggravate Kindra, aka Bridezilla. Trish stood there with her arms crossed, mentally ripping through her closet to find something to wear. "What time do we have to be there?"

"In fifteen minutes."

"Well, hell, go ahead without me. I've got to take a shower. It's only five minutes from here. I'll drive myself." Then she slapped her head. "Except that I left my car at Ryan's last night. Shit!"

She was already moving ahead to plan B, figuring she could take the bus or ask Caleb to drop her off, when Ashley flipped back her blond hair and narrowed her eyes. "Late night?"

Trish nodded.

"Is your shower running?" Violet asked, peering down the hall.

Ashley laughed, glee evident in her expression. "You have a *guy* here, don't you? We'll wait for ten minutes for you to get ready if you tell us who he is."

Since Ashley had parked her little floral-dress-covered butt on Trish's couch, she figured she might as well tell her. "He's one of Joe's friends—I met him at Ryan's last night."

"You just met him?" Violet sounded shocked, which irritated Trish.

"Ryan's known him for fifteen years, he wasn't just some freak on the street." She loved Violet, but she really wasn't one to talk. "And if memory serves, Dylan had you pregnant like ten minutes after you met."

Violet's face turned a guilty red. Good.

Ashley just laughed. "But this is cool, Trish. We're all part of a couple now. We can take vacations together and stuff. And go out to eat and to Cedar Point amusement park . . ."

As charming as that sounded, she needed to stop Ashley's couple train before it rolled any further. "Except that Caleb and I aren't a couple. His ex-wife is getting remarried today and he was just looking for a distraction. I provided one. I'm not his type."

Saying it made her feel like complete and utter dog crap, even though she knew it was true. Yet she wanted it not to be true.

Annoyed at her weakness, she stood there, leg out in defiance, and said firmly, "I'm the transitional woman. That's it. Nothing more." Only it had felt like a heck of a lot more to her last night when they had talked for hours. And this morning, just minutes ago, when he had been holding her, their bodies joined intimately.

Dammit. She should have just stuck to unconscious orgasms—they were a lot safer, though not nearly as satisfying.

Ashley's eyes darted past her, then went wide. "*Hello.*"

Violet put her fingers over her mouth. "Oh, my."

Trish turned and saw Caleb in the doorway, wearing only his jeans, water still running down his chest, hair sticking up like toothbrush bristles.

"So you felt sorry for me? The sex was your contribution to the Poor Caleb Fund?"

Her mouth worked, but nothing came out.

Ashley said, "That's one big, angry guy."

Which pretty much summed things up.

"Of course not! I'm not nice enough to run around having pity sex with guys. I *wanted* to have sex with you."

"But that's it?" His voice was quiet, tight, tense.

Shoot, shoot, he was hurt. She had hurt his feelings. This was why she couldn't make a relationship work. She was selfish and too blunt.

Violet tapped Ashley on the shoulder. "It's time for us to go. We'll meet you there, okay, Trish?"

Trish waved her hand in agreement.

Ashley looked disappointed to miss the show, but she followed Violet with one more peek back at Caleb's chest.

A Lake Erie–sized wave of jealousy flooded over Trish.

"I saw that, Ashley Andrews! Watch it or I'll tell Lucas." God, she sounded like she was twelve. And she knew darn well Ashley was head over heels for Lucas, which made her own reaction seem even stupider.

"What?" Ashley blinked innocent green eyes. "I was checking the clock."

"We'll see you at the shower," Violet said, and dragged Ashley out the door.

When it clicked in place, Trish turned to face Caleb.

But he was gone.

She found him in the bedroom, pulling on his T-shirt. "Caleb . . . I have to go to this bridal shower, but we need to talk first."

"About what?" He sat on the bed to pull on his socks.

"Us." She stood there feeling like a humongous jerk, somehow devastated by the idea that he was going to just leave and she'd never see him again.

"There is no us."

"Yes, there is," she snapped.

"No, you're just the transitional woman, remember?" He tossed her own words back at her calmly as he laced his gym shoes.

And her heart broke for the first time in her twenty-eight years of life.

Six

Caleb wanted to eat his words the minute they left his mouth. Trish froze, her hand dangling over her chest, her eyes huge.

He swore. Just because she had hurt him didn't mean he was justified in turning around and doing the same thing. And she hadn't said anything that was surprising. They hadn't discussed dating at all. They had just fallen into bed together.

Because it had felt so right, so perfect.

"I'm sorry, Angel, I didn't mean that the way it sounded."

Her hand came up in a defensive gesture. "No, no, you're right. I said it first. It's not like we could actually date or anything."

Jesus, there were tears in her eyes. He leaped off the bed, reached for her, hesitated.

"We don't have anything in common or, or, anything," she finished, turning away and blinking hard. "God, I'm just as annoying as your ex-wife must have been."

That's when he knew she felt the same as he did, and that they could get past this little blip, and be together. Because for some reason she had sat down on that stool next to him the night before, and he knew what that reason was. They were supposed to be together.

"We have a lot in common. We like bowling, lizards, and Harleys, and we believe the bad guy should pay for his crimes. We like the same books and movies and we've both been lonely. We like each other." He touched her chin, forcing her to look at him. "At least, I like you. A lot."

"You make it sound like it's easy."

"It can be easy, if we make it easy."

She snorted. "The only thing easy is me. I was about as subtle as a hooker this morning."

Caleb was momentarily distracted by the memory of her straddling him. "Did I look like I minded?"

"Caleb." She gave a sigh, all hint of tears gone. "Let's be practical. Maybe I wasn't tactful in what I said to Ashley, but it was the truth. I've confused you with great sex, but I'm not an easy person to get along with. And you still have feelings for your ex-wife."

The only thing confused was her logic. "Honestly, Trish, I do not." They needed to get that cleared right up. "What drove me to that bar last night was the fear that I was never going to find someone to share my life with. A woman confident in who she is, intelligent, passionate. And then there you were. All of those things, sitting down right next to me. That's not dumb luck, Angel. That's the universe telling us something."

Trish turned and went to her closet, sorting through her clothes. She shot him a rueful expression over her shoulder. "Telling us what? I don't feel illuminated. I feel confused as hell."

Anything he was going to say was forgotten when she pulled that nightshirt off and stood in front of her closet completely naked.

Her fingers plucked an orange-colored dress off a hanger and she turned and threw it on the bed, clearly not noticing that his tongue was on the floor and his dick had shot forward like a pointer dog at attention.

"I'm going to be late to this shower, which makes me a sucky friend. I have to get ready, Caleb. Kindra's important to me and I don't want to let her down."

He wasn't even going to acknowledge she was standing there naked, looking good enough to lick from head to toe. Because if he did, he wasn't going to be able to prevent his tongue from taking action.

"I'll drop you off." Caleb took a step toward her, palms itching to touch her. He shoved them in the pockets of his jeans. "But before you go, think about this. You said you're not sure marriage would ever be worth it. Well, this . . ." He gestured from himself to her. "This is worth pursuing. Because right now I'm feeling like if you let me, I could fall right into love with you."

Trish felt her nipples harden and her heart go soft like crème brûlée. She was naked and he was talking about love. How exactly did she get herself into situations like this?

Someone here had to be rational, and since he was giving her a lovesick look, it would have to be her. "You just think that now. It's called afterglow. You don't really mean that. We just met sixteen hours ago."

She expected him to give in. Maybe even look a little hurt and embarrassed.

Instead he took another step closer to her, eliminating the remaining space between them. His big hands landed on her arms and she thought taking that nightshirt off had been her stupidest move to date.

"We have something else in common, Trish Jones. You said you always get what you want. Well, so do I. And I want you."

Then he picked her up and held her so tight she expelled all her air and feared for the safety of her bladder. "Put me down."

"No. I want you and I'm keeping you and you can't do anything about it."

"You're nuts." And sexy as hell. Geez, she had it bad for him.

"Nuts about you, lawyer girl."

"I thought I was Angel." Her words came out breathier than intended since his hands were stroking across her backside and her breasts were pushing into his bare chest.

"That too." He kissed her chin.

"You know I'd love to stand here all day and chat, but I have a bridal shower to go to. You know, lots of gifts, cake, smiling so much your face cracks." Talk wasn't the only thing she had in mind when he started nibbling on her ear.

"Just tell me you want me, too, and I'll let you down."

"You know, if we're going to start dating, you can't just sling me around whenever you feel like it. It's rude."

"Sorry." His tongue slid into her ear.

Somehow her legs wrapped around his and a moan escaped her mouth. "Caleb, stop it."

"Tell me you want me, Trish. I need to hear it." His voice was soft, vulnerable, even as his nose nuzzled into her neck.

Trish couldn't think of any more good reasons to deny it. The man clearly had no sense of self-preservation. "I want you, too. There, I said it, and you'll be sorry, you know. I'm difficult to get along with. I'm aggressive."

He laughed. "That's one of the things I love about you. And the only thing I regret is that you have to put clothes back on your sexy little ass."

He patted the little ass in question and Trish felt sickeningly, grotesquely happy, and very glad he hadn't walked out of her apartment angry.

Caleb covered her mouth with his in a desperate, possessive kiss that rocked her to the tips of her bare toes. And she thought she might have an idea why Kindra, Ashley, and

Violet had been walking around with such smug smiles on their faces.

Finding a great guy was better than winning a court case.

She broke off the kiss. "Give me a ride on your Harley," she panted.

Caleb raised an eyebrow and gave her a wicked grin.

"No! I mean to the bridal shower." Then she thought about it and relented. "But maybe tonight . . ."

He groaned and dropped her to the floor. "Go, before I use my strength for evil purposes."

Trish darted away from him and went to her underwear drawer. "There's one good reason to go to the shower. I can order more pink condoms from Ashley. I anticipate us using these up quickly."

As she pulled on panties, Caleb said, "Order red instead. It's your signature color."

She laughed, while Caleb adjusted himself in his jeans. "What's the matter? Pants too tight?"

"Yes. You have no idea how you just looked wiggling into those panties."

"No, I don't." Trish shoved the panties back down to the floor and pulled them off. She stepped in front of her full-length mirror and lifted a leg, thoroughly enjoying the shocked arousal on Caleb's face reflecting back at her. "Let me see."

"You are going to kill me."

Trish pulled the panties up her legs, making sure Caleb got a nice view. "But you'll enjoy every minute of it."

Caleb nearly tore through the front of his jeans watching Trish display everything she had and then some. "Oh, hell, yeah."

When he pulled her into his arms again, Trish looked up at him, her brown eyes serious. "I do believe in love and marriage and a happily ever after, you know. I just never saw it happening for me. I'm still not sure it can."

Caleb thought it was ironic that a woman so confident, so successful, could doubt that she would ever find love. And he found it amazing that what he already felt for her seemed suspiciously like love.

"Trust me, Trish, not to hurt you."

She nodded without hesitation. "I do."

"Then let's go for a ride."

Trish grinned. "Can I drive?"

"Our relationship, my Harley, or in the bedroom?"

"All three."

"How about we drive the first together and take turns with the other two?" Though he felt a little pang at letting her drive his bike.

"Perfect." She threw her arms around his neck. "Now kiss me, you big lug."

"You got it, Angel." Caleb moved his lips over hers and sighed. She was a hell of a woman.

Which was confirmed when she grinned up at him. "Now let's get a move on. We have a bridal shower to be late for, and an ex-wife's wedding to crash."

WISH YOU WERE HERE

Amy Garvey

One

"It's lopsided."

Mackenzie Pruitt ignored her friend's observation and folded her arms over her chest, squinting thoughtfully at the structure in question. Crouched at the edge of the tiny backyard, the shed's paint was peeling and its roof seemed flimsy, but while it wasn't a thing of beauty, it wasn't as dilapidated as Susannah seemed to believe.

"It's really lopsided," Susannah insisted, nudging Mackenzie with her elbow. "Like, about to fall down lopsided."

Mackenzie sighed and shook her head before turning to narrow her eyes at her friend, who shrugged innocently, her blue eyes wide. "What?

"You really are a glass-half-empty person, aren't you?" Mackenzie said, shading her eyes against the bright June sunshine as she looked at the shed's side window. The glass was ancient, and the window itself was too small for what she needed, but if she was going to have the whole structure renovated as a photography studio, she could add upgrading the window to the list.

A photography studio. She smiled and turned her face up to the sky, which was clear as glass today, a sharp, blue flag over the ocean. It was a perfect day, and the beginning of a perfect summer. Inheriting her Aunt Letitia's house on Wrightsville Beach was a boon she'd never expected, and the opportunity to have a separate studio space was even more unbelievable. She'd been working out of the cramped second bedroom in her apartment in Wilmington for so long, the idea of living in this cozy little cottage with a studio out back was still like something out of a daydream.

Maybe Susannah couldn't imagine it, but Mackenzie could see the renovated studio in her mind's eye: the white paint fresh; new windows sparkling; the large room inside fitted out with a refinished floor and new storage for her files and equipment; a built-in darkroom; and a soft, warm color on the walls behind framed examples of some of her favorite photos.

It was going to be beautiful.

Even if it *was* a little lopsided, she thought, frowning as she realized Susannah wasn't wrong. The north side of the shed listed drunkenly to one side, and the rotted shingles along the bottom had buckled in the overgrown grass.

Susannah, bored with the view, had wandered back to the cottage and sat on the back steps, her long legs stretched out to catch the sun. She was examining them thoughtfully when Mackenzie joined her.

"Just think, Kenz," Susannah said with an affectionate smile, winding an arm around her shoulders. "A place at the beach. This summer is looking better and better."

"This summer is going to be about getting that studio renovated, and painting and cleaning the inside of the cottage," Mackenzie told her firmly. "I loved Aunt Tish, but there's a definite old-lady smell going on." She got up and dusted off the seat of her shorts—the back steps were no less dusty than anything else, and she'd only been given the keys two days ago. Aside from a cursory airing and a quick swipe with the broom, she hadn't done any serious cleaning. She'd been too busy making plans, calling a contractor, and trying to stop herself from jumping up and down in glee every other second.

Not that she was particularly joyful about Aunt Tish dying, of course, but the woman had been ninety-seven, and she'd lived a long, full, interesting life. Anyway, it was difficult not to celebrate when owning this place meant saying a blissful good-bye to her cramped Wilmington apartment, her skyrocketing rent, and her shiftless landlord. Paying the taxes and upkeep on the cottage wouldn't be easy, but it would be more than worth it. She hadn't planned on owning a place for years yet.

"You're entirely too excited about cleaning and painting," Susannah complained, following her into the cottage with a frown creasing her blond brow. "And not excited enough about being at the beach. The beach, Kenz! Lifeguards, hot guys. *Wet* guys. Is this ringing any bells?"

"You can ogle all the guys you want," Mackenize told her, shaking her head with an amused grin as Susannah tilted her head to one side, considering the possibility with a happy sigh. "Wet or otherwise. I've got work to do."

"You are hiring someone to work on that shack out back, right?"

"It's a shed. And yes." She looked at her watch, surprised that it was already nearly two. "He should be on his way, as a matter of fact. So if you don't mind . . ."

"All right, all right." Susannah scooped up her purse and dug inside it for her keys. "But the next good beach day, I'm here, so be prepared."

"As long as you bring your own towel," Mackenzie replied, absently flipping through the notes she'd made when she'd spoken to the contractor on the phone. She'd left the file on the kitchen counter beside the circa 1960 phone on the wall, and she made a mental note to buy a new portable to install.

When Susannah had gone, her Volkswagen's engine chugging out of the driveway, Mackenzie wandered through the cottage, her fingers trailing over the woodwork and the peeling wallpaper in the hall, letting her imagination transform the place from an old woman's summer cottage to the kind of house Mackenzie had always envisioned for herself. It was going to take a lot of elbow grease, and more than a bit of juggling, considering the jobs she already had lined up for the month, but she could work on the house little by little. It would be a pleasure, she thought, peeking into the bathroom and letting her imagination conjure up a cool white shower curtain around the clawfoot tub, and the tile floor freshly scrubbed and grouted.

Then again, maybe "pleasure" was taking it a step too far.

Outside, the sound of gravel kicking up in the driveway was followed by the rumble of a truck. Tucking her hair behind her ears, she ran down the hall to the front door, trying to remember what the contractor's name was. Leo . . . something. Leo Dawson! That was it. He'd sounded reasonable and competent over the phone, but that didn't mean much when he was the only contractor she could afford who was available immediately. And she had very specific ideas about what she envisioned for the studio, which she wanted to explain to him, so when she opened the door her fingers were crossed that he would be easy to work with.

She swallowed hard as she stared at him. Well, one thing was certain. Leo Dawson was very definitely easy on the eyes.

"Mackenzie Pruitt?"

She nodded without a word, stepping back to let him into the tiny foyer. She couldn't remember the last time she'd struggled for words, but her brain was too busy processing the man standing in front of her to form a single syllable.

She'd been expecting something else entirely—thinning hair, beer breath, grimy nails. Plumber's crack, probably. Apparently her imagination had heard "contractor" and taken a detour on Stereotype Street.

But Leo Dawson looked nothing like that. He was, in a word, beautiful.

More than six feet tall, he was tanned and gorgeously sculpted, his muscles clearly the product of hard work instead of weight lifting. His head was shorn to a light fuzz, outlining the shape of his skull, and his angular jaw was rough with dark stubble. A bright silver stud pierced one ear, and his eyes were a dark, intense green flecked with gold. In his jeans and T-shirt, his sunglasses dangling from one hand, he didn't look like a contractor at all. He looked like the kind of guy who roared up on a motorcycle and made your mother cringe. He looked . . . dangerous. A little bit bad. But a whole lot delicious.

"Ms. Pruitt?"

"Yes," she said quickly, fighting the hot blush on her cheeks. She shut the door and motioned to the sofa in the cozy living room just beyond them. "Please, sit down."

"Actually, it might be easier if we went out to the shed," he said with a smile, hooking the sunglasses into the collar of his black T-shirt. "It is the shed you want renovated, right?"

"Oh. Right." She led him through the kitchen to the back door, wishing she was wearing something other than grimy shorts and an old T-shirt, and cursing herself for not even bothering to brush her hair. Which was stupid, because this was business, not a date. Who would think to dress up for her contractor?

You will, next time he's supposed to show up.

But it was business, she reminded herself as they crossed the sun-warmed lawn to the shed. Even if the idea of watching him work, sweaty and gleaming, hammer in hand, was enough to make her a little breathless.

"Well, this is it," she said needlessly when they were standing in front of the structure in question. It looked even more lopsided up close, she noticed with dismay.

"Uh-huh." He cocked his head to one side, considering it, and started to circle around the little building, squinting and frowning.

"It's withstood hurricanes," she offered, noticing for the first time that the hinges on the door were rusted nearly through.

"By the skin of its very ancient nails," he replied, coming back to stand beside her, his arms crossed over his chest. He smelled freshly showered, clean and slightly spicy. "You sure you don't want to rip it down, start fresh?"

"That's always more expensive than renovating, isn't it?"

"Most of the time. Depends." He cast a wary eye back at the shed. "You wanted to use this as some kind of studio, right? All year round? You're going to need insulation, possibly heat, this close to the beach."

"It's going to be a photography studio, yes," she said, biting back a frown. Damn it. She wanted this shed renovated because she wanted to preserve some of its character. She didn't want something new. She could see what this one would look like finished, and even if it was going to cost her an arm and a leg, she'd just have to figure out how to grow new ones.

And right now, she wanted Leo Dawson, skeptical or not, to understand that.

She was working up to explaining it to him when he tilted his head at her, those clear lake-water eyes regarding her with what looked like amusement. And then he grinned.

It started slow, just a quirk in one corner of his mouth, but when it spread, it was warm and full and so incredibly sexy she suspected other women had actually melted under its influence.

Those eyes would look fabulous in a close-up black-and-white photo, she realized suddenly. And that jaw, too. All shadows and angles, the sun behind him . . .

"Okay. Show me around inside?" he said, one eyebrow cocked in invitation.

"Glad to," she replied with a rush of relief, opening the creaky shed door and brushing away a sticky net of cobwebs as he preceded her inside.

Maybe this summer's work was going to be closer to pleasure. Because a new idea was forming, and it involved her favorite Leica and Leo Dawson.

TWO

There were very few things as dangerous as a client who knew exactly what she wanted, without having any idea what it would entail. Especially one who was as sexy, and innocently persuasive, as Mackenzie Pruitt.

Mackenzie. It was a big name for a little person, but it fit her, he thought, cutting his glance sideways as she wandered toward the window, trailing one finger along its rotted casing. The name was unusual, but pretty, just like she was.

At least so far, he reminded himself, drawing a small notepad out of his back pocket and making a few notes with a capless Bic he'd shoved into another pocket. There was never any telling when a client would turn into a demon from hell, snarling and growling at every additional nail and every extra minute spent on a job.

He couldn't imagine Mackenzie Pruitt snarling, though. That lush little mouth wasn't made for it. Whatever it *was* made for was none of his business, though. She was a client. And that, as the saying went, was that.

She turned to face him in the gloom of the unlit shed. Her dark swing of hair fell forward over one shoulder as she rested a hip against the windowsill. "So we can do it?" she said suddenly, startling him.

Do it? Do what?

Oh. Crap, he was losing it. *Focus, Leo.*

"Yeah, we can . . . do it," he said, nodding. "I may have to adjust a few prices here and there, and I need to give you a detailed quote, but I can make you a studio. No problem."

She smiled, although the effect was muted in the dim light. "So what's next? The quote, I guess, and then . . . well, when do you start work?"

"You want to see the quote first," he told her gently, stuffing his notepad back in his pocket. "You always need to see the quote first."

She nodded, biting her bottom lip as she led the way outside, squinting in the bright sun. Out in the yard, the salt tang of the ocean was sharp. "I'm just excited to see it happen, you know?" she said, tilting her head to one side as she looked up at him. Her eyes were brown, he noticed. A deep, luscious brown, like very good chocolate, or polished mahogany.

"I know," he said, biting back a grin. "You can see it all now, right?"

She flashed him a curious look, her delicate brows drawing together. "I can, actually. I mean, I have this vision of what it's going to look like. I always do, though. It's the photographer in me, I guess."

He considered that for a moment, watching as she turned to glance back at the shed. Seeing it finished, taking a snapshot in her head, he guessed. Framing it, judging sunlight and shadow, making it perfect.

It was a dangerous thing to do. At least that was his take on it. Life very rarely cooperated with imagination or expectations, at least in his experience.

Before he could comment, she'd turned back to him, her

hands clasped loosely, a very dangerous smile on her lips. Dangerous in a pretty-please-don't-deny-me way. He'd seen that look before. And it was hell to say no, especially when the woman flashing that smile was as appealing as Mackenzie Pruitt.

"Speaking of photography," she said, her tone casual, "I have a proposition for you."

A warning bell went off in his head. Several, if he was going to stop to count them. A "proposition" could mean a lot of things, but one that involved a camera was a definite no.

She plunged on, ignoring what he was sure was the beginning of a scowl. "I'm branching out, or trying to. I want to do more than weddings and company brochures and birthday parties. I've had my work in a few galleries, and I've done a few commercial shoots here and there, but I'm . . . well, I'm boring you, I can tell." She smiled again, and he noticed a dimple in her right cheek.

Shit. She really was cute.

"The thing is, I just had a great idea for a photo essay," she continued. The muscle in his jaw clenched, and he folded his arms over his chest, waiting. "I'd like to take pictures of you working on the project, black and white, kind of an exploration of form and function, you working, the tools, the shed coming back to life . . ."

She finally trailed off, the dimple disappearing as her smile faded in the face of his complete lack of enthusiasm. "Mr. Dawson?"

"Sorry, but no," he managed, mentally subtracting the money he'd make on the job from his checking account. "I'm a carpenter, Ms. Pruitt, not a . . . model." He nearly choked on the word, it was so unbelievable. If she had any idea how long he'd worked to keep his face out of the papers . . . Christ, maybe she was talking about a magazine, something national.

"Well, I know that." She cocked an eyebrow at him, amused. "You wouldn't have to actually do anything, just whatever you need to do to the shed. And the PR could be great. I'm thinking of a local North Carolina magazine, but there are a few other places I'd love to try and—"

She bit off the last word when he held up a hand and shook his head. He struggled to keep his tone calm when he said, "No. I have all the PR I need—thanks, anyway. I'm not interested. And I think you'd better find someone else for the job."

He was already halfway across the lawn when she found her voice and raced after him, her fingers tentative on his elbow. "Wait! Look, you have to take this job. You were the only carpenter available on such short notice, and I need to get this place finished by the end of the summer. Please, Mr. Dawson."

He turned around, even though he knew he would be toast when he did. The pleading voice was hard enough to resist, but those eyes?

Yeah, there they were, big and round and innocent. Not even messed up with any of that mascara and other stuff women wore. Naked eyes, just the way they were meant to be.

He took a deep breath and shook his head as she gave him a sweet smile. Maybe if she promised . . .

He growled, "No pictures, though. No photo essay, or whatever you call it. I mean it."

Her shoulders slumped in relief. "You won't regret it. I promise," she said. Her dimple flashed, teasing him like a wink.

"You promise there won't be any pictures," he repeated, sticking out his hand there on the tiny lawn, with the breeze rolling off the ocean, warm and full of brine, riffling her hair away from her face like a glossy flag.

She stared at his hand for a moment, and although it didn't

seem possible, she managed to look even more innocent when she returned his gaze. "I promise," she agreed somberly, taking his hand and shaking it.

She had a nice, firm grip, businesslike and no-nonsense, he noted, holding her hand a moment longer than necessary, enjoying the feel of her soft skin against his palm, her long, delicate fingers against the inside of his wrist.

Not that it mattered, of course. Because no matter what she said, he didn't believe her for a minute.

Well, damn it, Mackenzie thought, leading Leo back to the house. She hated to shake on something when she had no intention of fulfilling her promise.

Not that it would stop her, of course. She wasn't going to paparazzi him and shoot film in secret, but she wasn't above a bit of persuasive wheedling. Even cajoling, if it was necessary. Begging wasn't entirely out of the question.

It was simply that she could *see* how gorgeous the photo spread would be, she thought, as Leo wrote up a quote at the kitchen counter, his brow furrowed over those amazing eyes, the pencil in his hand far too small for the size and strength of his fist. In her mind's eye, the photos were arrayed on a long table, all black and white, the muted grays and shadows giving dimension to the shed, and to the man. The juxtaposition of the sharply defined curve of his bicep against a straight-edge was so real, she almost believed she would find the shot in her camera later.

Why on earth would anyone be against something like that? It wasn't as if she was asking him to pose nude. At that thought, her cheeks heated, and she realized her gaze had rested on his ass. His very firm, very finely shaped ass. Which she could imagine all too well without its current covering of very well-fitting, faded blue denim.

"This is the ballpark," he said, and she yanked her head up to meet his eyes. "A few things may change here and there, depending on available materials and unexpected problems, but this is the figure you should expect." He slid the piece of paper across the counter toward her and she took it, amazed by the jumble of numbers and notations. The grand total was neatly circled at the bottom, and it wasn't too much more than she'd anticipated.

Of course, at this point she'd probably mortgage something just to get Leo Dawson and his tool belt into her backyard for a few weeks.

"It looks fine," she said, hoping her blush had faded. "When can you start?"

He folded his arms across his chest, and tilted his head at her. "Thursday, if that's good for you."

"That's great," she said, folding the quote and sticking it in the pocket of her shorts.

"Without photo documentation."

Damn it. "Of course," she said, making her expression as innocent as possible. It wasn't easy when those sexy green eyes were trained on her in suspicion. "I already told you."

"I'm going to hold you to it," he said, arching an eyebrow.

She didn't doubt it. But she was beginning to suspect that she'd be happier if he'd just hold her, period.

Three

Heaving his toolbox out of the back of his truck on Thursday morning, Leo considered Mackenzie's black Jeep, parked in the driveway in front of him. She was here, then.

He bit back a frown and opened the battered gate to the backyard, wiping his forehead with his forearm. Just nine o'clock and it was already steamy. The air was thick, nearly soggy, and the sun over the ocean was shrouded in haze.

It didn't matter if she was here. He had work to do, and he'd accomplished plenty of jobs with the homeowner around. It wasn't like he had anything to hide.

Except his face, he thought ruefully. Not to mention his curiosity about this particular homeowner and her adorable dimple. He'd actually dreamed about her the other night, and the dream definitely hadn't been rated PG. Not even PG-13.

He would just head out to the shed and start working—that was all, he told himself. If she wanted to talk to him, she could come find him. It was simple, really. She wasn't a problem.

And definitely not a temptation. She was a client. Even if she was an adorably sexy, fascinating one.

Just as he opened the door to the shed, though, a splintering crash from inside the cottage brought his head up in alarm. What the hell?

Muffled cursing followed, along with a dull thud.

Damn it.

Dropping his toolbox in the dewy grass, he covered the distance between the shed and the back steps in moments, and squinted through the screen door. "Mackenzie? You okay in there?"

Another thud. "Damn it! But yeah, I'm okay." There was a silent pause, then, "Leo?"

He shook his head in exasperation and pushed the door open, making his way through a mountain of cardboard boxes piled on the kitchen floor, and into the living room, which was littered with even more boxes among furniture that seemed to belong somewhere else. She was nowhere in sight. "Mackenzie?"

"Here." She popped up from behind a particularly big box, hopping on one foot. "I had a little run-in with a box of china."

That explained the crash, all right. It didn't exactly explain her outfit, which was an ancient pink T-shirt paired with a loose, floral-print skirt. The fact that the flowers were blue was the problem, he thought. For a photographer, Mackenzie seemed to focus on everything other than herself.

Not that she didn't look tasty, anyway. All that glossy hair was piled in a loose knot on top of her head, and her toenails were painted . . . was that purple?

Dragging his attention back to the problem at hand, he poked a tipped-over box with his foot. "This the china?" he asked her.

"Sadly." She lifted one corner of it with effort, and he winced at the sound of loose pieces jangling. "I think it's probably pieces for a mosaic now, though."

"Didn't you wrap it?"

Her chin came up in self-defense, and she sniffed as she said, "I ran out of newspaper. I wrapped other stuff, though."

He arched an eyebrow at her, and she shrugged. "I was trying to get it done quickly. My moving man, also known as my impatient brother, didn't have a lot of time."

"I can see he didn't exactly help you get this stuff organized, either," he said, pointing at a box marked "bathroom" which was wedged on the back of the sofa.

"Yeah, well." She'd perched on one of the sofa's arms to rub her injured foot, and stood up now, a sudden smile on her face. "So you're here! Beginning work on the shed, right?"

"You bet," he agreed, turning around slowly, glancing at the boxes stacked against the wall and lining the short hallway that led, he assumed, to the bedrooms. Stuffed laundry baskets and several black plastic garbage bags rounded out the wall of brown cardboard. "Although I could spare an hour if you want some help in here. I don't know how you're going to find anything until you get some of this into the right rooms."

She turned those huge brown eyes up to him in surprise. "No, that's okay. I mean, I know it's a mess, but you've got your own thing to do."

"What if I insist?" He hefted up a box marked "bedroom" and started down the hall. "Which room?"

"Mr. Dawson, really . . ."

"I thought you were going to call me Leo," he said, turning around to find her following him down the hall. She stopped short, her cheeks pointed with color and the beginning of a smile nudging her dimple into an appearance.

"Leo." She tilted her head, considering him. "And you'll call me Mackenzie?"

"I'll call you whatever you want if you tell me where to

put this box," he said with a smile, shifting the box in his arms. "What have you got in here?"

She frowned, squinting at the lettering on its side in the dim light of the hallway. "I don't remember. And it's that room, on the end."

There was nothing in her bedroom but a rumpled double bed and a serviceable pine dresser, and a laundry basket piled high with clothes. The wood floor was bare, as were the old casement windows. Wallpaper had been scraped away with what looked like effort, and the walls were rough with the remains of old paste and layers of paint.

"You take off that wallpaper yourself?" he asked, setting the box down near the wall. Pieces of tackless carpet strips meant wall-to-wall had been removed, too, and not professionally.

"It was awful," Mackenzie said, brushing a hand over the wall near the door. "I thought it would never come off, and I still have a lot of work to do before I can paint."

"That's an understatement." He crossed his arms over his chest, hearing the next words in his head before he uttered them, and wondering what the hell was wrong with him. He had enough work to do, here and elsewhere. "I can help you out, if you need it. Spackling isn't for everyone."

"You're beginning to seem too good to be true," she said, leaning against the doorjamb, her eyes thoughtful.

"You might not think so if I start unpacking your underwear."

She snorted, then bit her lip in embarrassment. Her cheeks were bright with color again, but her eyes were sparkling. "I'll take care of the unmentionables if you do the heavy lifting."

"Just point me in the right direction," he said, but when he started into the hall, she was slow to move, and they wound up together in the doorway, her chest brushing his arm. "Sorry."

"My fault," she said, turning toward the hall.

Just then he stepped back into the room, which suddenly brought them chest to chest. Her hair smelled like spring, light and green and vaguely flowery, and her skin, where his hand brushed against her arm, was warm and soft.

"Sorry." He should have moved, he knew it, but he didn't want to. He wanted to breathe her in for a while, and then he wanted to touch her some more. In a lot more places. On purpose.

"We seem to be stuck," she said, looking up at him. Her eyes had gone even darker, and the pale gold of her cheeks was hot with color.

"We won't get much done this way," he agreed, letting his hand come to rest on her hip.

Her head tilted to one side, her lips parting, and he felt her move closer.

Oh yeah. Tasting her would be even better than touching.

He bent his head, moving in—and the phone rang, a shrill jingle out in the kitchen.

She jumped, bumping against the doorjamb, and he stepped back.

"I . . . uh, I should . . ." She released a shaky, pent-up breath, and he nodded.

"Yeah," he agreed, and then she was off, running down the hall to answer the phone.

He leaned back against the doorframe as he heard her breathless "Hello?" and drew in a deep breath. So much for resisting temptation. Christ, he'd practically asked for it. *Can I help you move boxes?* That translated pretty easily into: *Can I hang around and look at you?* What the hell was he doing?

Helping her move boxes, he realized. There was no backing out now. And there was no denying that looking at her while he did was the payoff.

Oh, yeah. He was in trouble.

* * *

By noon, every box in the compact little house had been moved to its appropriate room. The box of broken china had been set out on the back steps until she could deal with throwing it away.

Wiping a stray hair off her forehead, Mackenzie looked around the much tidier living room and beamed at Leo. He was slouched against the kitchen counter with a bottle of water, his eyes following her, a weary smile on his lips.

"I really can't thank you enough," she said. "I don't even want to think about how long this would have taken me without you."

"Especially since a few of those boxes were heavy even for me," he said. He was sweaty, the skin on his arms gleaming. Watching those muscles in action had been an unexpected treat. No matter what he said, he had toted the cartons from room to room as if they contained nothing but feather pillows, stopping only to ask her where to put things when he came across an unmarked box or a laundry basket of odds and ends.

That wasn't actually true, she thought, stepping around him to get herself a bottle of water from the fridge. He'd stopped to lift an amused eyebrow at her collection of snow globes. He'd shaken his head at the explosion of bath salts and lotions that tumbled out of a box with a weak bottom. He'd examined a few of her summer dresses with an appreciative eye when he lifted them out of a laundry basket and hung them in her closet.

And he'd looked at her. A lot. The heat in his eyes alone was enough to make her long for air-conditioning.

Of course, after the almost-kiss in the doorway to her bedroom, it wasn't as if she hadn't been looking right back. Leo Dawson was a huge, gorgeous, solid wall of man. But it was more than that. As often as she'd found herself admiring the play of muscles in his arms or his back, she'd caught herself gazing at his face.

That was where the "more" came in. It was in the lines on his forehead, the shadows in his eyes, a sense of melancholy that lurked behind his smile. Leo Dawson gave every impression of a man who had lived hard, but who was much more than the rough-around-the-edges man he presented to the world.

Even if that man was so hot, she'd been trying to turn off her imagination all morning. It was disconcerting to find herself fantasizing about a man who was actually in the same room.

Not that he'd be in the same room much longer. He was probably going to head outside to the shed any minute, since that was what she was actually paying him for. The idea caused an unexpected pang of loss.

"Can I get you some lunch?" she said suddenly, turning to look at him. "You deserve some nourishment after all that work."

Nice going, Kenz, she told herself when he lifted a curious brow at her. *Not too obvious. Oh, no. Not at all.*

"I should probably get to work," he said slowly, but as he stood up and stretched, his eyes took her in, head to foot, lingering in all kinds of places.

As if he were hungry for something she definitely didn't have in the fridge.

"A quick sandwich might do the trick, though," he added, setting down his empty water bottle. "What have you got?"

"Let's see." She opened the refrigerator, grateful for the cool rush of air on her hot skin, and glanced inside. "Not much, unless half of a day-old bagel with cream cheese is your thing. Or some Fresca. I can run out, though. The deli over on Stone has great subs."

He shook his head. "Not necessary."

"I insist," she said, straightening up and going toe-to-toe with him, which forced her to crane her neck to see his face. "You've been working like a pack mule all morning, and not even at the job I'm paying you for. Do you want an Italian or a roast beef? Or something else?"

"Nothing, I swear," he said. "You go get yourself something and I'll get to work." He didn't move, though, and she was suddenly aware of how close their bodies were, and how warm his was.

She swallowed hard, fighting the rush of heat in her cheeks. It was going to be a long two weeks.

Two weeks of looking at him, and of inviting him in for a cool drink, since that was the polite thing to do when someone was working for you in the summer heat. Two weeks of having him close enough to touch, but not touching him. Two weeks of the throaty rumble of his voice echoing in her head, of remembering the moment when he had almost kissed her . . .

She stepped backward, angling for a little distance, a comfortable separation between herself and the heated, masculine smell of him, and bumped into the refrigerator.

Damn it. Why did the one contractor with time free have to be him? Why did he have to look like the embodiment of a fantasy bad boy?

And why-oh-why had she never realized she *had* a fantasy bad boy before now?

He wasn't her type, really. He was too gruff. Too rough around the edges. Too . . . blatantly masculine. He could probably do a pretty fair caveman imitation.

When he's carrying you off to bed.

To stop that train of thought in its tracks, she drew in a breath, speaking before she even knew what she was about to say. "You're pretty easygoing for someone who won't even let me take his picture."

In the suddenly deafening silence, she had plenty of time to examine his furious scowl.

It wasn't pretty.

"I thought we agreed on that." It was practically a growl. And he'd leaned forward, his arms crossed over his chest, making her wish she could back up even further.

"We did! I was kidding," she said quickly, trying not to squirm under his glare. His green eyes had gone muddy and darker. "Kidding. Really."

"I hope so," he said. "I'll be outside."

And with that the screen door banged shut behind him, his boots thudded down the wooden porch steps, and he was gone.

Four

For a Sunday night in early June, Buddy's was packed. Shouldering her way through the crowd with two fresh beers for herself and Susannah, Mackenzie wished for at least the dozenth time they'd found somewhere quieter to meet. She wasn't in the mood for noise, and the jukebox had been blasting since they'd arrived.

Susannah was loving it, though. She was perched on a stool, moving to a Gwen Stefani song and flirting with a guy across the room, who very clearly appreciated her moves. One more bounce from her and his jaw was going to drop open.

"Oh, thank God," she said when Mackenzie handed her the icy Corona. "I'm parched."

Mackenzie nodded, settling onto her stool and staring at the lime wedged into her bottle's neck.

"I'm beginning to get the feeling you're not having a good time," Susannah said, leaning closer to be heard over the music. "Are you still stewing over your hunky carpenter?"

"I'm not stewing," Mackenzie protested with a frown. "And he's not *my* carpenter."

"Semantics," Susannah said fondly, nudging her with one bare shoulder. She was wearing a sleeveless red blouse that set off her early tan, and her fingernails were painted to match. "You like him, you almost kissed, and then he bolted. So tell me the rest."

"There's nothing to tell," Mackenzie said, running a finger along the side of her cold beer. "I haven't seen him since."

"But he's been there working, hasn't he?"

Mackenzie nodded, fighting the cold knot of unhappiness in her chest. "Friday and Saturday, as planned. But I left Friday before he showed up, and I had to leave Saturday while he was out—I think he had to run to Home Depot. And both days he was gone by the time I got home."

Which was fine, really. He was working for her, after all, despite the almost-kiss. And he was working hard. She'd wandered out to the shed today, his day off, to find that he'd already torn away the rotted siding, replaced it with fresh lumber, and started preparing for the plumbing and electricity hookups. Then there was the small fact that for a photographer like her, it probably wasn't the brightest idea to get involved with a man who seemed to be pathologically opposed to cameras.

But she couldn't help wondering what he was hiding. And there had to be something. Every time she remembered the guarded sadness in his eyes, not to mention his entirely negative reaction to the possibility of having his photo printed somewhere, she came to the same conclusion. And she'd been letting herself remember his face an awful lot over the past few days.

"Maybe he's in the witness protection program," Susannah offered, her eyes wide. "Maybe the mob is after him!"

"You've been watching too much HBO," Mackenzie told her, rolling her eyes. "Real world here, remember?"

"Hey, the mob is part of the real world," Susannah argued. "So are other criminals. And murderers! Oh God, what if he killed someone? What if he's on the lam?"

Mackenzie spluttered beer on the table, narrowly missing her shirt, and sighed. "I don't think crazed killers 'on the lam' establish carpentry businesses and come with good recommendations."

"Well, you never know," her friend sniffed. "Truth is stranger than fiction, and there has to be some reason this guy doesn't want you to take his picture. Either way, you should talk to him. Just ask him, for heaven's sake. What's he going to do?" She considered her words for a moment, and added, "If he's not a murderer, I mean."

Mackenzie laughed and took another swallow of her beer, shaking her head. "It doesn't matter. I mean, yeah, I'm curious, but it's not really my business, is it? And he's not even my type."

Susannah didn't bother disguising her snort of disbelief. "For someone who's not your type, he's definitely managed to work his way into your imagination. Hell, he's working his way into my imagination, and I've never even met him."

Mackenzie restrained the urge to glare at her friend, but she couldn't help frowning at the ship's lantern hanging on the wall opposite her. Leo was clearly hiding something—or maybe protecting something?—but he wasn't a criminal. He certainly wasn't a murderer. It didn't matter how little she knew about him, she knew that much, deep down. Crazed killers didn't help you move overstuffed boxes and hang up your dresses. They didn't gently tease you about your collection of *Little House on the Prairie* books, or admire photographs you'd taken of your family. There was something soft under Leo's crusty exterior, all right.

It was a shame she'd probably never get to it.

"What is your type, anyway?" Susannah asked, crossing

her arms over her chest and tilting her head. "I'm trying to work it out based on Peter and Tom, but they're nothing alike."

Mackenzie definitely didn't want to talk about ex-boyfriends, especially Tom. The big, shaggy blond jerk. He'd been more attached to his PlayStation than he'd been to her.

"They're not the same physical type, no," she said, thinking about the two men with a grimace. "But they're both the kind of guy I think I'd like. You know, if they hadn't turned out to be totally wrong for me."

Susannah frowned. "And the kind of guy you'd like is . . . ?"

"It's not always about looks, you know," Mackenzie chided her with a lift of her chin. "I want someone stable, someone who will be a good dad, someone who wants the same things I want, like a home and a family, a dog."

Susannah stared at her, her mouth pursed in a frown. "And you're looking for this guy where? The Mr. Bland Yellow Pages?"

"Not bland," Mackenzie protested, kicking her friend's calf with the toe of her sandal. "Responsible. Reliable."

"Yeah, well, it doesn't mean you can't have a fling with your mysterious carpenter in the meantime, you know." Susannah stood up, hooking her bag over her shoulder to go to the ladies' room, and gave Mackenzie an affectionate smile. "As long as he's only mysterious in a sexy way."

Mackenzie was still thinking about that an hour later, when she and Susannah parted ways outside the bar. She'd refused the offer of a ride home. The night air was sultry and soft, and walking would give her a chance to enjoy it.

And to think.

Susannah didn't have a five-year plan. In all the years Mackenzie had known her, which dated back to high school, she couldn't remember her friend even coming up with a five-day plan. Five minutes, maybe, but that was pushing it. She'd bounced through college, somehow emerging with a degree in education, and she was a wonderful first-grade teacher, but she seemed to enjoy the fact that her students changed every year. And when it came to dating, she was all over the map—in the last two years alone, there had been a pediatrician, a mechanic, a software designer, and a navy lieutenant who was scheduled for an overseas tour in the coming year.

Taking life as it came worked for her, Mackenzie thought, breathing in the salty air as she walked along North Lumina and letting the breeze blow her loose hair off her face. But Mackenzie had always had a firm idea about the way her life would end up, or at least the way she wanted it to, and a moody carpenter with a secret didn't exactly fit the picture. He was a loner, that much was clear. And fitting a baby seat into his pickup probably didn't figure into his plans.

And she wanted a baby seat, with a baby to put into it, someday. She wanted the kind of guy who was thinking long-term, who wanted a partner. It was what she'd always seen when she imagined her life—herself branching out from wedding photography into gallery shows, with a husband in a white shirt and tie coming home at the end of the day with a kiss, helping to give the kids their baths, offering to make her tea, talking to her as she loaded the dishwasher and got ready for bed . . .

No matter how tempting it was to think about what it would be like to spend a night with Leo, he didn't exactly look like the kind of guy who had marriage and fatherhood on his mind.

Which made it that much more surprising when she realized that the man walking out of the drugstore just a dozen feet away was Leo.

With his arms full of diapers, and what looked strangely like baby shampoo.

* * *

Fumbling with the slippery package of diapers and the bulging bag from the pharmacy, Leo swore under his breath as he reached for his keys. At the sound of footsteps on the sidewalk, he looked up—and nearly dropped everything.

Mackenzie.

And she looked good.

He'd spent the last three days trying to hammer the sight of her, the scent of her—the *feel* of her—out of his head, which wasn't easy when he was doing it in her backyard.

She was dangerous, that was the thing. Dangerously curious, dangerously stubborn, and very dangerously tempting. Not a good combination, not for him. He'd finish the job on her shed because it was the right thing to do, but he'd been stupid enough to hope he could do it without seeing her again, at least not for more than a minute or two.

Stupid. Stupid, stupid, stupid.

Because here she was, close enough to touch and looking like she'd just walked off the beach in loose white pants and a little blue T-shirt that hugged her breasts, her hair long and loose around her face. Tousled, a little sleepy, and unbelievably sexy.

"Hi," she said. In the street light, her eyes were nothing but a soft, dark gleam.

"Hey."

She was fidgeting, dragging the toe of one sandal along the sidewalk, her mouth working as if she had something else to say. She looked so uncomfortable, he couldn't take it. Juggling his purchases, he said, "Can I give you a ride home?"

Her mouth opened in surprise, a round pink *O*, and she blinked at him. "I . . . all right."

Oh yeah, this was the way to keep his distance.

He motioned her around to the passenger side, and she held out her hand for his packages when he climbed into the driver's seat beside her.

"Shopping?"

Girl didn't miss a trick. "Yeah."

"For . . . diapers." It wasn't a question. She held the bulky package up to the light. "Newborn, I see."

"They're for my neighbor," he explained, turning the key in the ignition. The truck rumbled to life. "She just had a baby and her husband had to go out of town. Death in the family or something. I said I'd pick up a few things for her."

When she was silent, he cast his eyes in her direction and found her biting back a grin. "What?"

She shrugged helplessly. "It's just . . . well, it's a little like seeing your grandmother revving up a Harley. I didn't expect to see you with . . . this." She held up a fuzzy duck washcloth he'd snatched off the rack on a whim.

"My grandmother does drive a Harley," he said, keeping his eyes on the road as he pulled out of the parking space.

She laughed, stuffing the washcloth back into the bag and setting it on the floor. "I'm sorry. It's just that you don't look like the warm, fuzzy type."

He grunted. "Oh yeah? What type am I?"

She didn't answer immediately, and he cut his eyes sideways as he turned onto her street. This early in the season, most of the houses were dark; her porch light was a warm glow in the distance.

"I don't know," she said finally. She was staring out the window, but her fingers worked the strap of her bag unconsciously, twisting and untwisting it. "I didn't mean anything by it. It's just your hair, your earring, your . . ." She trailed off, but he saw that her gaze was now fixed on his bicep. "You have a kind of dangerous air. Rock and roll, not nursery rhymes."

He pulled into her driveway and cut the engine and the lights, sliding his arm along the seatback behind her. She thought he was a bad boy, or whatever women called them today. He had to restrain a bark of amazement. Rock and roll. She had no idea.

But all he said was, "Dangerous, huh?"

She nodded, and despite the darkness he knew she was blushing. "Not really. Not like you'd hurt me."

Not physically. Never. But the violence of the lust rushing through him was almost frightening. He turned her on. He could hear it in the husky whisper of her voice, feel it in the heat and tension of her body. And that turned him on.

"Of course I wouldn't hurt you," he agreed, getting out and walking around to her side of the truck. He opened the door and offered her a hand. "You probably wouldn't expect this, though, would you?"

"Probably not," she admitted. Her hand felt small in his—small and delicate and very warm.

He led her down the driveway and through the gate to her back porch. After the first day he'd come to the house, he'd never seen her use the front door. The shadowed shelter of the little porch was better for what he had in mind, anyway.

"You'd probably expect a guy like me to take instead of asking, huh?"

She'd backed up against the door, and he braced his hands on the frame on either side of her. In the velvety darkness she was nearly indistinct, but he could sense her body, warm and alive, trembling slightly.

"Maybe," she said. The word was a breathy whisper.

"Definitely," he told her, and leaned in, covering her mouth with his own.

It was hot and soft, her tongue a wet surprise, spiking his arousal even higher. She tasted so good, felt so good, and when her purse dropped to the floor with a thud, her hands crept up his chest, fingers tightening in the fabric of his shirt.

She didn't know from dangerous. She didn't have any idea how easy it would be for him to sweep her up and carry her inside, tossing her down on that rumpled, lonely bed in her room. Get her naked, fill his hands and his mouth with her, the silky heat of her skin, the rich, dark taste of her body. Fill *her*, with his cock . . .

She whimpered when he tangled his fingers in her hair, angling her head back to give him easier access to her mouth and the slender column of her throat. She was melting against him, nearly boneless already, and he hadn't even touched her.

But he was going to. Oh yeah. Didn't matter how stupid this was, how dangerous it was for him to get close to a woman who was too curious for comfort. Mackenzie Pruitt had gotten under his skin.

She groaned, a low vibration of pleasure against his mouth, when he slid his other hand under her shirt. His fingers were firm and sure against her back, her ribs, the sweetly curved underside of one breast beneath her bra. Squirming, her fingers clutched at his shirt again, pulling him closer.

He let go of her hair and dragged her up against him, inhaling the scent of her hair and her skin, and cupping her ass with one hand. Soft, round, and so fucking sweet.

She was holding on now, arching into him, and he pushed her T-shirt and bra out of the way so he could lower his mouth to her breast. The skin was flushed with heat, the nipple ripe and firm already, and he fastened his mouth around it, drawing hard, his cock responding to her moan of delight.

Bracing her against the door, he slid his hand into the loose waistband of her pants and then into her panties, smoothing his palm over the curve of her ass, and then moving around to stroke her thigh. She murmured something wordless, an incoherent sound of pleasure, and he twisted his hand to delve between her legs as he licked the hard, hot point of her nipple.

"Leo," she said breathlessly, and he smiled against her breast. Her heart was pounding beneath it, a frantic drumbeat, and she was already wet, creamy and hot.

He slid a finger through her folds gently, lingering at the dark center of her, circling it before sliding up to stroke her clit. It was swollen, already pulsing, and she was panting now, shudders of pure need racing through her.

One finger, then two, thrusting inside her, stroking hard, the way he wanted to thrust. The urge to take her, to devour her, to fill her was overwhelming, but not yet.

Now, what he wanted more was to feel her break, to watch as she gave herself up to the pleasure, and with one long, sure stroke against her clit, she did. Knees buckling, mouth opening, she arched into his hand, the only sound she made a desperate, breathless groan.

Holding her close, he buried his face in her hair, stroking her down, rearranging her pants, her shirt, waiting for her trembling to stop. When she looked up at him, eyes full of moonlight, he kissed her hard, sating himself on the taste of her tongue.

When he pulled away, she drew in a shuddering breath and opened her mouth to speak, but he shook his head. It was too much—it was crazy. He wanted her in ways he hadn't wanted a woman in a long, long time, and that was bad. He wanted her in ways that had nothing to do with lust, and everything to do with a far deeper need. Maybe she expected him to take his fill, maybe she wanted to give that to him, but he couldn't do it. He shouldn't have done this.

"Good night, Mackenzie," he murmured, reaching down to pick up her bag and hand it to her. He didn't trust his voice—it was rough with need. "Sleep well."

And then he was striding toward the truck, cursing himself and everything he couldn't tell her. Stupid. He was so fucking stupid. He'd wanted to keep his distance, and instead he'd opened himself up to her, or at least to her curiosity.

Mistakes. He was so fucking good at them.

Five

By eleven o'clock the following morning, Mackenzie had decided that watching the clock truly didn't make time go any faster. If anything, she felt as if she'd been planted in front of the damn thing for about three days instead of nearly three hours.

Thank God it was the microwave clock. If she'd been monitoring a timepiece that ticked, her head would have exploded by now.

She glanced out the kitchen window as she took a pitcher of iced tea from the fridge. The sky was a dull slate, and the air was swollen with the promise of a storm. But Leo had pulled into the driveway just after eight, truck tires crunching the gravel. By eight-fifteen, she'd heard the groan of old wood being torn away from its studs, and the metallic clatter of tools in use.

What she hadn't heard was hello. After those wild minutes on the back porch the night before, she'd sort of figured it was the least she could expect.

So she'd waited, scrambling out of bed and into the first clothes she stumbled across. She'd brushed her teeth and made coffee, all with an ear cocked toward the backyard.

She'd ditched her shirt for a different one—okay, a prettier one—and she'd brushed her hair and slid lip gloss over her mouth, certain she'd be interrupted any minute.

Wrong. It had been the longest three hours of her life.

Stirring a spoonful of sugar into her iced tea and swallowing down half of it in a single gulp, she made up her mind. She couldn't very well hide in the house all day, just because she didn't have an appointment scheduled. Not that she was hiding, of course. No, she was waiting. Well, she couldn't wait all day, either. She wanted to clear the air. She wanted to discuss what had happened between them.

She wanted him to kiss her again.

Taking a deep breath, she set down her glass and marched outside, swallowing hard when she saw that Leo was in the yard outside the shed. One confrontation, no waiting, she told herself, fighting the hot flush creeping up her neck to her cheeks just at the sight of him.

He was breaking apart old boards, throwing them into a loose pile outside the shed, and he was already sweaty. The sun was only a suggestion of light behind the clouds that had amassed over the ocean, but it was hot and sticky, the air full of moisture and the faint, burnt smell of electricity.

He looked up when he heard her crossing the grass, and nodded curtly. "Morning."

"Morning," she echoed, waiting, wriggling her toes in the damp grass.

Well, this was awkward. He'd turned back to his task, the cut-off sleeves of his dark T-shirt giving her an unobstructed view of the muscles in his arms. His hands were encased in heavy work gloves, his feet in dusty construction boots.

What to do . . . She stood there, impatient, irritation beginning to tingle along the back of her neck. *Turn around*, she wanted to say. *Talk to me.*

Kiss me again.

As if he'd heard her unspoken thoughts, he glanced at her over his shoulder. "You need something?"

Did she *need* something? She took a deep, calming breath, willing her voice to remain steady. She needed something, all right. She needed some answers, some clarification.

Almost as much as she needed him to finish what he'd started last night.

"I . . . need to talk to you," she said finally, taking a step closer.

"Can it wait?" he said, not looking at her, breaking a splintered piece of siding apart with a single blow. "I'd like to get this done before it rains."

She glanced at the sky, which was even darker now, an ominous near-black. Somewhere in the distance, thunder rumbled.

"It will only take a minute," she insisted, jumping when he threw the pieces of wood onto the pile with a sharp clatter.

He sighed and turned around, stripping off his gloves. Beneath his furrowed dark brow, his green gaze pinned her to the spot. "What is it?"

He had to know what *it* was, didn't he? Why was he making her try so hard? Why was he being so goddamned difficult?

"Mackenzie?"

She cleared her throat, feeling like every kind of fool on earth, and straightened her spine. "It's about last night."

He ran a hand over his head, bristling the barely-there fuzz. "Okay."

Crap. Now what? If only her heart would stop banging so violently, maybe she could think of something intelligent to say.

"You're not making this easy," she said finally, taking another step closer and looking him in the eye.

"Making what easy?" he asked, shrugging. But he ran his hand over his head again, as if he were restless. Possibly uncomfortable.

Huh. She went closer still, nearly close enough to touch him. "Last night was . . . well, it was unexpected, for one, but it was also wonderful. It would have been more wonderful if you'd come in." She stopped, the double entendre occurring to her too late, but Leo ignored it.

"I don't sleep with my clients," he said flatly.

"But you do . . . that?" She waved vaguely at the porch, baffled.

"No." He practically growled it. He was staring past her at the gathering mass of clouds, and his eyes were just as stormy.

"But you did," she protested. "With me."

"You're not like most of my clients." He shook his head and crossed his arms over his chest. "You're not like most women I've met lately."

Oh. Well. "I'm going to take that as a compliment," she told him, covering the final few inches between them with one step and laying her hand on his forearm. His skin was hot, the rough hair dark and bristly. "I don't know what happened last night, but I liked it. I . . ."

Her heart was in her throat as she looked into his eyes, which had gone dark and hungry. She wanted him so much—not just his body, but him, the man he was and the man he was hiding. And she wanted to tell him that, wanted to say the words aloud, but all she could feel was his heartbeat, drumming in time with her own, and his soft release of breath as he bent his head to kiss her.

And then the sky opened with a magnificent clap of thunder, lightning streaking the sky with blue light. The rain pelted down, stinging her bare arms, and without warning Leo grabbed her and pulled her into the shed.

The door banged shut behind them, and for a moment

they stood facing each other, silent and panting, shaking off the rain. Just as Leo reached for her, lightning crackled outside in a crazy flare, and she found herself wrapped in his arms, his mouth hot and urgent on hers.

God, he tasted so good—dark and strange, all man. The rough stubble on his chin and jaw rasped against her skin, and the sturdy denim of his jeans brushed her thighs, and she loved it—this was real, this was right now, Leo's solid body the only thing anchoring her to the moment.

He stumbled backward, taking her with him, and dropped onto a wooden crate. Tugging her between his spread thighs, he hooked his fingers into the hem of her shirt and stripped it off.

She shivered, still damp, but hot beneath the skin. So hot—she wanted his mouth on her, everywhere, wet and demanding. "Leo," she murmured, without any idea what she meant to say.

"Right here," he murmured back, and then he unhooked her bra with a sharp click and tossed the delicate scrap of silk to the floor.

Bare to him from the waist up, she had never felt more desirable. His eyes swallowed her up, and his hands were possessive when they stroked over her breasts. "Gorgeous," he said, and then he was tasting her, his tongue just as wet and urgent as she'd imagined.

She groaned as his mouth fastened around one tight, aching nipple, his tongue pushing against its underside as he suckled. It was almost too much—the sensation rippled outward like a stone in a pond, until she felt its echo in her belly and between her legs.

He kept suckling, but his hands were busy. Before she knew it, he was sliding her shorts and panties over her hips, pushing two fingers between her legs. She whimpered as they thrust inside her, filling her, stroking her, coaxing the flame higher, hotter.

But she wanted so much more. Struggling free of his hands, she reached blindly for his jeans. The air in the shed was too close, humid and stale, and the floor was gritty beneath her bare feet. It was dark, too, with the rain drumming on the flimsy roof, but she didn't need to see to unbuckle his belt.

It was his turn to groan when she'd fumbled it open and tugged down his zipper—she reached inside and curled her fingers around his erection. Smooth and hot, gloriously hard, it rose to her touch when she ran her thumb over the velvet head.

When she climbed into his lap, straddling his rigid thighs, she could have sworn he growled.

She reached between them for his cock, but he was already there, stroking through her folds, spreading the creamy wetness, his free arm wrapped around her waist.

Now. Please, now. She raised up to take him in, and Leo muttered, "Damn. Can we? I don't have—"

"I'm on the pill," she bit out, and slid onto his cock, taking him deep.

He growled again, thrusting up into her, the whole breathtaking length of him. They set the pace together, hard, fast, deep, her arms around his neck, his hands on her ass.

Nothing mattered, nothing but the feel of him inside her—not the rain or the shed or the conversation they hadn't really gotten around to, not his secrets or her growing suspicion that her "type" might be exactly like Leo. No other man had made her feel what he did, inside and out.

And right now she felt deliciously full and so incredibly alive, every part of her awake to his touch.

He pulled her closer as he drove inside, thrusting home again and again. She groaned. The pleasure was coiling tight now, drawing in on itself, but it was going to burst, soon now, so soon . . .

His lips fastened on her throat, and he licked the damp skin before drawing it between his teeth in a startling, possessive bite. She came in a dazzling starburst, a surprised gasp of pleasure escaping her lips. It went on and on, that widening ripple, sharp and bright and endless.

And Leo followed with a gruff shout, arms tightening around her as he spilled, his body shuddering with release.

She leaned her forehead against his, still panting.

"Bet this isn't what you had in mind for this shed," he said, his voice still rough.

She laughed, and settled against his chest to lay her head on his shoulder. He was like a furnace, hot all over, and his arms around her felt like the only thing holding her up. "Right now," she whispered, "I can't think of a better use for it."

So much for keeping his distance, Leo thought a few hours later, in Mackenzie's bed. She was asleep beside him, sprawled facedown in the tangled sheets, her hair a dark, glossy fan on her bare back.

He lifted a strand of it, rubbing it between his fingers, remembering the way it whispered against his face as she arched over him.

He'd stripped off his T-shirt and wrapped her in it before sprinting through the rain and inside, and once there they'd only blinked at each other in amazement before winding up in her bedroom. He couldn't get enough of the feel of her against him, the little incoherent sounds of pleasure she made when he touched her, the complete lack of inhibition in her response.

Mackenzie had a wild thing inside her. And experiencing it only made him want more.

Despite the fact that he'd gone and done exactly what he'd said he wasn't going to do. Last night had been torture, at least when it came to walking away before taking his pleasure—walking away from her now, after this afternoon, would be impossible.

But he couldn't ignore the knot of uneasiness in his gut. If Mackenzie had met him a few years ago, there was every chance that she not only wouldn't have been interested in him, she would have been appalled. And she would have been right to be. The man he'd been in those days wasn't anyone a woman like Mackenzie would want in her home, even as a carpenter, much less in her bed.

Mackenzie was forthright, responsible, focused. And, yeah, she was kind of a strange dresser, and he really didn't understand the snow globe collection, but the woman, at her core? She was good where it counted, and she was beautiful.

She was also curious. And that was a problem all on its own, at least for him.

She shifted in her sleep, turning over, and then stretched and opened her eyes. "Hi, there," she murmured, blinking. "So . . . that wasn't all a very lovely dream, huh?"

"Not a dream," he said, sliding down to scoop her up against him, burying his nose in her hair. "Not by a long shot."

"Well, that's good." Her words were muffled against his chest. "Because I've never been able to rerun a dream."

He laughed, and she untangled herself to look up at him. God, her eyes were so gorgeous. It was more than the rich dark brown color, it was what he could see in them—pleasure and drowsiness and surprise.

"Are you hungry?" she said suddenly, sitting up, heedless of the sheet. "Because I'm starving all of a sudden. Apparently, you give me an appetite."

"You give me an appetite, too," he whispered, and leaned forward to circle one soft, flushed nipple with his tongue.

"Someone will find us eventually, I suppose," she murmured, closing her eyes as he teased the nipple to life. "Starved, near death, but incredibly satisfied."

"I guess I could let you eat if you promise to let me bring you back to bed later," he said, pulling himself away from her body with effort. The taste of her skin was the only thing he could focus on at the moment—that, and the awful knowledge that he was digging himself in deeper with every word, every kiss.

He hadn't been this drawn to a woman in years. And he certainly hadn't been this reckless, either.

You have a job to finish, he told himself. As if that were the real reason he wasn't hightailing it out of her house right now, truck tires screeching on the pavement as he gunned down the street.

Maybe it would work out between them, he thought as he pulled on his jeans and followed her into the kitchen, where she stared into the fridge with interest, muttering to herself about the packages of deli meat in the drawer. Maybe she wouldn't care if he admitted to her why he didn't want her taking, and publishing, photos of him.

Maybe pigs would fly. He grimaced, an image of his mother's face flashing before him at the remembered words.

But it was very tempting to hope that maybe, just once, he wasn't going to fuck up his life completely.

Six

"Hold still, buddy!"

The blond two-year-old in question gave Mackenzie a look of supreme condescension and ducked behind his mother's sofa again.

"I'm so sorry," Ellen Mather said. She was bright red and wringing her hands like the heroine of a Victorian novel. "He usually loves getting his picture taken! I just had no idea . . ."

At a gleeful giggle from behind the couch, she cringed and spread her hands in surrender.

Mackenzie turned off her camera and motioned toward the kitchen, just down the hallway from the bright, spacious living room where she had set up her equipment. Ellen followed her, but not without a glance back in the direction of her mischievous toddler.

"Give him a minute," Mackenzie said, sitting down at the kitchen table. "It could be the novelty. He's used to having Mommy or Daddy behind the camera, but not some strange lady with lights and backdrops and all kinds of funny equipment."

"If you think so," Ellen said doubtfully, hovering at the

counter, where she had set out iced tea and muffins, both of which Mackenzie had already indulged in.

She stared out the wide bay window at the backyard, which was probably four times the size of her whole property, house included. A wooden play set was already in place on the manicured lawn, although little Jamie Mather probably wouldn't be able to use it for another year or so.

In her mind, it was going to be at least that long before she could convince the toddler to sit for a portrait that wouldn't make his mother cry, pack up her things, and get across the bridge and home, where Leo would be waiting.

Her home, of course. It wasn't as if he'd moved in, although just days after that first unbelievable afternoon it almost felt as if he had. She'd never met someone she'd felt such an immediate connection to, even if so much of him was still a mystery.

Even if he was nothing like the kind of man she'd always thought she wanted.

They were beginning to behave like an old married couple already, she thought, aware that a satisfied little grin was beginning to form. When she came home from appointments with clients, he was there waiting, hammer or hacksaw in hand, sweaty and usually shirtless, ready to kiss her. And then kiss her some more.

And the days when she had no scheduled outside appointments were even better.

Yesterday, for instance. They'd spent most of the morning in bed, for one thing, but then she'd pulled out a kitchen drawer in search of a teaspoon, and the whole thing had fallen on her bare foot. After Leo had done his best to kiss it and make it better, he'd tackled the rotted track and repaired it. That had led to a discussion of the fact that the cabinets needed repainting, which had detoured into a conversation about the color—which had been a kind of faded hospital mint green—and before she knew it, Leo had talked her into an earthy red, which she had to admit looked wonderful against the butcher-block counters.

Especially since he'd taken off for the home center and come back ready to wield a roller.

The shed had taken a backseat, of course, but she didn't care. He was taking as much of an interest in her little cottage as she was, and what was even more surprising was how bold, and how creative, he was. In her mind, kitchens were supposed to be white. Clean, simple. She'd never imagined cabinets the color of a ripe tomato could look so right. So gorgeous, in fact, especially with a deep yellow on the walls. Standing in the tiny kitchen this morning, she'd felt like she'd been plunged into the heart of a ruby.

But then, he'd already questioned her idea for the storage she wanted in the studio, too, and his solution was . . . well, better. More creative, a little different, and much cooler than what she'd pictured. It was startling, actually, to realize that she was pretty rigid about the way things were "supposed" to be. Leo was affecting her in ways she hadn't anticipated, none of them bad.

Even if she was still curious about his past. If he was rigid about anything, it was his tendency to clam up whenever she asked a personal question that dug deeper than his favorite movies or what kind of food he liked.

She dragged herself away from her thoughts when Ellen set a fresh glass of sweet iced tea, garnished with a very pretty sprig of mint, on the table in front of her and sat down.

"It's too quiet in there," she said, her warm brown eyes troubled. "Maybe I should check on Jamie."

As if she'd said the magic words, tiny feet thudded down the polished wood floor in the hall and a moment later a blond head was looking up at Mackenzie from the safety of his mother's side. The child's round blue eyes were serious.

"Pitcher?" he said dubiously.

"Picture," she agreed, restraining a laugh of relief.

Ellen sighed and stood up to take the child's hand. "There's a cookie in this for you, buddy," she said in a stage whisper.

Catching the toddler's amazed smile, Mackenzie said, "Keep saying that. The Christmas card will be priceless."

She grinned at him as she picked up her camera. If the kid cooperated, she was one step closer to home—and Leo.

Leo set down a dripping paintbrush and reached for his bottle of water. He'd discovered that morning that Mackenzie's tiny kitchen pantry was a mess—the shelves uneven and some partly rotted, the shelf paper peeling and stained.

Somehow, between running to the home center to buy lumber and paint, and cutting and installing the new shelves, he'd never gotten around to working on the shed today.

Of course, the longer he took finishing the shed job, the longer they would be together. Neither of them had mentioned the future, that big gray area that existed just beyond the moment he showed her the completed studio. Part of him didn't doubt for a moment that Mackenzie considered this weird rhythm they'd fallen into the beginning of a relationship, but a bigger part of him—the smart part, he reminded himself—believed that if he confided all the things she wanted to know about him, she would say good-bye without a second glance.

He sank onto the stool at the counter, guzzling the cold water and wiping his brow with the back of one hand. Installing air-conditioning would be high on his list of priorities if the house were his.

But it wasn't. And every day, as she unpacked yet another cardboard box and continued the process of making the cottage her home, he doubted just a little bit more that it would ever be a place she'd want to share with him permanently.

Mackenzie was smart, and funny, and warm, and deliciously sexy, but she also viewed the world out of her own unique lens. In Mackenzie's world—a world which wasn't at all unlike that of lots of women like her—things had a place, a time, a proper function. She'd raised her eyebrows in disbelief when he suggested that the miniature hall closet could double as a bookcase if he took down the door and installed shelves. He'd convinced her it would take better advantage of the space, in the end, but it had taken a good fifteen minutes of discussion.

It was a stupid little thing, nothing earthshaking, but every time he found himself looking at that quirky collection of snow globes, his heart sank a little further. That was the life she was looking for, when it came down to it. Perfect, encapsulated, pretty. Everything, and everybody, in its place. What was more, she was willing and able to work for it, honestly and as hard as she had to.

He was willing to bet his left arm that she'd never envisioned an ex-rocker and recovering alcoholic in her picture-postcard fantasies of her life.

The water bottle drained, he stood up and tossed it in the recycling bin beside the back door, stretching. The pantry looked good. Bright white, clean. Mackenzie would love it, he hoped. And if she didn't . . . Well, he could paint it again, build different shelves.

And that would give him another day of not working on the studio, which meant another day before he had to face the future. Denial, he thought wryly, was working just fine for him at the moment.

He looked up at the sound of her car in the driveway and a moment later she was pushing open the screen door, hands full of white plastic bags.

"Hey there, Mr. Carpenter," she said, giving him a teasing smile. Her hair was twisted up behind her head with some kind of clip, and her loose white blouse was untucked and wrinkled. "You look like you could use a good meal."

"I certainly wouldn't say no."

"Well, you're in luck." She set down the bags on the table, rustling plastic as she removed the take-out containers. "After toddler-wrestling most of the afternoon, I didn't feel up to cooking, so I stopped at The Lobster Pot and got dinner." She looked stricken suddenly, and faced him with wide eyes. "Tell me you're not allergic to seafood."

He laughed, taking a Styrofoam container from her and opening the lid to peek inside. Crab cakes. Awesome. "Not at all. You better tell me more about this toddler-wrestling, though. Sounds dangerous, and possibly sticky."

She was rummaging in a drawer for silverware, and turned around to make a face at him. "My afternoon was spent with a photo-shy two-year-old. I'm thinking of charging his mother double."

"Hey, you were two once," he said, sitting down next to her after he'd made room at the table. The air was thick with the aroma of fresh seafood and garlic, spices, the tang of Caesar dressing on two leafy green salads. "I bet you weren't always a model of good behavior."

She considered that as she bit into a fat crab cake, and tilted her head when she smiled at him. The curve of her lips was a wicked temptation. "Well, there are definitely times when it pays to be bad."

He nearly choked on his food, and stood up to get another bottle of water from the fridge. The conversation had taken a wrong turn, and it wasn't one he wanted to follow, not now. There was bad in Mackenzie's world, and then there was *bad*.

"Are you okay?" she said, scrambling out of her chair and laying a hand on his back.

"Fine." He kissed her forehead, then her nose, and finally her mouth, lingering as he tasted her. Her arms snaked around his waist, her soft breasts pressed against him, and he had to resist the urge to slide everything, food and all, off the table and take her right there.

Before it was too late. Before it was over.

"Hey," she said when he finally broke the kiss. "I forgot—I bought wine, too. Let me get it."

Fuck. He sat down as she withdrew a bottle of chenin blanc from a brown paper bag. "Crap," she muttered, opening a drawer beneath the counter. "I forgot this meant I'd have to find my corkscrew."

He focused on his food, squirting lemon juice over his crab cakes. What the hell was he going to say? And why hadn't he thought about it before now? People who were dating were known to have a few drinks. So were people who were just sleeping together, or whatever it was he and Mackenzie were doing.

"Leo? You sure you didn't swallow your tongue?"

She was teasing, but he could see the question in her eyes when he glanced at her.

"Yeah." Oh, good. Monosyllabic answers were sure to convince her everything was fine.

"Triumph!" she cried a moment later, holding up a corkscrew and carrying it and the bottle to the table. "You want to do the honors while I dig up some glasses?"

Here's your chance, he told himself. "Just one glass, babe," he said, keeping his tone light.

"You don't like wine." Her shoulders slumped. "I should have asked. I can run out and get some beer, if you like. And I think I have some vodka in the cupboard . . ."

She was rummaging again, her back turned, and he closed his eyes in defeat. "No, it's not that." *Just say it, you coward. You had to in AA meetings. Can't forget that.* "I'm . . . I don't drink, Mackenzie. Not . . . ever."

There was a moment of electric silence, weighted with all the things he hadn't said, and she didn't turn around to face him immediately. When she did, her expression was carefully neutral, compassionate.

God, she had no idea how much he didn't deserve that.

"I didn't know," she said softly. She bit her bottom lip. "Obviously. I'm sorry."

Now she was apologizing. He didn't think it was possible to feel any worse. "It's my fault. I should have said something."

"Why?" She sat down and reached for his hand across the table, her slender fingers a whisper against his skin. "It's not like telling someone your name. It's not required. I just wish I hadn't made you feel uncomfortable."

If only she understood. He was uncomfortable because she was. He'd put her in a bad position, and when she finally insisted on hearing everything else he'd carefully left unsaid, it was going to be downright awkward.

Hell, "awkward" didn't even begin to cover it.

"You didn't," he reassured her. "It's my issue." Then, because he wanted to feel her against him and because he definitely didn't want to talk about it anymore, he reached over and grabbed her up, hauling her onto his lap for a long, deep kiss.

She returned it, brushing her palms over his skull, wriggling until her breasts were crushed against him, warm and giving, and he was glad. Because while kissing her accomplished both of the things he'd wanted, it also meant that he could avoid the questions in those deep brown eyes of hers for a little while longer.

Seven

If Mackenzie had thought Leo was gorgeous in his jeans and sweaty T-shirts, she should have considered what he would look like in a well-cut suit.

Strange that the gray pin-striped affair looked so absolutely perfect on him, and all she wanted to do was rip it off his body.

"Stop staring," he said, running a finger around the inside of his stiff collar. "I feel weird enough as it is. I haven't worn this in a while." He'd shaved, although a dark shadow of stubble was already present along his jaw, and he'd taken out his silver stud. She kind of missed it.

"You should wear a suit all the time," she said, tilting her head as she examined the elegant cut of the jacket's shoulders. "You look . . . well, beautiful."

He lifted an eyebrow and stepped closer. He smelled of soap and cool water, and faintly of pine, but the clothes couldn't mask the heat of his body. Ignoring the trembling thrill of lust in her belly wasn't going to be easy. She eyed the hallway which led to the bedroom, where the bed was still unmade, waiting patiently for them. They had at least thirty minutes before they had to leave for the wedding, after all . . .

"Do you want to go now, beat the traffic?" Leo said, fumbling with his tie, which already looked fine.

"Stop that, you're going to ruin it," she said, smacking his hands away and smoothing the front of his jacket. "And what traffic? We have plenty of time."

"Okay." He dropped onto the sofa, his eyes far away, his shoulders rigid with tension.

She bit her bottom lip as she sat down beside him. Maybe this had been a mistake. Bree was a friend, and even though Mackenzie was technically working at this wedding, Bree had been bugging her for at least two months to bring a date.

"You're my friend," she'd said. "I want good pictures, but I want you to be able to enjoy the day, too. You should at least have a little fun."

And nothing had sounded like it fit the bill as much as bringing Leo along. To thank him for all the extra work he'd done in the cottage, to make sure he had an afternoon off with nothing but celebration and good food to enjoy. And, okay, to simply be with him, instead of at a wedding by herself, wielding her camera and trying to remember exactly what you were supposed to do during the Electric Slide.

But Leo hadn't been thrilled when she'd broached the subject. Actually, "not thrilled" was an understatement of nearly epic proportions.

He'd agreed—almost right away, actually—but not before a handful of emotions flickered in his eyes. She hadn't understood any of them—not the shame, not the weariness, and particularly not the fear. It was a wedding, for heaven's sake, not a public execution.

But what had convinced her not to drop the issue was the brief flash of what looked like pride that touched his hard, masculine mouth in a hesitant smile. He was touched that she'd asked him, she would bet on it. Which meant there was no way to rescind the invitation, not that she wanted to, anyway.

She wanted him there. She wanted him everywhere—in her dreams, in her life, in her bed. He was already in her heart, whether she liked it or not.

And days like today, it was hard to be sure. There was so much she didn't know about him, so much he seemed unwilling to share. She wished she could convince him that nothing mattered but the here and now, that she truly believed kicking an addiction to alcohol was courageous, but there was never an opening, never a way to tell him so.

And there were, she had to admit as she studied his sharp profile, all those unsettling unknowns. She knew in her bones that Leo would never hurt her on purpose, but it didn't mean she wouldn't get hurt, period.

He slid his hand into her lap and twined his big fingers around hers. "Sorry," he said. His voice was gruff. "I'm not always real comfortable with a lot of strangers."

Why did she suspect that was a lie? A little one, to be sure, but no matter what, it wasn't the whole truth.

She decided to ignore it, and squeezed his hand. "Stick with me, buddy," she said lightly. "You'll do fine."

Picking at the moist chicken marsala on his plate three hours later, Leo glanced up at Mackenzie, who was across the room taking pictures of the flower girl. The child couldn't have been more than four, a tiny blond thing with a headful of curls and the most enormous blue eyes Leo had ever seen. Her dress was wrinkled, its lavender sash untied and trailing behind her, but she smiled for the camera as if she'd been posing for photos all her life, and he heard Mackenzie's laugh of delight.

"Thank you, Shelby," he heard her say above the chatter

and the DJ. "I think that's going to be the best picture of all."

She'd barely taken the time to eat. Beside his, her plate was heaped with food she hadn't touched. But he'd never seen it affect anyone less—she was all over the place, bending down, stretching up on her toes, crouching, catching the wedding party and the guests in pairs and groups, laughing and talking and dancing. She was tireless, and she was good. She'd caught a quiet moment between the bride and groom, seated at their table, the groom running his knuckles over his new wife's cheek as she looked up at him from beneath her lashes. If the couple didn't cherish that picture, they didn't deserve a photographer like Mackenzie.

He'd brought his own camera, a small digital, since he'd figured it would be cool for Mackenzie to have some pictures of herself with her friends. He'd caught a couple of her with the bride and groom, and one of her and Bree and their friend Susannah, but she'd been so busy otherwise, he'd only had a view of her back.

A moment later she sat down next to him, placing her camera in the empty seat on the other side of her, and sighed happily. "Almost over," she said, laying a hand on his knee. "Why aren't you eating?"

"I could ask you the same thing."

"I'm saving room for cake," she said with a smile, leaning toward him to bump shoulders.

So casual, so familiar. As if they'd known each other forever. As if their lives were entwined for good.

God, how he wished.

He was an addict, that was the problem. After years of not dating, barely even looking, he'd fallen off the wagon with a deafening crash when it came to Mackenzie Pruitt. And just one taste of her had been his undoing. He wanted her nonstop, not just her body—though that was pretty fucking wonderful—but her. All the time, every day, forever.

Forever. God, it had been almost that long since he'd even let himself think about a relationship. And now he was poised to be with the one woman he wanted, and the one woman who would run the other way when she discovered what and who he was.

At least no one at the wedding had recognized him. Yet. He'd caught a few questioning glances, but there was no way to know if Mackenzie's friends were curious about her choice of a date, or the kind of sharp-eyed people he'd been avoiding all these years.

Beside him, Mackenzie idly forked up a piece of chicken as she watched the guests on the dance floor. The DJ was decent—he'd kept the music going, picking lighter, softer songs during the meal, and the bouncier, really danceable stuff now that the party was in full swing. And without, thank God, resorting to the Electric Slide or the Chicken Dance.

Suddenly the bride was beside them in a cloud of billowing white satin, her cheeks flushed with exertion. "Did you get pictures of the cake?" she asked Mackenzie.

"You bet," Mackenzie replied. "It's gorgeous, too."

"Well, good," Bree said, taking her hand and smiling at Leo. "You're off duty until the whole cutting and feeding portion of this program. You two need to dance, have a little fun."

She tugged Mackenzie to her feet despite her protests, and leveled him with a dictatorial gaze. "Come on, buddy, get your butt on the dance floor and show my very good friend a good time."

There was no arguing with that, however much he wanted to. He stood and tipped an imaginary hat at the bride, who beamed, and took Mackenzie's arm, leading her through the swaying bodies to an empty spot on the polished parquet floor.

"At least this way I get to have my hands on you," he murmured in her ear.

"I'm all for that," she whispered back, leaving a kiss on his jawbone just before the music started.

But it wasn't a slow-dancing kind of song. It was the Commodores' old hit, "Brick House." He watched in horror as the groom's mother began gyrating, her silk-clad bulk jiggling as the song funked up.

Mackenzie bit her bottom lip to restrain a giggle and steered him backwards, moving her shoulders in time to the music. "Loosen up, Leo," she shouted over the music. "Show me your moves."

"I'll show you all kinds of moves later," he replied, turning and nudging her toward the hallway to the restrooms and the kitchen. The music throbbed around them, and Mackenzie kept bouncing in time until he pushed her against the wall and leaned down for a kiss.

She tasted good, as always, and beneath her simple, hot-pink linen sheath, her body was warm and mobile, grinding against him as his tongue swept inside her mouth.

After a moment, her arms twined around his neck, and he growled in appreciation when her breasts pressed against him. Stupid suit coat. He wanted it gone, wanted her body bare and open against his.

He deepened the kiss, losing himself in the taste of her mouth and the soft curves of her hips as he slid his hands over them. On the dance floor, most of the guests were singing along, shouting, "Brick! *House!*" during the chorus, and, he hoped, oblivious to what he and Mackenzie were up to just a dozen feet away.

The waitstaff, however, was a different story. "Oh, excuse me," a young girl in a white shirt and black bow tie exclaimed when she backed into the hall a moment later, bumping into him, a huge tray of discarded dinner plates wobbling in her hands.

Mackenzie blushed a deep rose and nudged him away from her, managing a sheepish smile for the girl. "Our fault. Sorry. Come on, Leo."

She grabbed his hand just as the song ended, leading him back to the dance floor, but he froze as the DJ cued up the next tune.

There was no mistaking that familiar bass beat, the raunchy growl of the guitar. Two solid CDs and a spectacular crash-and-burn later, and "Making Time" by Joe's Garage was still in heavy rotation, not quite a one-hit wonder, but close.

He swallowed hard, dropping Mackenzie's hand. "I have to go to the men's room. I'll be . . . back in a minute."

He didn't even wait to gauge her reaction, just took off, brushing past a waiter with another tray, nearly stumbling into the men's room and into a stall, slamming the door shut behind him.

Damn it! No matter what he did, that song at least was going to follow him till the day he died. He couldn't even complain, not really, since royalties still came in on a regular basis. It was one of the reasons he'd been able to keep Dawson Carpentry small, picking and choosing his clients from the limited population of the Wilmington suburbs and Wrightsville Beach. The goddamn song had paid for rehab, for God's sake.

But every time he heard it, he knew that someone with a sharp eye would do a double take and figure out that, yup, he was the former guitarist for Joe's Garage, nineties wonder band gone wrong. He was the guy the tabloids had loved to gossip about, between the booze and the women and the parties. He was the guy who had self-destructed when his band mate had OD'd. He was the guy who had disappeared from the face of the planet, holed up somewhere no one would look for him . . .

He slammed his fist against the stall in frustration. Just because no one was looking didn't mean he'd never be found. He'd known that five years ago, and he knew it now. And every time a "where are they now" program ran, every time someone wrote an article on rock-star excess and fallen idols, he waited for the phone to ring. He didn't want any part of it. He wasn't that man anymore.

The song was ending—he could hear the last chorus, Mike's voice rasping, "'Making time for us to share, making time's become so rare . . .'" The music vibrated through the walls, a clatter of drums and his own sliding guitar riff, and then it was over.

He took a deep breath and reached for the stall door when he heard footsteps. Two men, it sounded like, over by the urinals. There was a metallic hiss as a zipper slid down.

"He looks familiar, doesn't he?" one of the men said. "And so . . . Well, he's not exactly Mackenzie's type, you know?"

Hand on the door's metal lock, Leo froze.

"Yeah, Bree said he's working for her, building a photography studio or something." Another zipper, the telltale sound of urine splashing against tile. Bree's new husband, Mark. It had to be. "She usually goes for the white-collar types."

"I wish she'd go for me," the other man said over the sound of flushing. "She's so freaking cute. That ass, man. But she gives pretty stern cold shoulder, you know?"

A flame of rage, hot and dangerous, licked through Leo. Her *ass?* White-collar types? He restrained the urge to burst out of the stall and shove the guy's words back down his throat, with his fists.

Like he needed any extra attention now. Already, the asshole who'd been ogling Mackenzie had pronounced him "familiar."

He had to get out of here. As soon as they cut the cake and Mackenzie took the requisite photos, he was taking her home.

And then he was taking her to bed. Before she started asking questions, and he would be forced to say good-bye.

Eight

Leo drove home like a man possessed. Strapped into the passenger seat of his truck, Mackenzie eyed him warily as he gunned across the causeway. The windows were open, and the sultry night air on her face felt good. Or it would if it wasn't rushing by quite so fast.

The minute she clicked the last photo—Bree throwing her bouquet of overblown white roses—Leo had practically kidnapped her, helping to stuff her cameras and equipment into their appropriate bags, gathering up her purse and the special favor Bree had made her, a painted picture frame.

"I have to say good-bye, Leo," she'd protested. He'd only scowled, and gone to wait in the truck for her.

So much for her good-time wedding plan. He'd looked like a torture victim through most of it, even if he hadn't behaved that way, but at the end? What was that? What was wrong with him?

The obvious solution was to ask him, of course.

But in this case, the obvious solution seemed like the perfect way to get her heart broken. Whatever he was hiding, he could hold onto it for a little while longer.

Even if that made her a coward.

She opened the door when Leo pulled into the driveway and cut the engine. "So much for my hair," she said lightly, reaching up to touch the elaborate knot she'd made that afternoon. During weddings especially, she didn't need her hair swinging into her eyes or the lens, but the wind had effectively made hay of it. Loose strands blew around her face in the evening breeze.

"It looks pretty," Leo answered, gathering up her equipment and following her inside. "Sexy, in fact."

"Thank you," she said, flipping on a light and setting down her purse. "I think."

If she had any sense at all, she would send him home. Give herself some time to think about what they were doing, and what they were going to do when he finished the studio. To wonder why he'd never invited her to his house, why he preferred staying in to going out. To contemplate the way a song had spooked him, the fact that he'd once had a drinking problem.

But when she looked up at him after kicking her shoes off, she knew the truth. When it came to Leo Dawson, she apparently didn't have any sense at all. Because all she wanted to do was hold him.

Well, okay, not "all," but close.

Turning, she walked past him down the hall to her bedroom, switching on the little lamp on her dresser. It cast a soft glow in the darkness, throwing shadows over the unmade bed and the comfortable, rose-patterned easy chair she'd found at a flea market.

She knew Leo was behind her, even though he hadn't said a word. Without turning, she reached for the zipper of her dress and slid it down, letting the garment drop to the carpet. Next came her bra, and then her panties, both items tossed recklessly toward the open door of the closet, and the hamper inside it.

A rustle of movement, a muted groan from the floorboards beneath the carpet, and then Leo's hands were on her, framing her waist as his mouth traveled the back of her neck and across her shoulder. Her body responded with an electric thrill of anticipation, her skin waking to his touch, tingling with pleasure already.

He snapped the clasp of her barrette, and her hair tumbled over her shoulders. She shook it out as he turned her around and set her away from him, his eyes hungry.

"So beautiful. You don't even know," he murmured, and she felt a hot flush of arousal on her skin, from her breasts to her belly.

"You're pretty beautiful yourself," she whispered, stepping backward until her thighs hit the mattress. She sat down, then slid onto the bed, lying back against the mound of pillows at the headboard.

Her nipples were already erect, rigid with excitement. He was swallowing her up with his eyes, which were nothing more than vague shadows beneath his brow in the gloom. She was dying for him to touch her, to get undressed and climb onto the bed with her, but there was something wildly exciting about being on display this way, just for him.

He shrugged off his jacket, but he didn't throw it on the chair. He reached into the inside pocket first, withdrawing his camera and setting it on the dresser.

A hot flame of arousal licked at her belly. He wasn't going to . . . ? Oh, but he was. Loosening his tie and rolling up his sleeves, he picked up the camera again. And aimed it right at her.

"Leo . . ." she began, but her voice was strangely breathless, hardly audible.

"I've never been much of a photographer," he murmured, "but I think now might be a perfect time to try again." He crouched at the foot of the bed, aiming the camera up at her. "You're so beautiful, just like this. I want to remember you this way." He pressed the button and the flash went off, a shocking flare in the dim room.

Oh God. He'd really done it. He'd taken a picture of her, naked.

And it was . . . exciting. Slightly naughty, in a completely innocent way. It was Leo, after all. She trusted him. And she had a feeling that she wasn't the only one turned on.

She took a deep breath and wriggled up on her elbows, thrusting her breasts farther forward. "What about this?"

Had she really said that? Was she really doing this?

"That's . . . very good," Leo said, his voice catching in his throat as he snapped another picture. He sat at the foot of the bed, his face only partially visible behind the slim silver camera, waiting. "Show me how sexy you know you are, babe."

She twisted, tilting her head and parting her thighs just a little bit, teasing him with the glimpse of curls. *Click*. Then she sat up, eyes wide, her heart hammering in her chest, and let her legs fall open completely, one hand on her thigh. *Click*.

Oh God. She couldn't take much more of this. She was wet already, and so hot inside she was restless. She wasn't even thinking of the few nude centerfolds she'd seen—she was just doing what came naturally, opening herself to him, to the camera, reveling in how lovely her naked body felt against the rumpled sheets, fluid and soft, deliciously curvy.

Suddenly her hands were on her breasts, cupping them, holding them up to him, and the camera hit the floor with a thud.

"Photo shoot is over," Leo growled, crawling over her and pushing her back on the bed. Before she knew it, his mouth had fastened on one ripe nipple, suckling hard, and she groaned in relief.

He was still dressed, though, and that had to change.

Now. She reached for his tie, but his head was in the way, and when his teeth closed on her flesh, she gave up, the sharp, thrilling surprise of the bite echoing through her.

He moved down her body, his mouth hot and wet on her skin, biting, kissing, sucking, tasting. She shivered with the pleasure, the racing sensations skittering over her breasts, her belly.

He left one sucking kiss just above her curls as he nudged her thighs apart, wide and then wider, sliding his arms under them and gently spreading her folds. He murmured something she couldn't hear, and then his mouth was on her, his tongue licking through the creamy, wet flesh.

Oh God. Oh God oh God oh God, it was good. So hot, so very hot, and so wet, his tongue, her folds, a burning point, a dangerous blaze . . .

She came without warning, gasping out loud, her thighs tightening, but he didn't stop. He slowed down, licking her softly, but he kept at it until she was sure one orgasm was rushing into the other, waves of incredible pleasure rippling through her over and over.

When he finally lifted his head away from her, she was weak, panting, and his mouth glistened in the soft lamplight. Then he was getting up, stripping off his tie and his shirt, unbuckling his pants and letting them drop before sliding his briefs off. He was already hard, gloriously so, but she didn't have time to admire it—he was climbing on top of her and sliding inside.

He grunted, and she wound her arms around him, holding him tight, hanging on as he thrust in and out, harder and faster than he ever had before. His urgency was exciting—her fingers dug into the muscles of his shoulders, and she tilted her pelvis up, seating him even deeper.

"So good," he murmured. "You're so good, so beautiful . . ."

She answered him with her body, straining as his cock

thrust home, tightening around him, those fierce interior muscles milking him. He raised above her on locked arms, his eyes dark with abandon as he stared down at her.

She met him thrust for thrust, that sweet spot far inside throbbing with the delicious sensation. He filled her so completely, she whimpered when he pulled out, and sighed when he slid inside again, slowly, the gorgeous friction igniting her arousal all over again.

And then he sped up again, plunging, and she hung on, eyes fixed on his face. He was still watching her, and she knew he saw it when she broke, her mouth opening in a startled O of pleasure. He followed, spilling inside her with a hoarse cry, sliding a hand under her ass to keep him as deep inside her as he could go.

A moment later he collapsed, falling to one side and rolling her with him. She curled into his damp chest, still panting.

In the comfortable silence that followed, his gruff voice was a surprise. "It's good between us, isn't it?" he murmured. "Perfect?"

She never could have imagined anything as good as what they shared. Perfect? Hell, yes. At least in bed.

"Of course it is," she whispered, angling her head up to look at him. His face was shadowed, his eyes dark in the dim light. "It's wonderful."

He hugged her tight, dropping a light kiss on the top of her head. "Good."

There wasn't anything more to say. But as she dropped off to sleep in his arms, she remembered what he'd said when he'd taken the camera out. *I want to remember you this way.*

She was right here. Why would he need to remember her?

Nine

Four days later, Mackenzie was seated at an outdoor café she and Susannah liked, the sun on her face and the air sweet with the scent of roses, waiting for her friend to arrive.

If only the rest of her life was as picturesque, she thought with a moody swat at a fly determined to share her iced tea. Ever since Saturday night after the wedding, she'd seen less and less of Leo. He was . . . well, fading out. Taking himself away from her in bits and pieces, little by little, especially as the studio neared completion.

Sunday he'd claimed laundry and chores at his house, leaving her place by noon and not returning until the next morning. Monday and Tuesday he'd been busy with the subcontractors who were installing the plumbing and electricity, and she'd had appointments with clients, anyway. This morning he'd called to say he had a few appointments with prospective clients and not to expect him until tomorrow, and when she'd wandered into the studio before leaving the house, she knew it was only a very brief matter of time before he would be finished with the shed completely.

The basic shell had been refurbished and shored up, with

a new roof and a new door, and the larger window she'd wanted. The Pergo floor was down, the cabinets installed, the darkroom sink was working, and her countertop desk was waiting to be assembled and installed. Once that was done and the sheetrock was painted, including the trim, the studio would be finished.

A dream come true, actually. Gorgeous, functional, and all hers.

Except for the fact that she didn't give a damn about the studio anymore, not if it meant that Leo would be gone.

"I'm here," Susannah said, leaning down to kiss her cheek. "Sorry I'm late. Traffic was a bitch."

Mackenzie made a vague noise of understanding and handed her friend a menu. "No problem," she said.

"What's wrong? You look like you lost your best friend, and that's not possible because I'm right here." Susannah waved the laminated menu at her, her bracelets rattling as she did. "Spill. What's up?"

"Nothing," Mackenzie said, bending her head toward her own menu and trying to focus on the selection. "I'm thinking about chicken salad. What are you going to get?"

"I'm going to get annoyed if you don't tell me why you look like you're about to burst into tears." She reached across the table and laid a gentle hand on Mackenzie's arm. "Is it your hunky carpenter?"

Of course it was. Although part of the problem was whether or not he was really hers.

She started with the wedding and went on from there, explaining everything—without mentioning the naked pictures, of course. "It's just that I don't know where this is going," she said as Susannah waved the waiter away, hissing at him to come back later. "We weren't supposed to get involved in the first place! I didn't think it was a good idea to sleep with someone who was working for me, and he apparently doesn't usually sleep with clients, and, well, he's not even my type! I thought, hey, loads of sexual attraction, this could be a fling, but it's so much more than that now, and I don't want to lose him, but I don't know what he wants, or what he's hiding, and—"

"Whoa! Slow down, babe," Susannah said, biting back a grin. "Take a breath. I'll wait."

"I know," Mackenzie said miserably, sighing. "I'm a mess. I'm panicking. And I'm not supposed to do that. I *don't* usually do that! But this thing with Leo is so *different.*"

And why was it different, she asked herself as Susannah gave in to the impatient waiter and ordered their lunch. Because Leo had shown her that maybe the life she'd always envisioned for herself was a little bit lacking. All these years she'd been picturing a nice guy, but he was, she saw now, boring. Faceless, in fact. A piece of the puzzle, and not necessarily the most important one.

How awful. It was like the Christmas sweaters her grandmother gave her every year. She didn't want another red—or blue or pink—cashmere cardigan, but she knew she'd get one. And she'd actually begun to plan her wardrobe around them. She might have secretly wanted a black leather miniskirt or a vintage denim jacket, but cashmere wasn't bad. It didn't suck.

Every year, she'd settled. And somewhere along the line she'd settled for a life that was likely. A life that was normal, if not spectacular or unique or what she truly wanted. And she didn't even have it yet. She'd settled in her imagination for a guy who was nice enough, unthreatening, a bit bland. How pathetic was that?

What was worse was the fact that she didn't have any idea how Leo felt. Did he want them to be together? Did he want children? Did he want children with *her*?

And how ridiculous was it to worry about any of that when he seemed to be easing his way out of her life, step by step? When she'd never even been to his house, or knew anything about his family, and certainly not the secrets he seemed so determined to keep?

"You're going to have to fight for him, if you want him," Susannah said, squeezing lemon into her diet soda. "Maybe he's just scared. Maybe it's that whole commitment thing."

"I know," Mackenzie said, smiling at the waiter when he set down her plate of walnut chicken salad. "And I intend to."

She pulled into the driveway at home a little after three, determined to rope Leo into a conversation if necessary. Except he wasn't there.

The weight of disappointment was palpable, but it didn't matter. He'd be back at some point. If she had to, she'd track him down. She could show up at his house, even.

Or she would if she knew where he lived.

Inside, she kicked off her shoes and decided to catch up on everything she'd let fall by the wayside over the last two weeks. She'd never missed an appointment, but she hadn't been scrupulous about keeping up with e-mail, or with the mail. She had bills to pay and bills to collect from clients, she was sure, not to mention a mountain of developing to do in the makeshift darkroom she'd set up in the spare bedroom.

She opened her laptop and booted up, horrified to see nearly twenty e-mails waiting to be read, not counting spam. Those she axed immediately, and then scanned through the others trying to decide which was the most important. A message from Bree's husband caught her eye— wasn't he on his honeymoon?

She clicked it open, her heart sinking as she read the message. "Check out this link," it read. "There's some interesting stuff about your new boyfriend here." The URL was www.joesgaragefans.com.

Joe's Garage? They'd been a band a few years back, she thought, although she'd never kept up with new music. Her heart was with U2 and Dave Matthews, and she could never keep track of every must-hear song on the radio. What did Leo have to do with the band?

She clicked it anyway, and her mouth dropped open when the home page revealed photos of the band. There was Leo, front and center, a guitar strapped across his chest, his hair a bit longer, his earring a bit more prominent, in a scruffy gray T-shirt and black jeans, a sexy scowl on his face.

The sexy scowl she knew and, she had to admit, loved.

Leo had been a member of Joe's Garage?

She clicked through the site, her heart pounding like a drumbeat in her chest. She remembered this now—even someone as uninterested in the music scene as she was knew what had happened to the band in its final days, a year after the release of their second CD. They'd been the big new thing, and the press had followed their tour because the stories of their outrageous partying had been legendary. And then the lead singer, someone named Mike Ruggierio, had OD'd, and the band had fallen apart.

It was all on the Web site, in black and white, with pictures and anecdotes and links to news stories. This was what Leo had been hiding. This was why he didn't want her taking his picture and publishing it anywhere. The Web site even spelled it out: "Leo Dawson, former guitarist for the band, has disappeared from public life. Attempts to track him down have been met with hostility. Please leave the guy alone—he deserves his privacy and the peace and quiet of his new life."

She stared at the screen, aware that she'd slumped back in her desk chair, her mouth literally hanging open.

He hadn't told her. Not once in all the intimate moments they'd shared. Hadn't trusted her enough to keep his identity, and his privacy, to herself.

And no matter how much she cared about him, she couldn't love someone who didn't trust her. Not when she'd given him every reason to believe in her. She hadn't pushed, hadn't pressed, hadn't asked for an explanation when he admitted that he was an alcoholic.

She pushed away from the desk, pacing the living room, trying to ignore the tears sliding down her cheeks. Everywhere she looked, Leo was there. Here in the living room, where he'd helped her move boxes. In the kitchen, where he painted her cabinets and flirted with her. In the bedroom— God, the bedroom, where he'd almost kissed her that first day, and where he'd made love to her as if his life depended on it just the other night. She could picture him in the shower, wet and soapy and flashing that come-here-baby smile, and frying bacon at the stove, explaining patiently that her arteries, and her waistline, could take it. The house alone would always carry memories of him.

She'd opened herself up to him, body and soul. And right now, imagining losing him, imagining the things she'd want to say when she saw him again, it seemed like the biggest mistake she'd ever made.

Pulling out of the Home Depot parking lot at seven that evening, the bed stacked with lumber, Leo turned off the radio in the truck. Joe's Garàge, again. What was it about that fucking song this week?

He didn't want to hear it. Hell, he barely listened to any post-1985 music anymore. Too many memories. Of the band he and Mike had wanted to form, all those years ago in that Philadelphia suburb, of their rock idols, of the people he'd met when Joe's Garage started to play seriously. He remembered when the music was all that mattered, writing it, playing it, letting it weave its spell over him and the others, and their audience. And he'd shot that all to hell.

Some days it seemed like he was going to have to find a

dark cave somewhere if he wanted to avoid the fallout from that time in his life forever.

Maybe that would prevent him from creating new fallout, too. Like the fallout he knew was coming with Mackenzie. It was like smelling a coming storm in the air, the faint scent of electricity and the gathering damp. It was coming, all right, and he was pretty sure it was going to be a category five.

He was also pretty sure Mackenzie wouldn't want to live in a cave with him. It would make him, and possibly stalactites, her only photography subjects, for one.

He braked at the stoplight, staring out toward the ocean. Dusk was falling, and the sun was a pink-gold smear on the horizon. It was a perfect day. Except for the fact that he hadn't seen Mackenzie at all. He was going to have to get used to that, and soon.

When the light changed, he turned onto Lumina and then onto his own street, the faint jingle of an ice cream truck somewhere close by. He smiled. He and his brother had raced the truck in their neighborhood every night in the summer, hoarding sofa-cushion dimes all day to pay for their rocket pops and creamsicles. There was a memory he didn't have to hide from, at least.

But his smile faded as he neared his house. Because there in the driveway was Mackenzie's Jeep. And there on the porch steps was Mackenzie herself, arms folded over her chest, her hair scooped back in a no-nonsense ponytail, her brow, he saw as he drove closer, furrowed in a frown.

Shit. Well, that storm certainly came up faster than he'd expected.

He pulled into his driveway, parking behind her Jeep, and climbed out. Here it was. The end. *Fuck.* Suddenly he wanted nothing more than to make love to her one last time, imprint her scent and the feel of her body and the sound of her voice in his brain.

Wasn't going to happen, he knew. Not when her expression was made entirely of thunderclouds. So he asked the first question that came to mind. "How'd you find me?"

"You left an invoice in the studio, and it had your billing address on it," she said simply, her voice flat and tired. "I wasn't above snooping. Especially after I discovered just what you've been keeping from me."

Fuck. Fuck fuck fuck. So much for telling her himself. As if he hadn't had a million opportunities he'd been too chicken to take.

"Do you want to come in?" he asked, stepping around her and fitting the key in the door, trying to keep his voice level. "I'd like it, if you would. If you'll let me explain."

She followed him without a word, and stood inside the dark front room of the house as he closed the door behind her, taking in the big nothing he'd done with the place. An old black leather sofa rested against one wall. A huge TV was set up opposite it on a cheap entertainment center he'd picked up at discount place, and an old trunk served as the coffee table. One lonely floor lamp stood in the corner.

It was embarrassing, now that he saw it through her eyes. It wasn't a home, it *was* a cave. If she saw the empty field of the mattress in his bedroom, the only furniture there, she'd probably pity him.

"I don't know what there is to say, Leo." She sat down suddenly, and when he looked at her he saw her eyes were full of tears. "I thought . . . well, I guess I thought you trusted me. I don't know why you couldn't tell me what had happened to you. I still don't know why you're hiding it."

He tossed his keys on the trunk, and sat down next to her. He couldn't touch her—she was holding herself rigid, protecting against some kind of blow, even if it was only an emotional one.

He opened his mouth to speak, although he had no idea what he was going to say, but she beat him to it, the words rushing out through her tears. "I know you didn't plan this. I know I didn't. I know what happened between us was a surprise. But I can't help thinking that you knew all along it wasn't going to last, that when you took those pictures and talked about remembering me, you knew it would end. And I don't know *why*. Why, Leo? Why couldn't you trust me with this?"

Fuck it, he was holding her now, even if she fought him off with a stick. Sliding closer, he hauled her against him, murmuring into her hair. "You've got it all wrong, Mackenzie. I do trust you. I was ashamed. I'm not what you want. I don't fit into the life you're trying so hard to build for yourself. Do you want some fucked-up ex-rocker with an alcohol problem standing beside you in a church, saying 'I do?' Raising your children? Hiding from the press in case someone wants to revisit the crash-and-burn of Joe's Garage on a slow news day?"

She wrestled away from him until she could look him in the eye. The disbelief in her expression nearly killed him.

"That's not who you are, Leo." He'd never heard her voice quite so fierce before. "Those are things you did, things that happened to you. The man I know is no one who should be ashamed of himself. He's a hard worker, and he's kind, and he's loving and imaginative and generous—"

He cut her off with a barking laugh, and got up from the couch to pace the length of the room. She didn't see, she didn't want to. She was so much more than he deserved, because her heart was the generous one.

"You don't want to know how much of those stories are true, Mackenzie," he said, his back to her. "You really don't. I drank, I used drugs, I was out of control. High on the celebrity thing, fulfilling every stupid expectation of a rocker I'd ever heard. I cheated on every girlfriend I ever had, because I had hot-and-cold-running women every day. I made my mother cry, for God's sake. I made her terrified that I would OD. I crashed my car, I broke promises. I fuck-ing self-destructed, okay?"

He winced at the feel of her hand on his back, soft and warm through the sweaty fabric of his T-shirt. "And then you put yourself back together," she whispered. "And you did a damn good job."

"Did I?" he said, turning around and fixing her with his gaze. If she touched him again, he would break. "I'm hid-ing. I wasn't honest with you. At first I was so worried about what would happen if you went through with taking photos of me, I couldn't think about anything but more press, more local reporters. And then you meant so much to me, I couldn't bear what you would think if you knew the truth."

She shook her head silently, her eyes full again, tears rolling down her flushed cheeks. But he wasn't finished.

"Don't you get it, Mackenzie?" he said, walking across the room, away from her, away from the grief and the pain in her eyes. "Even after I figured out I was falling for you, I kept going. I kept drawing out the work on the studio, find-ing things to fix in the cottage, so I could have you to myself a little longer. Even when I knew you would never want a man like me if you knew the truth, even when I figured out I was hurting you by staying . . ."

"You're not making sense," she murmured, following him, taking his hand and forcing him to look at her. In the half light, her eyes were incredibly dark, but they were full of emotion. Understanding, compassion. Love.

"Aren't I?" he said. "Didn't I do those things?"

"Maybe," she said, winding her arms around him. Her body's soft, giving curves felt so good against him. "Everyone makes mistakes, Leo. Not everyone tries to cor-rect them."

Had he done that? Or had he just hidden? Sure, he didn't

drink anymore, and he worked hard at an honest business, but what about the rest? All those years ago, he'd done whatever the hell he wanted to, whatever felt good, because no one told him not to. A little excess was practically a pre-req for a rocker. And no one had cared about him, not re-ally—no one was interested in Leo Dawson, the man. They wanted Leo Dawson, the rock star, the guy with money and influence on the music scene, the guy with bottles of scotch to burn and no second thoughts about doing the craziest thing anyone could propose. They wanted the scent of fame to rub off on them. They wanted stories to tell their friends. They wanted the perks, the photo ops, the backstage passes. And the few people he'd cared about—his family, his long-ago girlfriend, the one who'd been there when Joe's Garage hit it big—had paid the price. He wouldn't do that to Mackenzie.

Not that she was giving him a choice, apparently.

Tugging him toward the sofa, she pushed him back onto it and climbed in his lap, straddling his thighs and smooth-ing her hands over his skull.

"I could tell you so many things," she said, leaning down to kiss his jaw, his cheek, his forehead, feather-light kisses that were tenderness as well as desire. "I could explain the things I've learned about myself, the things I've figured out about life and love, just in the past few hours. But I'll keep it to this. I don't want perfect. I don't want a picture-post-card life, or what's traditionally expected of a woman like me. I want you. I want the . . . eating seafood together, and making love in the rain, and crazy-sounding red cabinets that look awesome, and showing you my photographs, and maybe, just maybe, hearing you play the guitar. I want to be together, no matter how hard it gets, because it's going to be worth it. Love always is."

Love. His heart thudded against its cage, and a knot of

emotion formed in his throat. She loved him. She knew who and what he was, and she loved him. He could spend the rest of his life showing her how much he loved her.

"A life with you is more than worth it," he said between sudden, hot kisses, his hands tangling in her hair. "Always, only with you. I love you, Mackenzie Pruitt. I may have saved your shed, but you saved me. From myself."

"I had ulterior motives," she whispered, stroking his chest, her cheek warm and soft against his jaw. "I want you around for good, Leo Dawson. I want to spend my life with you."

He couldn't believe he was actually hearing those words. Couldn't believe that it wasn't over between them, that she loved him no matter what. It was almost too much. And he was going to prove to her, every day, that she hadn't made the wrong choice. That loving him was going to make her happier than any other woman on earth.

He stood up, bringing her with him, her legs wrapped around his waist, her arms around his neck, desire coursing through him in a hot wave. "I want to start the rest of our lives right now," he murmured. "In my bedroom."

She kissed him, hot and urgent, as he made his way toward the bed. "I thought you'd never ask."

Here's a peek at Karen Kelley's
HELL ON WHEELS.
Available now from Brava.

Cody sipped her beer, her legs stretched out with her boots propped on one of the four chairs circling her table. The bar was dim; only a few low-watt overheads kept the room from total darkness.

It was the middle of the week and not very crowded—two men sat on stools at the bar while three women on the prowl lounged at one of the scarred tables closer to the door. Cody had already seen them turn down the two men as they waited for something better to come along. Apparently, they were picky about who they screwed.

She couldn't fault them for that.

She rested her beer against her lips and tipped the bottle. The Bud Light was already room temperature. Hell, she didn't know why she was still there. A week of little sleep, living on crackers smeared with peanut butter and drinking flat soda had taken its toll on her. She should be at home in bed. Tiredness seeped out of every pore.

When she glanced up, the reason she'd hung around strolled through the door looking dangerously attractive. Like her, he'd gotten rid of his vest. The deep green T-shirt molded to each sinewy muscle while his jeans hugged every inch of his sexy thighs. He could put Calvin Klein male models to shame.

He surveyed the room until his gaze landed on her, and stopped. The little half grin that always sent tingles down her spine appeared—as well as the tingles down her spine.

Crap, she should've left. But then, maybe he was worth a little self-torture.

Casually, she watched as he came toward her. The three women zeroed in on him, their antennae going up. She could almost see the drool running down the sides of their mouths.

One of the three stood. Apparently, the leader of the pack. A frizzy-haired blond bimbo with *fuck me* flashing on her forehead. She wore a tight black leather skirt up to her ass cheeks and a knit shirt so low her silicone-enhanced boobs practically spilled out. She went so far as to stand in Josh's path.

Cody had to give Josh credit—he walked around the woman as if she wasn't even there and didn't seem to notice when she flounced to the bar to order another drink.

He stopped at Cody's table. "You waited."

"Yeah, right, in your dreams," she said with a very unladylike snort. "As soon as I finish this I'm out of here. Sorry to disappoint you."

He pulled a chair out, flipped it around, and straddled it. He didn't look a bit put out by her rudeness as he rested his chin on the top chair rung and stared at her.

What the hell had she been thinking? Hanging around the bar this long had been a terrible idea.

She'd reached her self-torture limit, and then some. Josh was one of the bad boys. The ones who enjoyed the chase almost as much as they did the victory.

Foreplay. That's all it was to them. She'd seen too many females fall prey to a man in low-slung jeans, boots, and a cowboy hat. Josh had left his hat behind, but he might as well be wearing it the way the three women had given him the once-over.

"Can't we just talk?"

"Your kind never wants to just talk," she countered.

"I won't even touch you." He straightened, opening his hands in supplication. "Talking, that's all we'll do."

"Talking?" She didn't trust him, but then, she didn't trust anyone.

"Yeah, don't you feel it?"

He continued before she could ask what exactly she was supposed to be feeling—other than sexually starved.

"You know, the rush of adrenaline that quickens your pulse when you bring down a skip. It takes me at least a couple of hours to unwind. Help me out. Just talk."

Bad thing was, she knew exactly what he meant. She might look calm on the outside, but on the inside she was wound tighter than an eight-day clock. She doubted talking would help, but he was right. She didn't want to go home to a cold, empty apartment.

She nodded toward him. "You talk, I'll listen."

"Fair enough. What do you want to know? Ask me anything and I'll tell you."

Yeah, right. Let's see how long it would take him to clam up when she got personal. "Why do you date so many women, but never stay with one longer than a month?"

He grinned. "So, you have been paying attention."

Have a look at
AUSSIE RULES
by Jill Shalvis.
Available now from Brava!

From the other side of the aircraft, the door opened. A set of stairs released. A moment later, two long legs emerged, clad in dark blue trousers, clean work boots, and topped by a most excellent ass. Not averse to enjoying a good view, Mel stayed in place, watching as the rest of the man was revealed. White button-down shirt, sleeves shoved up above his elbows, tawny hair past his collar, blowing in the wind.

Yep, there were a few perks to this job, one of them catering right to Mel's soft spot.

Pilots. This one looked more like a movie star pretending to be a pilot, but you wouldn't hear her complaining. And just like that, from the inside out, she began to warm up nicely.

The man held a clipboard, which he was looking at as he turned, ducking beneath the nose of the plane to come toe to toe with her, a lock of tawny hair falling carelessly over his forehead, his eyes shaded behind aviator sunglasses.

And right then and there, every single lust-filled thought drained out of Mel's head to make room for one hollow, horror-filled one.

No.

It couldn't be. After all this time, he wouldn't *dare* show his face.

His only concession to the surprise was a raised brow as he lifted his sunglasses, his sea green gaze taking its sweet time, touching over her own battered work boots, the dirty coveralls, the fiery, uncontrollable red hair she'd piled on top of her head without thought to her appearance. "Look at you," he murmured. "All grown up. G'day, Mel."

Yeah, he'd grown up, too. He was bigger, broader, and taller than the last time she'd seen him, but she couldn't mistake the smile—of pure, devilish, wicked trouble.

Australian accent, check.

Heart-stopping green eyes and long lashes to match the long, thick tumble of light brown hair falling in said eyes . . . check and check.

Curved mouth that could invoke huge waves of passion or fury . . . *CHECK*. "Bo Black," she whispered, getting cold all over again.

Cocking his head, he let out a slow smile. "In the flesh, darlin'. Miss me?"

Miss him? Yeah, she'd missed him. Like one might miss a close call with a hand grenade. "Get off my property."

As if he had all the time in the damn world, he leaned back against his plane, slapping the clipboard lightly against his thigh. "No can do, mate."

"Oh, yes you can." Staggering at a strong gust of wind, she planted her feet more firmly as she pointed to his plane. "You just get your Aussie ass back inside that heap of junk and fly it the hell out of here."

"Heap of junk?" Instead of being insulted, he laughed good over that, the sound scraping at her belly because it'd been a long time since she'd heard it.

Of course, she hadn't seen him in ten years, and the last time she had, he'd been eighteen to her sixteen, all long and lanky, not yet grown into his body.

He was grown into it now, damn him, and how. Reaching back, he lovingly stroked the steel of the plane, making the entirely inappropriate thought take root in her brain: *did he stroke a woman like that?*

Clearly she needed caffeine.

And a smack upside the head.

"You know exactly what kind of plane this is," he noted easily. "And how valuable."

"Fine," she granted. "Your toy is bigger than mine, you win. *Now* you can go."

Tossing his head back, he laughed again, and she made no mistake—he was laughing *at* her.

Nothing new.

And finally, here is a portion of a wonderful,
new magical romance that is the first
Zebra trade paperback,
WHEN YOU BELIEVE
by Jessica Inclán.
Available now.

The men had been after her for a good three blocks.

At first, it seemed almost funny, the old cat calls and whistles something Miranda Stead was used to. They must be boys, she'd thought, teenagers with nothing better to do on an Indian summer San Francisco night.

But as she clacked down the sidewalk, tilting in the black strappy high heels she'd decided to wear at the last minute, she realized these guys weren't just ordinary cat-callers. Men had been looking at her since she miraculously morphed from knobby knees and no breasts to decent looking at seventeen, and she knew how to turn, give whoever the finger, and walk on, her head held high. These guys, though, were persistent, matching and then slowly beginning to overtake her strides. She glanced back at them quickly, three large men coming closer, their shoulders rounded, hulking, and headed toward her.

In the time it had taken her to walk from Geary Street to Post, Miranda had gotten scared.

Now Post Street was deserted, as if someone had vacuumed up all the noise and people, except, of course for the three awful men behind her.

"Hey, baby," one of them said, half a block away. "What's your hurry?"

"Little sweet thing," called another, "don't you like us? We won't bite unless you ask us to."

Clutching her purse, Miranda looked down each cross street she passed for the parking lot she'd raced into before the poetry reading. She'd been late, as usual. Roy Hempel, the owner of Mercurial Books, sighing with relief when she pushed open the door and almost ran to the podium. And after the poetry reading and book signing, Miranda had an apple martini with Roy, his wife Clara, and Miranda's editor Dan Negriete at Zaps, but now, she was lost even though she'd lived in the city her entire life. She wished she'd listened to Dan when he asked if he could drive her to her car, but she'd been annoyed by his question, as usual.

"I'll be fine," she said, rolling her eyes as she turned away from him.

But clearly she wasn't fine. Not at all.

"Hey, baby," one of the men said, less than twenty feet behind her. "Can't find your car?"

"Lost, honey?" another one said. This man seemed closer, his voice just over her shoulder. She could almost smell him: car grease, sweat, days of tobacco.

She moved faster, knowing now was not the time to give anyone the finger. At the next intersection of Sutter and Van Ness, she looked for the parking lot, but everything seemed changed, off, as if she'd appeared in a movie set replica of San Francisco made by someone who had studied the city but had never really been there. The lot should be there, right there, on the right hand side of the street. A little shack in front of it, an older Chinese man reading a newspaper inside. Where was the shack? Where was the Chinese man? Instead, there was a gas station on the corner, one she'd seen before but on Mission Street, blocks and blocks away. But no one was working at the station or pumping gas or buying Lotto tickets.

The men were right behind her now, and she raced across the street, swinging around the light post as she turned and ran up Fern Street. A bar she knew that had a poetry open mic every Friday night was just at the end of this block, or at least it used to be there, and it wasn't near closing time. Miranda hoped she could pound through the doors, lean against the wall, the sound of poetry saving her, as it always had. She knew she could make it, even as she heard the thud of heavy shoes just behind her.

"Don't go so fast," one of the men said, his voice full of exertion. "I want this to last a long time."

In a second, she knew they'd have her, pulling her into a basement stairwell, doing the dark things that usually happened during commercial breaks on television. She'd end up like a poor character in one of the many *Law and Order* shows, nothing left but clues.

She wasn't going to make it to the end of the block. Her shoes were slipping off her heels, and even all the adrenaline in her body couldn't make up for her lack of speed. Just ahead, six feet or so, there was a door or what looked like a door with a slim sliver of reddish light coming from underneath it. Maybe it was a bar or a restaurant. An illegal card room. A brothel. A crack house. It didn't matter now, though. Miranda ran as fast as she could, and as she passed the door, she stuck out her hand and slammed her body against the plaster and wood, falling through and then onto her side on a hallway floor. The men who were chasing her seemed to not even notice she had gone, their feet clomping by until the door slammed shut and everything went silent.

Breathing heavily on the floor, Miranda knew there were people around her. She could hear their surprised cries at her entrance and see chairs as well as legs and shoes, though everything seemed shadowy in the dark light—either that, or everyone was wearing black. Maybe she'd somehow stumbled into Manhattan.

Swallowing hard, she pushed herself up from the gritty wooden floor, but yelped as she tried to put weight on her ankle. She clutched at the legs of a wooden chair, breathing in to the sharp pain that radiated up her leg.

"How did you get here?" a voice asked.

Miranda looked up and almost yelped again, but this time it wasn't because of her ankle but at the face looking down at her. Pushing her hair back, she leaned against what seemed to be a bar. The man bending over her moved closer, letting his black hood fall back to his thin shoulders. His eyes were dark, his face covered in a gray beard, and she could smell some kind of alcohol on him. A swirl of almost purple smoke hovered over his head and then twirled into the thick haze that hung in the room.

She relaxed and breathed in deeply. Thank God. It *was* a bar. And here was one of its drunken, pot smoking patrons in costume. An early Halloween party or surprise birthday party in get-up. That's all. She'd been in worse situations. Being on the floor with a broken ankle was a new twist, but she could handle herself.

"I just dropped in," she said. "Can't you tell?"

Maybe expecting some laughs, she looked around, but the room was silent, all the costumed people staring at her. Or at least they seemed to be staring at her, their hoods pointed her way. Miranda could almost make out their faces—men and women, both—but if this were a party, no one was having a very good time, all of them watching her grimly.

Between the people's billowing robes, she saw one man sitting at a table lit by a single candle, staring at her, his hood pulled back from his face. He was dark, tanned, and sipped something from a silver stein. Noticing her gaze, he looked up, and smiled, his eyes, even in the gloom of the room, gold. For a second, Miranda thought she recognized him, almost imagining she'd remember his voice if he stood up, pushed away from the table, and shouted for everyone to back away. Had she met him before somewhere? But where? She didn't tend to meet robe wearers, even at the weirdest of poetry readings.

Just as he seemed to hear her thoughts, nodding at her, the crowd pushed in, murmuring, and as he'd appeared, he vanished in the swirl of robes.

"Who are you?" the man hovering over her asked, his voice low, deep, accusatory.

"My name's Miranda Stead."

"What are you?" the man asked, his voice louder, the suspicion even stronger.

Miranda blinked. What should she say? A woman? A human? Someone normal? Someone with some fashion sense? "A poet?" she said finally.

Someone laughed but was cut off; a flurry of whispers flew around the group and they pressed even closer.

"I'll ask you one more time," the man said, his breath now on her face. "How did you get here?"

GREAT BOOKS,
GREAT SAVINGS!

When You Visit Our Website:
www.kensingtonbooks.com
You Can Save 30% Off The Retail Price
Of Any Book You Purchase!

- **All Your Favorite Kensington Authors**
- **New Releases & Timeless Classics**
- **Overnight Shipping Available**
- **All Major Credit Cards Accepted**

Visit Us Today To Start Saving!
www.kensingtonbooks.com

All Orders Are Subject To Availability.
Shipping and Handling Charges Apply.